CLOSES AT DUSK

Kim Paffenroth

CLOSES AT DUSK

by

Kim Paffenroth

2nd Edition 2018

1st Edition Trade Paperback 2012

All Rights Reserved

Dark Recesses Press
657 Craigen Road
Newburgh, Ontario
Canada K0K 2S0

Edited by Jodi Lee
Cover & Interior design by Bailey Hunter
https://baileyhunterdesign.wixsite.com/home

Library & Archives Canada ISBN
978-1-988837-13-0

ALSO BY KIM PAFFENROTH

Gospel of the Living Dead:
George Romero's Visions of Hell on Earth

Orpheus & The Pearl

Dying to Live

Valley of the Dead: The Truth Behind Dante's Inferno

Dying to Live: Life Sentence

Dying to Live: Last Rites

PRAISE FOR CLOSES AT DUSK

"Paffenroth just keeps getting better and better. I have devoured all his books, and watched with delight and awe as he stamps his intelligence and unique insight onto his stories. Here, in Closes at Dusk, *we have Paffenroth's personal De Profundis, in which he brings the full power of his intellect to bear on the nature of suffering and redemption. This is a beautiful book on all fronts, and in my opinion, a masterpiece."*

-Joe McKinney
Bram Stoker Award-winning author of *Flesh Eaters* and *Inheritance*

ACKNOWLEDGMENTS

The number of beta readers for this book has greatly expanded over that of my previous novels. Helping me once again with their able and timely criticism were Robert P. Kennedy and Christine Morgan. Joining them for this volume were Louise Bohmer and Carole L. Lanham. Nick Mamatas also offered comments on the first part of the manuscript. I repeat my heartfelt thanks to all of them. I asked each of them to assist, based on their own writing and knowledge. They have all done an excellent job and improved the work immensely.

The inspiration for the setting is a poignant one, to which I think many of my readers can relate. The Enchanted Mill Forest takes details from three now defunct storybook lands of the northeastern United States: The Gingerbread Castle of Hamburg, New Jersey; The Fairy Tale Forest of Oak Ridge, New Jersey; and The Enchanted Forest of Ellicott City, Maryland. The Gingerbread Castle was the one I most remember from childhood, while my wife visited The Enchanted Forest when she was small. The Fairy Tale Forest was the only one of these to survive long enough for us to take our own children there twice before it closed. (*Histories, and pictures of happier times, can be found for these and other such places at http://www.roadsideamerica.com.*)

It is to me a sign of the spiritual impoverishment and literal disenchantment of our world, that such simple and charming places are now gone, paved over for another mall or self-storage facility. Certain details of the story are taken from each of them, and perhaps a little of their magic can now live on in this story of familial redemption.

It is a morbid part of my writing process, when I get a certain ways into a story, and have it thoroughly outlined and have fallen in love with the characters, that I am suddenly overwhelmed by the fear that I will die before finishing the book. I therefore always name someone to finish each novel, if such a situation should occur. The designated writer this time was the Reverend Maurice Broaddus. I hope the themes and ideas herein appeal to him, even though he didn't get to finish writing it.

Kim Paffenroth
Cornwall-on-Hudson, New York

TABLE OF CONTENTS

PART ONE

PART TWO

PART ONE

CHAPTER 1

Friday, April 6, 2007 – Northern New Jersey

Darrah put her big, pink sneaker on a thick root, grabbed the trunk of the tree, and pulled herself up. She turned back, smiling down at her little brother, Nathan, as she extended her hand to him.

"Come on, Nat," she said. She pulled him up next to her, then brushed him off with her other hand. Not enough to tease or upset him—he'd get mad if he thought she was babying him. But with eight years to her fifteen, he still needed some help when they horsed around outside. This hillside was the highest and steepest on the property, and he'd slipped a couple times on the way up, plastering some of last fall's leaves to his red, plaid jacket; the arms of the jacket had some streaks of rust colored, clay mud on them, too.

Darrah got the jacket looking better with just a few slaps of her hand. She could throw it in the wash while their mom was still at work, if he got any dirtier this afternoon. No sense bothering her—she always wanted the laundry and other things around the house done just so, but she usually didn't get around to doing them herself, to her own specifications. For the last couple years, as she got older and more aware and adept at maneuvering around her parents' overt idiosyncrasies, as well as their hidden tensions and wounds, Darrah had found it easier just to do such housework herself.

She gave her brother a little shove with her left hand and pulled on his hand with her right, wrenching him around in a playful tussle. Big for her age, while he was a bit small for his, she had the size and strength to manhandle him however she wanted. He pulled his hand free as he swung at her with his other fist, giving her a good-natured bop on the shoulder. Darrah laughed. Nat lunged and she fell back a little—her partial surrender letting him join her in laughter.

"Nathan Hahn—pioneer, explorer, mountain man!" he said as he stepped past her, climbing further up the hill. "He pushes past his Indian guide and is almost to the top of Mount Hallicott, claiming it for the settlers!"

"Indian guide?" She let him stay a half step ahead, so he'd reach the top first. "Where'd that come from, Natty-Bo?" Their dad had nicknamed him that when he was a toddler, after the short, brown bottles of National Bohemian beer he sometimes bought if they went over the border into Pennsylvania.

Darrah considered her little brother's bobbing head. Both of them had wavy hair that could be described as reddish-brown, but his was several shades darker, almost all the way to russet or even dark brown, while hers was much lighter. He looked kind of blotchy today, and she hoped he wasn't getting sick again. Nat was prone to colds that lasted over a week, stomach upset, ear aches, and nosebleeds. He was also given to these random, slightly disconcerting fantasies, into which he would fit the people around himself.

"Indian guide—all the great explorers had one, and it was always a girl," Nat said simply, huffing a little, his short legs pumping to stay ahead of his sister as they made it up the last bit of steep incline. "Lewis and Clark. Captain John Smith. Probably lots more we don't know about it. Girls are good at that, but the man has to get ahead of her, before they reach their goal."

Darrah laughed again. "He does? Why's that?"

Nathan lunged forward to stand on a flat rock at the very top of the hill. "He just does. Or she won't respect him. And he won't like her. That's how it works. People don't ask why. It's just the way it is." He looked over his right shoulder at his sister, with a face that softened slightly as he met her bright green eyes; his were dark brown. "But you can come up here now. You earned it. Now it's your turn."

The ground dropped off steeply in front of the rock Nat was standing on, so Darrah grabbed his shoulder as she pulled herself up. Puffing more than she really needed to, she made it seem like she needed her brother's shoulder for balance and to steady herself, while carefully avoiding any hint that she might be holding him back from falling off the small cliff and hurting himself.

"I see," she said as they looked down at the lands below them to the south. She looked sideways at her brother. Most of the boys she knew in high school were much worse sexists than her sometimes odd eight-year-old brother, so she didn't feel like she had to raise his consciousness or anything. At least he thought the timid female guide and the great male explorer should both be on the top of the mountain at the end of the story.

Some of the trees on the hill beneath them still had little buds and flowers, a few were even showing the small leaves of the new season. It was grey and cloudy, and still quite cool for this time of year. The exertion of the climb up had warmed them enough that Nat unzipped his jacket and Darrah unbuttoned her heavy flannel shirt, as they took in the scenery below.

The hill sloped down to a high, wooden fence that enclosed the property. Her dad had been working on it since the weather had gotten better, and from somewhere off to their left, obscured by trees and the contours of the land, she could hear him hammering, fixing the holes that teenagers sometimes made in the barrier. Beyond the fence was a small, gravel parking lot, pocked and rutted in many places. Darrah's father and grandfather never seemed to have the money to pave it, but only repair it enough each spring that cars could come and go.

Just past the parking lot was Route 23. It was two lanes—double-yellow, here in front of their property—but less than a mile east the road widened out to four lanes. A few miles past there it was divided by a concrete barrier and cars couldn't make left-hand turns on it, but had to double back with one of the "jug handles" at the infrequent intersections. Further east, Route 23 intersected with 180 and led on to the George Washington Bridge. If there was no traffic—and east of the hill they stood on now, there was hardly ever a minute, day or night, when there was no traffic—you could be in Manhattan in about an hour.

Or, to turn it around as Darrah now did in her mind, and as she had heard her father and grandfather daydream about it so many times: in about an hour, any of those millions of people in New York City could be here, where it was quiet, calm, and beautiful. A place where, with the television and radio turned off, one didn't have to feel anxious and sick about hostages, 9/11, or Katrina; Vietnam, Iran, El Salvador, Bosnia, Somalia, or Iraq; Watergate, the Contras, or Whitewater; the dot com or housing bubbles; anthrax, ebola, or e-coli; one's high cholesterol or low credit rating. Here one could escape all such things for an afternoon, with just a short drive. Such had been the hopes and dreams the previous two generations of the Hahn family had expressed to her, and from where she was standing, on a day like this, they didn't seem as unrealistic as hard reality had shown her they were.

"Look, Natty-Bo!" Darrah said when a sudden movement caught her eye. She pointed to the top of the big sign in the parking lot, where a black bird landed and settled down into a long rectangular box that Darrah's grandfather had built there a half century before. Also at the top of the sign he'd built a replica of a medieval-looking mill, with a water wheel; from where they stood, if you looked really closely, you could still see two tiny figures in the door and window of the mill, though their paint was so faded, they looked like small, grey ghosts. The box the bird landed in had been meant to catch water as it spilled from the water wheel above it, but the mechanism had been broken even when Darrah was a small child. Now birds made nests in it every spring, a spectacle perhaps more wondrous than the little water wheel. "I think it's the same momma bird from last year."

Nat watched and nodded. "Yeah. They're cute. Cats can't get up there. Raccoons do sometimes, but they usually get run over on the highway. Then they don't bother the birds. But the baby raccoons are cute, too."

Darrah glanced at him. "I'm sure the baby raccoons are okay, too, in the forest. We just don't see them as much. They hide better."

"Maybe. They're pretty smart. Hiding is smart. Bats do that, too. I only see them in the summer, right after the sun goes down. And they never get run over."

Below the birds' nest and faded mill were the large letters of the sign, which read *The Enchanted Mill Forest* in yellow on a dark brown background, repainted recently by Darrah's father. Beneath that were the faint outlines of other words that in the past few years had been painted over several times, though without fully obliterating them: *And Holy Book Land.*

Whether it was scenes from the Bible, or Mother Goose and the Brothers Grimm, Darrah had never seen many people visit the carvings and buildings her grandfather had so skillfully and meticulously crafted. She had heard tales from him, about how many people used to come out there, away from the dirty, noisy, sinful city—cars filling the parking lot while happy families walked on every trail, smiling and laughing at all the displays. Of the few people she had ever seen there, most all of them said they remembered coming there when they were little, and now they brought their own children. Perhaps the rest had moved away, or else they did not crave the simplicity and peace of the place; or perhaps her grandfather's recollection of the number of visitors was not entirely accurate.

The partially obscured letters of *Holy Book Land* made Darrah look to the left, past the end of the parking lot, east down Route 23. She remembered when she was very small, long before Nat was born, the parking lot and fence had extended further in that direction. That's where Holy Book Land had been. The mill that the Enchanted Mill Forest was named after had been located on the other side of Route 23. It was already closed and boarded up even before Darrah was born, though it had been the original reason for people settling in this area; the town was still named Hallicott Mills.

Darrah did have some memories of Holy Book Land, however—especially of a big, black whale that didn't look at all like the ones you'd normally see in children's books, bright blue and smiling, with a little spout of water shooting out the top of its head. The one in their lake had been an ugly, savage, primal creature. When people came close to it, something—a hidden motion detector, though little Darrah didn't know it at the time—would set off a grainy, crackling loudspeaker that emitted a horrible, gurgling roar. If the visitors were brave enough to get even closer, they could see poor Jonah, bathed in a hideous red light, far down the monster's gullet, his hands upraised, his desperate cries to God apparently drowned-out by the Leviathan's song of triumph.

Darrah had since read the Bible story—not from any devotion, but just out of curiosity—and had found that Jonah was supposed to be the model of repentance and confidence in God's mercy. The figure she remembered from her childhood looked more like a soul in hell, crying out in never-ending torment and anguish. She still had nightmares about it.

Now, to the east of the Enchanted Mill Forest, instead of the Hallicott Mills Bakery and Holy Book Land, there were two nearly identical strip malls staring listlessly at each other across the black and yellow strip of asphalt. Darrah had been in enough places in New Jersey to know how generic such little enclaves could be. Their new neighbors here consisted of two sets of four stores each. Across the highway there was a weight loss center for women, a tax preparation office, an insurance office, and a store offering baked goods just past the expiration date.

Although the latter sold outdated bread and snack cakes made by all different companies, it was—along with the Enchanted Mill Forest—the only real, physical remnant of Hallicott Mills left in the area. The company had relocated its downsized operation to a cheaper location in Pennsylvania; stale examples of its few remaining successful products could often be found in the thrift store that stood on its original location.

On their side of Route 23, there was a store in which each item cost a dollar, a nail salon, a Chinese take-out place, and one empty store front that had rented videos, before one of the big chains moved in down the road and drove it out of business. Darrah had no pleasant memories from any of the stores, other than the occasional meal from the Chinese restaurant—at least those dinners when her parents would put on a good face and not fight or sulk—and the four of them would laugh together at the cryptic or fantastical fortunes in their fortune cookies. When he was still alive, her grandfather would sometimes join them at those meals, though he didn't like Chinese food as much as the younger people.

She smiled again at her brother. He narrowed his eyes a little at her, before returning a more tentative smile to her. Then he looked up to the circle of lighter grey in the clouds, where the sun partly shone through. "What time did Jesus die?" he asked matter-of-factly.

Darrah looked at him, trying to hide her shock. Their mom and dad had raised them to be agnostics, not so much decrying or criticizing religion, as ignoring it as much as possible—the same way one would avoid mentioning other awkward topics, like flatulence or sex or mental diseases that run in the family. For them, religion was not a scandal, it was an embarrassment. Neither Darrah nor her brother had ever set foot in a church except for a couple weddings and funerals.

"Well, um, let me think," she started slowly. "We have today off from school because people believe he died today, but I don't know what time. I guess it was later in the day. I think."

Even though her answer seemed vague and tentative, her brother seemed satisfied with it. "Yeah. I think you're right. Later. But not all the way dark."

"Did somebody ask you at school or something?"

"No. I just thought of it. I bet it wasn't as cold that day, either."

"No. I guess not." She felt relief when it looked as though Nat was going to drop the subject. It'd been a weird line of questioning coming from him.

Darrah leaned her head back and breathed the cold air in through her nose. It was early in the afternoon, right around lunch, and normally the smell of overheated peanut oil from the Chinese place would hit you pretty hard, wherever you were in the area. Maybe it was the wind, which was blowing the clouds in from the west, but she didn't smell the usual aroma from the restaurant. What was in her nose instead was cinnamon and cloves—a faint smell, but unmistakable. Not warm and smothering, like the oil, but a little burning and prickling. She had heard many stories from her father and grandfather, and even from some of the visitors to the Enchanted Mill Forest, about how exquisite the gingerbread was that used to come from the ovens at Hallicott Mills. She heard how it was as soft as butter and clouds, as sweet as sugar and icing on your birthday cake, how it'd fill your whole mouth and head with the spice, and warm every part of you from your toes to your throat.

But all that was before her time. All Darrah could know was that this smell was, to her, not at all as pleasant as the Chinese people's smoking grease. What she took in now filled her with the same dread and pity as poor Jonah inspired in her, when she saw him in the awful, powerful, implacable whale. The smell was, in some barely perceptible way, a hint of something fearful and unknown.

"Ow!" Darrah heard Nat squeal next to her. "Dam-buh!"

She came out of her confused reverie and whirled toward her brother. There was so much blood that it looked as if he'd plunged his entire right hand into a vat of it, and then smacked himself in the face. It poured most forcefully between his second and third fingers, though his cheeks and chin were covered too; it was running past his wrist and further down his arm, under the sleeve of his jacket. *That is definitely going in the wash as soon as we get back to the house,* Darrah thought, moving toward Nat.

Their mother could never get used to his nosebleeds, no matter how many times doctors reassured her they could find nothing seriously wrong and the condition would almost certainly stop soon. She would always act as though her son did it to spite her, or as if it were a judgment from elsewhere on her fitness as a parent.

Nat yowled and moaned, as Darrah caught him behind the neck with one hand and crammed a fist full of paper towels into his face with the other. Wherever they went, she always had one pocketful of paper towels and one of tissues. This definitely looked like the kind of gusher you needed to start treating with the paper towels before switching over to the tissues.

"Come on, Natty-Bo," she said in a honeyed voice. When he was sick or hurt were the only times Nat would let anyone baby him, and he actually seemed to prefer his sister's ministrations, though she'd never heard him admit it, and knew she probably never would. She pushed his head back with the paper-toweled hand. "You know to lean your head back, tough guy."

He snuffed and gurgled as his hands took the place of his sister's to hold the paper towels against his face. As angry as Darrah got with her mother for not helping out more during these attacks—and for even acting exasperated and hurt during them—when she heard the wet sounds of mortality her brother made, she could half-understand their mother's aversion. Darrah couldn't imagine any sucking chest wound or death rattle could sound much worse than her little brother did at those moments, when it looked and sounded as though he was just going to drain out all over the ground in a smoking puddle of crimson.

And the blood... the feel of it was even worse than the shocking red color. Silky and scalding hot at first, with that metallic stink that burned your eyes, and then quickly turning cold and sticky, as though it were something trying to trap you and peel your skin off, like when you touched a piece of metal in the winter.

Darrah's right hand was a mess, so she took her other hand from the back of Nat's neck and fished around in her pocket for the tissues. "It's okay, Natty," she said. "Just a little too much, that last climb to the top. You'll be fine." He'd even let her make those shushing noises that he'd never tolerate any other time. She brought the tissues up to his face as she took away the soaking wet clump of paper towels. "Clean up on aisle three," she said to encourage him as he pressed the new wad to his face.

They stood there a few seconds, before Nat silently nodded his signal that he could move. The tissues were soaked, but it looked as though the bleeding had slowed down enough for them to get home and clean up. Darrah held the paper towels away from herself as she put her other hand on her brother's thin shoulder and helped him down the hill by an easier, less steep way. They came to the little paved trail and followed it past the Old Woman in a Shoe and Rapunzel, before they got to the entrance gate. They stopped there for a second, and both of them instinctively looked up to check on Humpty Dumpty, precariously keeping guard, forever poised on the edge of a doom from which no horses or men could save him, but nonetheless always grinning and never falling from his faithful post.

Next to the entrance, a small sign read *Closes at Dusk*. They had plenty of time before then, or before their mother got home. Darrah rubbed her brother's shoulder and felt him relax some; his breathing was steadier and more even, too, not the ragged pants that always convulsed him when the blood started pouring out of him. She steered him along ahead of herself, and thought that with some lunch, a couple loads of laundry, maybe a game of Monopoly, it'd be a good afternoon anyway.

CHAPTER 2

Wednesday, November 9, 1938 – Darmstadt, Germany

David was a young father, still mesmerized by the motions and sounds his children made—always fascinated and seldom alarmed. Fussiness, crying, even a stream of warm, creamy baby vomit shooting onto the front of his shirt—all seemed to him routine problems to be worked through, not signs of anything more dire. They were the growing pains of new immigrants adjusting to their unfamiliar surroundings, small irritations that were much more easily alleviated than those of long-time residents of this imperfect world.

So when both their children began to fuss at once and neither would go down for an afternoon nap, David did not hesitate or mind at all to take their one-year-old son out for a walk, while his wife stayed at home and tended to their older daughter. He had quickly and efficiently bundled his son up and loaded him into the large black pram, wheeling it out the front door and lowering it down the steps to the sidewalk, its front wheels up and its back ones gently thumping down each step. Even the jerking, swaying motion down the stairs had served to calm the baby, who had stopped crying halfway down.

David looked down at the baby and made the silly faces and cooing sounds that parents always make at such times, and the boy responded with the wet giggles and awkwardly waving arms befitting his part. It was a cold, grey afternoon, so the baby's hands were covered in light blue mittens, which caught his attention; his father didn't mind that his son now ignored him and set about trying to remove the mitten with his mouth.

Like the contortions and splutterings of infants, the weather also didn't bother David. Other people—especially other Germans, he'd often thought with a smile—always complained about the weather, particularly in the autumn and winter. Then they'd turn around and reminisce about how much worse it had been at such-and-such a time, "Now that was real cold!" they'd say, before going back to more complaints about the current conditions. But to David, most days like this one, were approximately what they ought to be. It was early November in southern Germany, and therefore it was cold. The sun was obscured by the usual grey clouds, and it would be dark early—again, as usual.

If these were the conditions in August, it would be cause for alarm. It might be cause for complaint, if one didn't have a warm coat, along with a warm home and supper waiting at the end of the walk, but David had all these things, together with two healthy children and a beautiful, young wife, so he could only feel happy and satisfied with what the heavens offered that day.

However, as they crossed the street and entered the park there, the sight of four black-shirted young men at the corner reminded David that the bodily dissatisfactions of infants and the supposed shortcomings of the weather were nothing compared to the destructive, senseless activities of adults. Those would always fill him with rage and fear, and he usually had no idea how to react to such vileness, except to flee it with revulsion. Being careful not to turn or show any recognition, David observed the group from under the brim of his hat, noting their uniforms and ranks, guessing that the eldest—the leader—was in his early thirties, if that; the other three were early twenties. Schutzstaffel. The brown-shirts had been dangerous—like a crowd of unruly boys or a pack of dogs was dangerous—noisy, violent and unpredictable.

The SS were more insidious, crafty, sneaky, sophisticated, and so much more official. They were the police after all, and people— especially German people—always taught their children to run and tell the police if there was a problem. No one knew now what to do if the police were the problem.

Most times, the pram was enough to make them ease up a little and go looking for trouble elsewhere, but the walks to the trolley to go to work or the store had become repeated threats of randomness and brutality. Many days were uneventful, but one could always be singled out for nearly any absurd inquiry, backed up by physical violence. David was glad his eyes had always been strong and he didn't wear glasses: one could always be pulled aside and cuffed about for being an "intellectual." If there was nothing else on the brutes' minds, they could just say "What're you looking at?" the way little boys did to taunt and provoke other boys.

As David walked further into the park without any direct confrontation with the four SS men, he relaxed and returned his attention to his son. The baby had gotten one mitten off, though it was still held on to his sleeve by a piece of yarn, and he flapped this about so the mitten hit him in the face, making him laugh. David gave the boy his finger to hold instead, and the baby took it with his uncovered hand as his intense stare moved from the finger to his father's face and back. David stared back and nodded, wondering if his son would one day be a carpenter, like him, with big, callused fingers and always smelling of sawdust and linseed oil.

It was a good life of gratifying work, and like most every father, David found it overwhelming, even intoxicating, to think that his son might do the same work as he. But also like nearly every father, he found himself almost immediately hoping for something more for his son. Why think the boy would work in wood and nails? How primitive. The world was constantly advancing, quicker than ever before. There'd be cures for every disease soon, and flights to the moon in just a few years, so why think the boy would be something as archaic and medieval as a carpenter?

That thought led very quickly to fearing that his son would have much less than he, that the cures would not come but the diseases and famines still would—and worse than before—while the rockets would not go to the moon, but would crash down on flaming cities and screaming people. David pursed his lips as the baby held on and they remained like that for a few seconds, as that nearly inevitable train of thoughts ran through his mind. The baby suddenly let go and resumed flapping and laughing, and David joined him with a little chuckle, forgetting his more somber reflections of a moment before.

As they walked further, two boys in school uniforms passed by. Their yarmulkes labeled them as Jewish, and David bristled at them more than he did at the SS. If his feelings for them did not contain the fear he felt at the sight of the SS, they contained just as much revulsion and confusion. These were educated people in an advanced, modern society—how could they hold on to such fairy tales and superstitions, together with such odd customs? It didn't make sense, and only invited more abuse from the other barbarians.

David turned the pram around and began heading slowly back toward home. He went a different route through the park, so as to pass further from the SS men. From a block away, David could see that the crowd of four had grown to a dozen. He pushed the pram past the little sign on the fence that read Closes at Dusk, and for once he blamed the early twilight, not just crediting it to the normal cycles of late autumn, but feeling deep down that it had some much more sinister significance.

That night David tucked his son in, as explosions and shouting beat at the walls of their building, and a dull red glow seeped through the lacy, white curtains. Both the Orthodox and Reform synagogues of Darmstadt were destroyed by the fires that night, as were many other homes and buildings, the flames reflected in the seemingly infinite shattered glass that lay everywhere.

David put his hand lightly on his son's chest as tears welled up in his eyes, for he knew that his reason and patience were wholly powerless against either brutality or superstition. He had inadequately armed his child, thinking the world merely imperfect when in all reality, it was evil. The feeling of failure oppressed him, and he did not know how he would atone for the terrible mistake he had made in evaluating the world.

CHAPTER 3
Friday, April 6, 2007 – The Sublunar Sphere

He knew he must be in hell, because he had seen Lee Harvey Oswald there. Not that Christoph Hahn had ever been particularly enamored of the papist adulterer Oswald had killed so long ago. Mostly, when he'd think of the crime and its victim, he'd think how leaders didn't use to act like Kennedy. Even if they were violent or wicked, they knew to behave with some dignity and discretion. Kennedy was rich and spoiled, and besides being Catholic, those were two of the worst qualities Christoph could imagine.

As distasteful as Kennedy might have been, Christoph was like everyone of his generation, and he couldn't help but remember the day of the assassination—all the weeping, all the increase in fears and anxieties, and all the unrest and further assassinations that followed. Even if Kennedy hadn't been a virtuous man, the presidents since him had been noticeably worse, in Christoph's estimation—as ignoble as he was, but without any wit or charm. Terrible speakers, without any vision or goal other than their own ambition. A leader, even a very wicked one, should at least have a vision for his country. And discretion.

So Christoph was no great admirer of Kennedy, but that was not why he thought his assassin must surely be in hell. No, it was the cowardliness of the act, the senselessness of it. And the children. His own son, Benjamin, was just over a year old when it happened, and he couldn't imagine doing that to anyone's child, no matter how wicked the father might have been.

Besides everything else, he had heard that Oswald had some connection with communism, and Christoph—raised in Germany during the war—could never abide any sympathy for communism, a thing clearly worse than being spoiled with excessive wealth. A coward, capable of senseless violence that accomplished nothing other than the orphaning of two children, and a communist on top of it? For Christoph Hahn, that was a good enough description of the most likely occupant of hell. So, having seen Oswald, he knew he himself must be there.

He had first seen Oswald several months ago. Christoph guessed that was when he himself had died, though he didn't remember that event distinctly. He remembered Christmas and was sure he had been alive then, because the rest of his family—his son, along with Ben's wife, Ruth, and their children, Darrah and Nathan—had all spoken to him, laughed and eaten dinner with him. And now, in this place, no one spoke to him, he never ate, and he certainly had not laughed once. He wasn't quite as certain that he had still been alive at New Year's, but he might have been. It had been decades since he had stayed up till midnight on New Year's Eve, so the fact that he couldn't remember that event proved nothing. He might have made it to 2007, he might not have. He couldn't tell now.

At first, before he'd met Oswald, he'd been completely alone in this place. It was an odd feeling, being there, but the place didn't have any of the qualities he'd been expecting of either heaven or hell—no flames, no clouds, no torments, no choirs of angels—not much of anything. Christoph had thought maybe it was purgatory, and that idea made him feel much worse.

Though raised nominally as a Lutheran, he'd been a devout Congregationalist since coming to America, and it terrified him much more than any lake of fire, to think that that the papists might've been right about something and he'd found himself in their twisted, corrupt idea of an afterlife. But he soon got over this fear, because the place didn't seem like any idea of purgatory he'd ever heard of, either. There should be tortures in purgatory, but this place, almost regrettably, didn't have any. Just bland sameness, tedium, boredom; nothing inflicted on him from outside, but merely unpleasant facts of his present situation.

It wasn't particularly bright in this place, but it also wasn't totally dark. The light brightened and dimmed periodically, Christoph assumed in time with the cycles of day and night, though he could see neither sun nor moon nor stars. The physical world near his home in New Jersey was visible to him in some indistinct way. Sort of. Sometimes. But not all the time. Even when he could see the objects of his former life, the sights came through hazy, as though he were seeing them through gauze or smoked glass, and the sounds were wet and warbly, as though he were under water.

The only thing that was substantial and consistent and undistorted was Christoph himself. He appeared solid and—he was thrilled to notice at first—as he had been when his son was born, when he himself was twenty-five years old. His clothes, whatever they were made of in this place, were from that time period as well; the grey seersucker pants, white short sleeve shirt, and black leather shoes he'd often wear on his days off in the spring or summer. As exhilarating as it was to have the shape of a healthy, virile young body for the first time in decades, it became almost more of a burden, with no one else around.

When Christoph had first met Oswald, all he could feel was the natural joy that any creature feels at finding another of its kind after a long solitude. At such a meeting, even a cold-blooded fish or reptile would show some excitement appropriate to its nature, and the joy of a man—or the spirit of a man, at least, for Christoph still wasn't sure what he was now—was necessarily much greater. He stammered and tried to speak, but immediately thought better of it, for he didn't know the decorum, or whether other people here got frightened or angry.

And, if this really were hell, as he was beginning to suspect, then the punishments for breaking any rules were probably much worse than the simple boredom he had suffered so far, as oppressive as that had been. His upbringing had long impressed on him the necessity and desirability of following the law, and always finding out about any unknown restrictions before proceeding, so he contained himself and considered how to approach his new companion.

He had immediately recognized the pale, slightly balding young man: like anyone who'd been an adult in 1963, he had Oswald's face impressed on his memory, frozen there as a morose-looking twenty-four-year-old, who now seemed to move about right in front of him. As Christoph studied him closer, he saw that Oswald did not appear as tangible as he himself, though more real and substantial than the Wishing Well or any of the surrounding physical landscape. Oswald was somewhere in between, both as to solidity and color. On the one hand, he had some of the grey and washed-out appearance that the physical world now held for Christoph, but he wasn't as translucent as corporeal objects; he seemed solid like Christoph, but lacked some color or reality, at least, to Christoph's eyes.

Much more disconcerting to Christoph than his different appearance was his demeanor, for the other man didn't seem to perceive his presence at all. Oswald just sat there on a bench by the Wishing Well, reading a book. After watching and waiting for what seemed a very long time, and working himself up into an increasing anxiety, Christoph finally risked addressing him.

"Hello," he said softly, from a few feet away. When his companion did not react at all, he tried the same greeting a little louder and took a step closer. His spirit leapt when Oswald stirred, but Christoph saw it was only to turn the page and change his position slightly. Several more greetings, but still the young man kept reading without any sign of recognition. It didn't take long for Christoph to satisfy himself that Oswald did not sense he was there, and so he gave up trying to communicate with him.

He sat on another bench near Oswald and tried to identify what he was reading. The book appeared as pale as its owner, and the words were too faint for Christoph to make out. *Probably some communist garbage*, he thought, and looked with more disgust at the other man.

After that first encounter, they sat there like that again and again, for several days. Sometimes Christoph would get up and move around again, but he always returned to see if the other man was still there, and he was. He tried to reason why, of all people, Oswald would be here with him, or why he would be in this particular place at all.

Christoph knew why he himself was here—New Jersey had been his home for over half a century, the great majority of his life had been spent here. He couldn't remember where Oswald was from, but he was pretty sure it wasn't northern New Jersey. He did remember Oswald had gone to Russia briefly in his youth, and maybe after death he kept wanting to wander about, as he had then. Christoph also thought how criminals often were abused or neglected and had no home they felt attached to. Maybe Oswald was like that, so he didn't feel like staying in any one place and had ended up here.

Maybe.

Whatever had brought the man here, he didn't seem to feel any need to move on, but just sat there, day after day. Christoph didn't know if he kept reading the same book or he had some way of getting new ones. They sometimes looked a little different, but their appearance changed slightly even when Christoph looked directly at them, so he couldn't be sure. He supposed he could stay there all the time and watch Oswald more closely, to see if he ever changed books, but wondered what the point would be of such an investigation.

So Christoph continued his daily wanderings, always ending up back with his unresponsive companion, wondering what it all meant.

It was on one of those afternoons that he had reasoned through how he must now be in hell, how Oswald's presence here proved that this was hell. Christoph was sitting with his elbows on his knees, looking down as he came to that depressing realization, and nearly fell off the bench when his previously motionless partner picked exactly that moment to stand up. Christoph watched Oswald with wide eyes, amazed, as he simply walked down the path and out of sight. He wondered why he didn't get up and run after him: he had been, after all, the only other person he'd met, and his departure now plunged him back into his previous loneliness.

Although Christoph could wonder at his own inaction, he knew somehow that he would do nothing about it. Not that he couldn't, really. It wasn't that he *couldn't* move, but it just didn't seem right. Like drinking when you weren't thirsty or scratching a part of you that doesn't itch—it's possible to do such a thing, but you just wouldn't. More than wondering why he didn't follow Oswald, he was consumed by the question of why Oswald would suddenly choose that moment to leave. What had changed to make him get up and walk away from the spot he had silently occupied for days?

Christoph looked around for any clue, any sign, any outward thing that looked different. He held out his arms and hands and looked at those, to see if anything had changed about him. He looked up at the featureless sky, or whatever it was that was above them. Then he realized that right before Oswald got up and walked away, the only thing that had changed in their environment was nothing visible or physical, but was the realization that he himself had come to—that they were in hell.

Oswald had been there to show Christoph that terrible fact, and with his purpose now accomplished, he had left.

All of this came upon Christoph with an overwhelming and undeniable force that demanded assent. It dragged him off the bench and down to his knees, for there was a further revelation contained within it. As mute and uncomprehending as Oswald had been, it was clearly not his intent to teach Christoph the name and reality of their situation; he doubted that Oswald himself was even aware of it. But if it were not *Oswald's* plan and purpose—though he had arrived and left in just such a way and at just such a time as to deliver this message—then he was an unwitting messenger from someone else, someone whose purpose could be thwarted by neither Oswald's obliviousness and ignorance, nor by Christoph's dullness of mind.

When someone like Christoph Hahn, a devout man his whole adult life, receives a message that he is certain is from God, then he falls to his knees and thanks God for the generosity and grace that He has shown by deigning to communicate with His unworthy servant. And this reaction of grateful prayer is automatic and unquestioning, even if that message is that the recipient is in hell.

Christoph did not bother to debate whether God hears the prayers of those in hell. He did not bother to consider whether a soul in hell has anything for which to be grateful. And he certainly did not meditate on the paradox that someone in hell would probably be incapable of gratitude toward or communication with God, so how could he even be praying in the first place, if he really were in hell?

No, all Christoph could do was pray in the way every devout person prays at some point in his or her life—with the terror and hope of a child who is convinced his parents are angry with him, and deservedly so, and have every right not to relent in their anger.

And he had continued in this kind of prayer, whether on his knees or walking about with upraised hands, every day, up until the present moment.

CHAPTER 4

Friday, April 6, 2007 – Northern New Jersey

Ben was fixing the fence at the eastern end of the property. Damned teenagers had pushed some boards in, then wriggled under.

He could still see where the leaves were brushed away and the red dirt was scraped along, like it had been a tight fit for some of them, and they'd pushed themselves through on their bellies in a commando crawl, or pulled themselves through on their backs. It would've been cold as hell, doing that on the damp ground at night in March, but teenagers will do a lot more to find a place to drink beer and make out.

As he worked, Ben thought how he didn't mind that much, cleaning up after the kids. They could've been real pains in the ass, spray painting shit or breaking the plaster statues or the glass windows in some of the buildings, never mind if they started a fire. Any of those things would cost real money to fix, and then he'd have to go and get the help of those lazy, dumbass cops—*sheriffs* actually, like they lived in goddamn Mayberry or somewhere, when really they were right outside New York City, where real crimes occurred—while they sat around and gave out speeding tickets for people flying down Route 23.

Black people, more often than not, Ben had noticed.

No, keeping the Enchanted Mill Forest out of the sheriff's jurisdiction as much as possible suited Ben just fine, for it meant the damage really was nothing to worry about, while it denied the sheriffs the satisfaction of thinking or bragging how they were fighting real crime, when they were not. Fuckers sat on their asses, while he, with a goddamn useless Ph.D. in English, did grunt work out in the cold and hoped that maybe, if he were really lucky, he might get to teach a class somewhere next fall.

He stepped back and admired his work. The exertion, with all the lifting and hammering, had thoroughly warmed him up, though he retrieved his flannel shirt from a nearby tree branch and put it on over his T-shirt. He also pulled on the pair of canvas work gloves he'd left on the ground nearby. Over the years he'd gotten good at these jury-rigged jobs, using the materials at hand.

The ground dipped at the point in the fence where he'd been working, and he had needed something to fill the gap between the fence and the earth, but Ben was as loath to give money to a building supply store as he was to give credit to the Hallicott Mills sheriff's department. So he had taken the wheelbarrow and hauled over several large, smashed-up chunks of concrete from a pile at the eastern end of the park. Hauling stuff away cost money, and you never knew when something might come in handy. They'd managed to salvage and reuse quite a bit of Holy Book Land when they'd sold off the property.

Goliath was now a perfect giant for Jack to climb his beanstalk and defeat; the cow Jack sold for the magic beans had previously been one of the animals present at the birth of the Messiah. And Cinderella's carriage was really a clever hybrid of the chariots of Pharaoh and Elijah; the pumpkin-hued flames of Elijah's heavenly vehicle had seemed almost destined for their final form and function. That job had been a particularly difficult one for just two men with no heavy machinery, and Ben remembered it fondly as one of the few times in his adult life when his father and he had worked well together, producing something with which the old man had been happy and proud, salvaging the remnants of his one dream to give a facelift and reprieve to what remained of his naïve little fantasy land.

Today, blocks of the former walls of Jericho were being given a second chance at usefulness. Ben smiled that the source didn't inspire confidence in their impenetrability, but they looked as though they'd do the job now much better than they had in Joshua's time. Besides, he knew for a fact that Joshua's trumpet was currently being held by one of the Red Queen's card-men on the other side of the park, and posed little threat. It was a good solution, and had cost him nothing but a couple hours work. As an adjunct professor with no classes this semester, time was one thing he had in abundance.

Other people would do volunteer work, so teenagers could play basketball or go on band trips to the Rose Bowl. He spent a few hours working out in the cold, so teenagers could catch a buzz and make out and feel the urgent need of someone else pressed up against them. Let them. They'd remember those times more than any sports or marching band; the memories of such simple, furtive pleasures might even carry them through the dark times that Ben knew lay ahead for them.

For it would be soon enough that the buzz wouldn't satisfy, the kisses – what few there were – would be tepid and half-hearted, or else bitter with guilt, and no one else would long for them anymore. He could almost feel happy for the teens of Hallicott Mills, if he were not so overwhelmed and oppressed by his own sickening self-pity.

He pushed the wheelbarrow away from the worksite, stopping halfway up a low hill to rest for a second. Looking around as he wiped his brow with the back of one gloved hand, he thought of his own kids for a moment and felt much less wretched. To think of those two made the other side of the ledger seem less damning. He ticked off the items on the "failure" side easily enough, having had frequent practice at it. A failed career, moving back in with his father to save money, a marriage that for years had consisted of little more than mutual recriminations—a long, slow simmer of venomous sulking and glares, punctuated by explosive spats and curses—and finally, middle age as the owner and manager of this grand piece of wooded bliss.

It was as pretty as it ever was, but never as popular as his father claimed it once had been, and getting less so with each passing summer. Even though all those things and the inescapable darkness with which they filled his heart didn't go away, somehow the brightness of those two kids burned so white-hot and dazzling that he could bask in it whenever he wanted and draw at least a smaller, reflected happiness from them.

Listening to the birds and the wind, Ben wondered where the kids were in the park, and how Natty-Bo was doing in particular. He seldom worried about Darrah, on the other hand. How could anyone? The kid was just so strong and capable. She had some of his features—the nose and chin especially—and she was big and awkward like him, but her eyes and hair were her mother's.

As Ben pictured her, he could almost remember how he used to love his wife. To think of how he had a part in creating a person of such obvious quality and potential as Darrah, he couldn't help but have more hope for the future, and fewer regrets for the past. At least, until he thought of how much his fighting with his wife must've hurt their daughter growing up. Then he burned with shame at himself and with rage against his spouse all over again, as he did most every day.

He took up the handles of the wheelbarrow again and continued pushing it up the hill, wheeling it behind the little make-believe church that sat atop the knoll. Ben stowed the barrow and tools in a shed hidden behind some bushes there, then returned to the church with a big, black garbage bag. This was always the last stop on a cleanup detail after teenagers broke in. The church was one of the few buildings in the Enchanted Mill Forest big enough for people to enter, with a ceiling just over six feet high.

There was no door covering the entrance; Ben had removed the old one because it was, in a way, daring the vandals to do more damage, challenging and defying their right to be there. Better to leave it open, and they could come and go as they pleased, which is what the teenagers did on their nocturnal romps. They did little more damage than leave beer bottles, most of which were intact, and he only had to pick up a few shards of green and brown glass with his gloved hands. The local kids really weren't so bad.

When he had finished, Ben stood up almost completely straight. He was a little too big to stand up to his full height, and he'd been in there enough times to stop right before he whacked his head on the ceiling. He looked at the pale yellow windows—when it was sunny outside, it was a truly astonishing room to be in, as warm and solid as a piece of amber. But today was as grey as the rest of his life.

The cross at the front of the room was a particularly light shade of oak, the kind with just the barest hint of gold to it. Ben remembered being dragged to his father's god-awful Congregationalist church and how ugly and plain all the decorations had been. Apparently his father's skill and pride at woodworking had counterbalanced the austerity of his chosen denomination, for the cross he had carved here was, like most all his work, intricate and ornate in the extreme. Sensuous curves and waves adorned every inch of the symbol, and at the center, where the vertical and horizontal bars crossed, the pattern created something almost like a heart.

His father had even worked around a natural knot in the wood at that point, so that the lines of his carving suggested the upward motion of flames from the heart, while a dark streak in the knot suggested a full, pregnant, endlessly painful drop of blood hanging down. Ben could not remember a time when he had believed in a single tenet or practice of his father's religion—as far back into childhood as his memory reached, all he could recall was how he was filled with incomprehension at his father's fear and blame— an incomprehension that sometimes flared up into revulsion, but usually settled down into sullenness and disdain. But that cross... it didn't make him believe, but it did make him think that the object of belief must be real, even if it were unattainable or unreceptive, in order for something so dreadful and beautiful to exist.

Ben had examined that cross many times growing up, and its effect had been more calming then, turning his incomprehension almost, but not quite, into wonder. Now, in his middle age, he had developed many defenses against wonder or anything else that would threaten the routine of his wretchedness. Besides self-pity, cynicism was the remedy to which he most often turned.

"Jesus," he said as he tied the top of the full garbage bag in a knot, not taking his eyes off the cross. "The guy had no wife, no responsibilities, everybody loved him. And he was dead by age thirty. No arthritis, ulcers, old age." He turned and ducked a bit to walk out the door of the church. "Fucker had it easy."

One empty, long-necked brown bottle still lay under one pew. For some reason, Ben hadn't noticed it when he was picking up. The wind blew across the top of the bottle and made a tiny, whistling moan, so slight that Ben probably wouldn't have heard it, even if he were still standing there, but he was already to the bottom of the hill, the large bag of bottles clinking as he walked.

CHAPTER 5

Thursday, December 5, 1940 – Darmstadt, Germany

Christoph Hahn had heard stories of violence and privations, but so far his life was more or less free of them. He could remember the air raid sirens once in the summer, but the few bombs had fallen far from his home and no one he knew had been hurt. For a few days after that, he could sense his parents' fear, but even they had now settled into a more ordinary existence and seemed happy and relatively free of care.

He was playing at the moment with some blocks and train cars in their small living room. His older sister, Greta, came running in, wearing her long nightgown and slippers. She barely avoided a collision with his blocks as she bounded up to him, then bent over, her bright blue eyes flashing under her blonde bangs. "Come, Tof!" she squealed. "Let's check our boots! I thought I heard something!"

Mr. Hahn smiled as his two children raced by him. Greta opened the door and Christoph pushed past her to get out on to the stoop and see what had been done with their boots. The cold air stung his face and hands, but did nothing to curb his eagerness and curiosity. He looked immediately to the two pairs of small leather boots next to the door.

There were no branches sticking out of them, so that was a good sign. Days before, Greta had given him the most solemn explanation, that Saint Nicholas gave bad children a tree branch instead of candy. And if that weren't bad enough, it was a branch that would then be used as a switch on their legs and bottoms. She had seemed more frightened by her explanation than her younger brother. He had, however, been concerned enough that he checked with his mother, if his behavior had been good that year. Her blonde hair was pulled back in a bun, but one loose curl bobbed as she shook her head. "I don't know, my love," she had said with a smile. "I think you were very good, but Saint Nicholas—well, he's a very hard man to please. We will just have to wait and see."

Christoph was about to pick up his boots to see if there were any candies in them, but before he could do so, his sister grabbed his arm. "Look!" she said softly. "I did hear something!" Christoph looked up and saw Saint Nicholas on the sidewalk below. His hair and beard were long and white, as was his robe, which was tied about his waist with a golden cord. On his head was a red miter with golden cross on it; the large book he carried in his right hand was also red with a golden cross. In his left hand he held a bulging burlap sack, slung over his shoulder.

The old man had started toward the next row house, but he now turned back to face the two children on the stoop above him. The cold had made his cheeks rosy and must have put some tears in his eyes, for they sparkled. He did not smile however, but cocked an eyebrow at Christoph and his sister as he set down his sack. "Ah, what do we have here?" he asked as he rose up to his full height again. "The two children who live here? I'm glad you came out! I couldn't quite make out my own handwriting here in my book." He made a big flourish of fingering through the pages to find the right entry. "I was going to inquire further whether you were good or bad this year."

Christoph turned from Saint Nicholas to Greta. The girl looked more amazed than her brother, and he had to tug at her arm to get her to respond. "I've been very good," she finally squeaked.

"I've been good," Christoph said. "My mama said I was."

Saint Nicholas closed his book, but still didn't smile. "Good, good," he said as he nodded. "That's what I thought I had you down for."

Christoph heard a rattling sound, followed by his sister's shriek as she grabbed his arm. He turned to see another figure approaching Saint Nicholas, who turned toward the newcomer. "Ah, my servant Ruprecht!" Nicholas exclaimed. "These children say they've been good! What do you think?"

The new figure was the opposite from Saint Nicholas in most every way. He stood up taller than the saint, and not hunched over from his pack, for the coarse, black bag he dragged on the ground beside him was empty. In his other hand he carried some long, thin sticks tied together in a bundle. His black clothes were all tattered, with pieces hanging off everywhere and tied at the waist with a large chain that hung down to the ground. That had been the rattling sound Christoph had heard.

Flaps of animal skins covered the man's hands, and he wore a black hat of some kind of animal fur. From under the hat spilled a huge mane of black hair, flowing down to a shaggy, black beard that hung to the middle of his chest. The skin of his face, where it wasn't covered by his overflowing hair and beard, was also black. The two slivers of his eyes were the only white patches anywhere on him.

"Do they say so, master?" Ruprecht hissed in a low voice. "Children lie, master. They always lie. It's one of their favorite things to do." He pointed with the bundle of sticks, first at Greta, who cowered back into her brother, and then at Christoph. Then he held up his empty bag. "Wicked, lying children—do you know what my bag is for?"

Christoph could feel his sister trembling as she pressed against him, and he was surprised she didn't answer, as she had explained the bag to him when she told him about the boots. "It's for bad children," Christoph said.

Ruprecht had ascended the first step, still gesturing with the sticks. "Ah, the little one is bold, master," the large, black man said. Closer now, Christoph could see his black skin had a slight, oily sheen to it, like coal. "Bold at lying, too, I'm sure.

"Yes, little one, my bag is where the bad children go. And I take them back to the cold, dark woods, so they don't bother nice people. Those who are just a tiny bit bad, I let them live in the woods and eat bark and sticks, 'til they learn to be good. The really bad ones?" His eyes narrowed, so he was almost completely black. He slowly raised the hand that held the bag, stuck his thumb out, and dragged it across his beard at neck level. "I find the deepest, fastest river, and I throw the bag into it, with the bad children inside, and they're gone forever."

"Oh, Ruprecht," Saint Nicholas said from the bottom of the steps. "Leave them alone. I'm sure they've been good. How can you be so certain they're lying?"

"Oh, I know, master. I can tell. And they know I'm right."

Ruprecht lunged up one more step and swatted Greta's arm with the sticks. She screamed and turned to run, pushing past her brother. As she dashed by Christoph, Ruprecht gave her another slashing cut across the backs of her legs.

Christoph was now alone on the steps with the large, dark man. The boy could hear his sister behind him, whimpering and being comforted by their father. Ruprecht slowly extended the sticks, until their tips were just in front of the boy's nose. "Frightened, boy?" he asked.

Christoph was cold, and confused, but he was not scared. He shook his head slowly.

Ruprecht lowered the sticks and nodded. "Oh, we do have a bold one here, master. Interesting." He raised the sticks again. "Stick out your hand, boy."

That command *did* frighten Christoph a little, but he stuck his right hand out, palm down, in front of himself. Ruprecht raised the sticks, then just barely touched them to the boy's outstretched hand, merely scratching and tickling his skin. "You'll learn to be scared of pain and the dark, boy. But not tonight. Not by me."

The black man turned and went back down the steps. "Well, master," he said, "these two check out all right. The big one has paid double for her crimes, and the little one is so bold that he'll have to learn his lesson another time."

"Good, Ruprecht," said Nicholas. "That will do."

The white and black figures continued to the next house, Christoph staring at them as they walked away. As he watched, the black one suddenly turned back and gave a quick grin, his wet, gleaming teeth flashing for a moment in the darkness. Christoph stood there another moment before picking up their four, candy-filled boots and taking them inside.

For some reason, Christoph Hahn felt strangely comforted by Ruprecht's smile. As he fell asleep that night, he was not thinking of the hard candies he had sucked on after supper, but was still wondering at the dazzlingly white teeth in their sooty frame.

CHAPTER 6

Friday, April 6, 2007 – The Sublunar Sphere

As Darrah and Nat were climbing the hill that afternoon, and their father was doing his repairs, their grandfather was also nearby. He was, as he had been for many days, praying fervently to God, though not to release him from that place; that would be blasphemous, to question God's judgment. Besides, Christoph did not think it made sense, to ask for release from a state that was not really that unpleasant, even if he now thought it was hell. Surely there could be a far worse place, where God put those who railed and complained against His decisions.

No, Christoph was still thanking God for revealing Himself and His will, and if he were making a request for anything, it was only that God continue to reveal himself in whatever way God saw fit. Christoph was always as meticulous in the wording of his prayers as he had been in his woodworking; he was also equally patient and perseverant in both activities. All these qualities of carefulness and persistence continued after the death of his body.

The Wishing Well was out in the open, and he liked to go there because it was slightly less grey than everywhere else in this dim world. Today though, he had gone to the church. It was, of course, the most appropriate place to pray, and he had spent much of the morning there. However, without the sensation of taking in and expelling breath, without the physical and sensual rhythms of speech, Christoph had noticed that it was sometimes harder to concentrate. He remembered those videos on the news, of Jews at their place in Jerusalem, bobbing back and forth like they were little clockwork dolls that'd been wound up too tightly. He had thought they looked quite ridiculous, but now he was the one who felt weak and silly, for he could not use his body to focus his mind.

The Jews he had mocked had learned a trick of concentration he would now dearly like to avail himself of, but no longer could. He felt unmoored and distant and not attached to the words he formed, and almost had to pull himself back down to them, as though he were floating away, the words and feelings he so desperately wanted to express were flowing beneath him in a cold, wet, living rush that he wanted to dive down into, but couldn't.

Ever since he had died and wandered freely about the park, Christoph was very careful not to go near the church when it seemed like it was night, for fear of what he might see or hear there. The thought of the depravity that went on there was too terrible, too disgusting for him to bear. It had been a few days since he noticed the bottles on the floor of the church, so his anger about them had abated somewhat. He thanked God for taking away his wrath, so that he could better pray to Him, and repented for letting it take him over and distract him as much and as often as it did.

As he mastered his anger, he felt it settling down into something more like a simmering hate, a kind of fascinated malice for the ungrateful heathen who drank and fornicated in the Godly building that he had built with his own hands. For years Christoph had fought against generations of them; they seemed to pour forth from Hallicott Mills in greater numbers than had populated Gomorrah at the height of its wickedness. He'd put a heavy door on the church, but they'd smashed the lock and gotten in. So he'd put it back up. It was their little back and forth, a running battle that would always be a stalemate. As long as they were strong enough to break down his door, he was strong enough to rebuild it. Christoph wouldn't call the police on them, not because he was trying to save them from any trouble, but because as he was growing up, his parents had impressed on him many times that calling the police wasn't always a good idea.

His battle for the church had raged like that for years, until his son and daughter-in-law had moved in. Ben had used his terrible logic to "prove" how locking up the building and trying to protect it actually did more harm than good. He had even raised the specter of the police getting involved, if the vandalism continued.

Christoph was sure his son knew how much that would frighten him. He had given in, letting his church be taken over by the wicked and their awful, boundless lusts. He cursed himself now for such weakness, barely keeping himself from cursing his son for using it so effectively against him. If he had thought about it, he might've remembered how many times he had cursed his son, to his face, when he was still alive. But he didn't think of it, just as he had not considered it all those times before.

Christoph gazed up at the wooden cross he had carved so long ago. He had often wondered why, during all their break-ins, the vandals had never touched it; there were people's initials carved in practically every piece of wood and every tree, all over the park, including the pews here. Sometimes he liked to imagine that the cross was impervious because of some supernatural power it had, even over the Godless, but deep down, when his anger had cooled and solidified into the icy stratum of lonely hate that lay beneath it, Christoph knew the real answer, and the real question, were quite different.

It was not a question of why the vandals had not damaged the cross. Christoph knew the bigger, more important question was why he had never moved it to a safer location, knowing vandals came in here most nights. And to that question, he did not have just pious or superstitious speculation, but a terrible certainty. He hadn't moved the cross, because he hated it most of all, and every night he secretly hoped it would be destroyed. It filled him with more hate for his teenage tormentors when they had refused to perform the one act of destruction for which he longed.

Christoph hated the cross, because he had made it wrong. The cursed thing was so damnably, culpably pretty. It was the symbol of God's suffering for mankind's sins, and therefore should be as plain and simple as the reality of sin, as ugly and necessary as an iron nail. But he had gussied it up so spectacularly, with all sorts of flourishes and swirls of wood that made no sense on the instrument of God's torture and death. Even though it was made from the hardest, most unforgiving oak, he had somehow made it look like something a baker would create from spun sugar, an object almost of longing and delight.

And that thing—that nameless shape in the middle—he still didn't know exactly what it was supposed to be, for it was such a maddeningly confused orgy of curves, that it almost seemed to leer at him like a hungry mouth, or some sickeningly sensuous flower. The dark, vertical scar made by the grain of the wood suggested something even worse. He begged God again for mercy for ever having created it, but at the same time, he remembered vividly that when he had carved the thing, he hadn't meant to put such decorations on it. His hands and the chisel had seemed to move on their own, with him only watching as the hideously beautiful shape grew in front of him, until it was too complete and too awful to change or discard.

The terrible thing stood there before him, once again, as the clearest and loudest indictment he could imagine. Christoph had made something that was a gaudy, flattering example of his own skill, rather than a testimony to God, an object that invited people to admire it, rather than remember the One who had hung on it. Christoph was especially exercised by this idolatrous element of the cross he had made, when he remembered the effect it had on his son as the boy was growing up.

So many times, he had needed to beat his son, in order to get him to read the Bible or go to church. Christoph tried to be lenient, since the boy's mother had died right after he was born, and he knew it must be hard and confusing, growing up without a mother. There was no excuse for shirking one's duties to God, however, and so the beatings continued as they were necessary.

But despite such a total lack of religious feeling, Ben could be found on many afternoons, sitting here, staring at the cross. The boy didn't believe or study anything of true religion, and yet he gawked at this abomination. Worse than creating an idol, Christoph had created an idolater out of his own son. Often he'd even catch the boy smiling at his idol; the child's beautiful, seemingly innocent face lit up by the golden light inside the church.

He had tried to be even more gentle than usual, when he beat the boy at those times, because he knew the idolatry was really his fault, leading the boy unwittingly to sin. But the beatings were still necessary, because one does not smile at God. One only prays to God with shame, as he himself now did.

Christoph heard his son hammering in the distance, and decided to leave the church for now. He knew Ben would come here soon, and he feared even in adulthood his son would commit idolatry with the cross. He knew that would be more horrible to witness than the animal ruttings of the teenagers, and so he moved on; he avoided coming near his son as much as possible in his wanderings around the park. His son's presence chilled him, more so even than realizing this was hell. Although he lacked any faith, Ben had always been diligent about cleaning and fixing the Enchanted Mill Forest. Christoph thanked God for giving at least that lesser virtue to his son.

He sensed his grandchildren were nearby. It was an odd feeling, the feeling he got from the living. Other than his son, who made him feel so terribly cold and alone, other people made him feel rather too hot, a sort of electrical prickliness came all over him. It was a pleasant feeling, that made him feel a little more real and alive and less grey and numb, but it could easily be overdone. When he'd first sense people, and when they were at a slight distance, it was exhilarating. If he stayed around them too close and for too long, however, the feeling would become overpowering, so that he couldn't think straight and all his feelings were in turmoil. Then he just had to get away.

For now, however, he wanted to feel some of that life force and current, so he moved up the hill to where the two children were. As usual, he couldn't make out what they were saying. They sounded like they were whispering at some distance from him, even though they appeared to be standing right beside him. Truth be told, he had long considered them a rather odd pair. Darrah was too much like her mother to please him very much, both of them being far too confident and assertive for women. It was unnatural and disturbing. And whatever the reasons for his son and daughter-in-law fighting so often, Christoph felt certain that her unfeminine, unyielding character was somehow behind it. He had to admit, though, that Darrah often seemed more careful and responsible than either of her parents, and today all her confidence expressed itself to her grandfather as an extra buzz of energy that pleasantly replaced all the anger and hate he'd been feeling moments ago. Perhaps there was some hope for her.

If Darrah were too much like her mother, then Nat was too much like his own son for his comfort. The boy was moody and quick to anger, just like his father. At least his father had had the decency not to express such unruly emotions until adulthood, while Nat had indulged his all his life, encouraged by those around him, by tolerating his outrageous, tyrannical behavior. He didn't even have the bodily health with which Ben had always been blessed.

Christoph had never seen his son or daughter-in-law hit either of the children, and he strongly suspected some beatings would've toughened up the boy's body, while taming his undisciplined mind and subduing his lawless spirit. The old man had said as much on several occasions, but no one had listened to him.

It was a source of pride and enjoyment to Christoph, however, that his grandson had always loved all the books and stories upon which the Enchanted Mill Forest was based. As unfocused and volatile as it might be, the boy's mind was amazing in its voraciousness. He had even caught Nat reading a Bible several times, and relished the look of consternation and confusion on Ben's face each time, though his own triumph was always short-lived. As soon as he asked the boy about it, the child would spout the most bizarre, blasphemous combinations of stories.

One time he had confidently and without the slightest hesitation told Christoph how Lot's daughters had escaped to Egypt with their babies and built boats out of reeds to sail back to Eden with the crocodiles they had tamed as pets, and they would stay there until Jesus came and got them all. Christoph felt easier when the boy stuck to other books.

As he followed his granddaughter's gaze, Christoph remembered the mill that used to be there, where he had first worked when coming to this country. At first, Hallicott Mills had produced some real treats—pfeffernüsse and gingerbread and stollen. Oh, those were real cakes and cookies. Those had life to them. You'd get them at Christmastime, and there was something mysterious and even a bit painful about their taste. A lot of things about Christmas were like that, he remembered. Americans didn't like to eat those kinds of things, however. They wanted bland and sweet cakes, too buttery and soft and without savor.

He wished he could smell the gingerbread again. When the bakery made it, the odor would be all over the town, like a warm, scratchy wool blanket. That gingerbread was something Christoph would've liked to share with his grandchildren. He wanted so much to give them those things he had made years ago, and he cursed the fact that the bakery had closed so long before. He even felt a little embarrassed now, for criticizing the children in his mind, because it suddenly occurred to him, that with all their oddities, they of all American children would perhaps appreciate and love the things others dismissed as weird and bitter. He felt quite confident and proud they would love the smell and taste as much as he did, and they'd be grateful he had made the cookies for them. He wished they had been there for that experience.

Christoph heard his grandson cry out in pain, and pain, like all the primal languages that do not require words—like love and hate, for example—carried between their respective realms, crossing the boundaries set between them with only a very slight diminution in its intensity. The blood was the first color he had seen since dying, and the sight of it felt as though it would burn him physically. It was so bright and searing, while the boy's pain and fear slammed into him like an explosion. He half-expected to see the trees around them flattened and charred, but only he was knocked backward, his mind reeling and crackling in confusion.

He slowly regained his senses and composure as he watched Darrah ministering to her brother. Gradually he could feel the panicked cacophony of the children's life forces settle back down to a steady, reliable hum, the two of them returning to the kind of harmony shared by two people who have weathered together the same storms, year after year, and have grown to need and trust one another without thought or words.

Christoph watched them leave, then he went to the Wishing Well to pray some more. The exact rules of his hell were becoming clearer to him. The time for sharing with his grandchildren was over. Now he could only cause them pain. With that as his reality, there was no need for actual flames or pools of lava or the screams of the damned.

CHAPTER 7

Friday, April 6, 2007 – Northern New Jersey

While her children and husband roamed about the Enchanted Mill Forest, Ruth Barber-Hahn sat in her office at Garden State University. It was a quiet afternoon, with almost no one else around the faculty office building. Ruth stared at her computer screen, reading over the last paragraph she'd written. It was part of a good article on folklore and gender. A good article, but certainly not a great one. The various dots of Little Red Riding Hood could only be connected in so many ways, after all. Once the rape subtext behind the story was accepted—as it was now, universally—she could only fiddle around with the wolf's cross dressing, bring in some issues raised by scholars of disability, and look at the different versions of the story. All of which she'd ably done, even with some nice turns of phrase and trenchant remarks, citing the relevant literature and acknowledging the points of debate.

But it all seemed so pat now, a little stale and dull. It wasn't like in grad school, when she first realized she could solve these intellectual puzzles, look behind things, and unlock some secret code. She remembered the first time she'd presented a paper to a group of six people—two of them the other panelists for their meeting, and a third the moderator—in a freezing basement conference room in February; the experience was exhilarating, making her stammer and her heart race. Back then she could imagine herself uncovering new interpretations and meanings every day for the rest of her life, all to the adulation of awestruck students and the praise of admiring colleagues.

The reality was that since then, she had seen her name in refereed journals and on the covers of books, and it had barely registered as anything other than ticking off boxes on a list of goals that needed to be fulfilled. She'd gotten tenure years ago, when Nat was still a toddler, and now there didn't seem much point in making those discoveries that had once seemed so important and thrilling. She'd need a few more publications to apply for full professor this year or next, but the pissant raise that would entail hardly seemed worth the effort. And what of the expected adulation and praise? Mouth-breathing boredom and sniping jealousy were about the only reactions her accomplishments had ever gotten, as far as she had observed.

Ruth took her gaze from the computer screen to look out the window. The clouds had broken up a bit, and the sunlight made her blink and take a second to refocus her eyes. The grounds here were landscaped nicer than the more urban campuses around the New York metropolitan area, with a lot of flowering trees and bushes visible from her window. She hadn't noticed if the trees back at the Enchanted Mill Forest were as far along as those here.

She watched one of the all-black squirrels that she'd only seen on the campus here, and once on a trip to Toronto. The odd little animals not only had shiny, coal-black coats, they even had pointy ears, increasing their diabolical appearance. The one she was watching stopped on a branch to chatter at something as it flicked its tail wildly back and forth. Ruth scowled and decided she'd skip coming in to the office tomorrow. It now seemed preferable to putter around the house and the forest with the kids. The article wasn't going to get that much better by wasting another day on it, and she knew it was already publishable in its present form. Polish it up some on Monday and send it off; check off the box. In the meantime, she'd neglect her children and responsibilities at home a little less. For the only time she could remember, Ruth thought the devil-squirrel looked kind of cute.

A light knocking on the open door of her office made her turn. Peter Middleman stood in the doorway, his usual sheepish look on his boyish face. Ruth's heart filled with revulsion so quickly and so violently she feared she wouldn't be able to conceal it, though really she didn't give a shit if she did or not. To be sitting there and thinking of all the embarrassments and disappointments of the last fifteen years, and then have the purest, most sterling example of them appear, that was galling enough to induce a complete lack of giving a shit.

"How's it going?" he said quietly with his usual half-smile. She felt sick to think she'd once thought it attractive and charming. She'd since found out he did *everything* halfway. "I saw your door open, you know, and thought I'd say hi."

"Hm-hmm," she said. "Hi."

She sized him up without moving her eyes. He hadn't put on weight. He probably still worked out once in a while. *Something boring, like an exercise bike or a stairmaster,* she guessed, *not a real sport.* Sandy blonde hair, kept longer than most men his age, skin with a bit more color than hers, fashionably mod glasses that actually helped his face, since his eyes were a tad on the beady side. Not stupid or unattractive, but just so darned uninspired. And when you let a man mount you and hump you in your office a couple times a week for almost a year, you should at least find him inspiring in some small way.

That's not about morality, that's just having some self-respect. But no, not this one. He had that bitterest, most damning quality of extra-marital affairs—convenience.

"Working on something?" He took a half-step into her office. It had been seven years since she'd last spread her legs for him, but she knew he was like any other man. He'd never stop sniffing around the territory he'd marked, seeing if maybe he could lay down some fresh pheromones. Might as well watch the sun come up or the leaves change in the fall as observe men's behavior, all such phenomena were unalterable and utterly predictable—and after a while, so fucking dull.

This was what she had gotten herself into. The job market the way it was, and both of them now with tenure at Garden State, she'd probably have to put up with him the rest of her life, a constant reminder of how weak and stupid she was. And that was if he didn't try something really crazy. If he were ever passed over for a promotion or raise or honor, he could conceivably dredge up their affair and accuse her of sexual harassment; he was sneaky enough to twist everything around and claim he'd been the one to break it off, and now she was retaliating.

He was sneaky enough to do something, but Ruth was ninety-nine percent sure he didn't have the balls for much of anything. She knew this because today – like any of the couple hundred other times he'd come mooning around after she'd told him to go back to banging his wife – she could stop him in his tracks with a glare. She didn't need to say anything, or even frown or raise an eyebrow. The slightest intensification of her gaze, and he didn't move his back foot forward, but instead withdrew until he was again, half in and half out of her doorway.

She'd started the affair; she'd ended it. He couldn't do a damn thing without her permission. Ruth felt a little better when she saw him retreat, and she wondered for about the ten-thousandth time what it must be like to have real, physical gonads, since she was so damned tired of being a woman who seemed to have a bigger pair than the men around her.

"Yes." Her gaze didn't soften at all. "I was just about to go home."

"Oh, okay," he said as he took another step back. "Well, have a good weekend."

"I will."

Ruth remained staring at the doorway after Peter left. All of the shit she'd stirred up had happened when she'd gone back to work, after Nat was born. She thought giving birth and going back would feel good, and she'd be able to get lots of work done for her tenure application that year. Instead, she had just felt bad all the time. While she looked okay in clothes, she knew she was a fright when she was naked, with stretch marks and boobs leaking milk. She didn't let Ben near her, no matter what he said or did. She couldn't feel right anywhere. If she were at home, she felt like she should be in the office working. If she were in the office or classroom, she felt guilty and wanted to go home to see the baby. She'd never been a big one for tears, but in those first months she felt like crying all the time.

And then there was a not-unattractive man at work, a man who complimented her on her writing and her looks all the time, one who dropped unsubtle hints that his own home life was not what it should be. The whole thing was just so darned easy. Hell, she could even leave most of her clothes on during it, and avoid that embarrassment.

It wasn't that the sex hadn't been good. Definitely not. It hadn't been good because of anything particular to him - or her, for that matter; it had been so good because she could close her eyes and get all heated up over the naughtiness of it. She could even protract that naughty feeling by wearing sexy underwear, which necessitated clandestine trips to Victoria's Secret in the Palisades, thereby further augmenting the delightful wickedness.

And all of it - the sex, the lingerie, the shopping, the sneaking around - all of it when and if she felt like it. On her terms.

That was the real intoxicant and addiction. All of it had been so pleasurable and liberating because for the only moments in her hectic, overwhelming life, no one was making any important or difficult demands on her, For a few minutes, no one wanted anything from her except what was between her legs, and it was easy and not unpleasant to make that available.

Ruth looked at the picture of Darrah and Nat from those bad, old days, when neither her family nor her affair satisfied her. It was up on a shelf now. She'd moved it there after it had fallen off her desk. Her butt had pushed it off one time when Peter was doing her with a bit more enthusiasm than usual. She frowned as she thought how, if her life were a novel, she would've broken off the affair when the glass shattered in the frame. Indeed, in the film version, the scene would've unfolded in slow motion, perhaps with a single tear hanging on her cheek after the symbolic event.

Instead, they'd finished fucking, she'd pulled up her Victoria's Secret French-cut bikinis, then she'd very calmly discarded the shards of glass and moved the picture to a safer location.

No, life wasn't propelled by such huge, weighty gestures, but it chugged along much more gradually and consistently. Little by little, Ruth had looked at herself with increasing disgust, at Peter with disinterest, and at Ben and her children with tinges of pity, regret, and even some longing. Then it was time to change, months after the picture had lost its glass covering.

In the picture, Nat was about nine months old. Darrah was holding him on her hip and giving her usual big, goofy smile. Ruth wondered, as she often did, if she loved them the "right" way. She hated listening to other people gush about their children. *God, what sickening, unbelievable bunches of bullshit people flung around.* Like anyone's going to admit they've had one less-than-ideal feeling about their kids, one moment of regret or disappointment. She had managed such confessions, but only to herself, in private, and they still hurt.

She knew Darrah looked far too much like Ben for her ever to feel totally comfortable or satisfied with the girl. Big and oafish, Darrah had never liked anything girly—and for all her ambition and assertiveness, Ruth had always kept herself pretty and feminine, disdaining women with other tastes and habits. She never understood women her own age who had all their hair shorn; hers wasn't as long as it had been in college, but she kept it down to her shoulders even now. Peter had always said how beautiful her hair was, and Ben used to as well. Not everything men said in order to get in your pants was a lie.

She wore a skirt most days, and her legs were still decent. Darrah's hair was short, and she was always in jeans and t-shirts. It was a flattering but not entirely welcome thought to Ruth that, even in a few years, with her daughter in college, she would probably turn more heads than Darrah would. The girl was an enigma to her mother, though Ruth was grateful to her for all her help with Nat. But being grateful just didn't feel as satisfying or natural as liking her daughter, and it filled Ruth with doubt and anxiety.

Nat was definitely preferable in some ways. You could really see the kid being an author or artist someday. *Wouldn't that be something— but my God, along the way it sure hasn't been much fun.* The kid had been hell on wheels since he was born. Worse temper than his father with less self-control, and his health problems threw Ruth into depressions almost as bad as when he was first born.

Like everything else in her life—career, marriage, affair—her children had not turned out to Ruth's expectations. If she could banish Peter to the far ends of the galaxy, she would. The same for Garden State University and all the bullshit of the MLA. She'd have a bit more pause about consigning Ben to the outer darkness, only because her thoughts of him were wrapped up so closely with their children, but she knew that most of the time, he just pissed her off, too.

As much as they upset her, Darrah and Nat weren't like that. She didn't like them, exactly, but that was about as meaningful as saying she didn't like her left lung or her liver. It wasn't a matter of liking it—it was a part of her and she couldn't live a complete life without it. She still didn't know if that was enough, or if it were the "right" way to be, but she knew it was the feeling that had overwhelmed and defined her since she'd given birth to those two.

Outside the window, the black squirrel had stopped twitching its tail, and now sat on a branch nearer to Ruth's office. She stared at its obsidian-shiny eyes a moment before she sighed and turned to leave.

CHAPTER 8

Monday, September 11, 1944 – Darmstadt, Germany

It had been a good day at school for Christoph—one of those days when the lessons seem easy, the play at lunchtime is free of shoving and tussles, and the teachers seem not so intent on being difficult or punishing the children.

After school on that warm autumn afternoon, Greta even wanted to play outside with him. She didn't play with him very much lately, preferring dolls to climbing trees or digging trenches in the dirt with sticks. Christoph was still young enough that he didn't totally disapprove of helping her play house or post office or tea party, but he thought she needed to compromise more than she did. She needed to play boy things sometimes, and she was getting far less agreeable about that. But today she had cooperated, and Christoph had gone inside to dinner in high spirits.

After dinner, Greta had also helped her brother by reminding him to pick his animal for the night. She needn't have bothered, as he would never forget something so important, but it was still nice of her to show concern. Since the war began, the tradition in the Hahn household was that every night Christoph would pick one stuffed animal and Greta would pick one doll, and those chosen would be put in the knapsack by the door. It was a cold, dark, and dirty spot, and when Christoph was very small, he'd thought how the animal must not like being crammed into the canvas bag and shut in.

Now that he was big, he understood the importance of this choice, and was sure the animal would know and appreciate it for the honor it was. The bag was the one thing their father would snatch on the way out the door during an air raid call. If their building were blown to bits, and they were lucky enough to get out in time, the things in that bag would be the only ones that would survive the bombing. Besides the two items the children chose each night, it contained mostly practical, grown-up things—wads of cash, mother's more valuable jewelry, a small packet of family photos, and some warm clothes. Making the choice was about the most important thing Christoph did each day.

Greta was less careful about the nightly choice than her brother. She would give some dolls more turns in the bag than others, sometimes she'd even put the same one in the bag two nights in a row. Christoph could not understand such haphazard, irresponsible behavior. He was always sure to have a plan and follow it precisely, especially about something important like this. One did not take lightly the choice of who was given a chance to live and who was marked for possible death. His animals were on a strict rotation, so that they each got the same number of nights in the bag, and always in the same order. He had always done his job with care and pride.

Tonight was turtle's turn, because it had been beaver's turn last night, and Christoph had made sure the two animals that lived in the water got their turns on adjacent nights. After that, the land animals would have their turns in descending order of their size—bear, rabbit, and mouse. Then the rotation would start over, since he did not have that many animals, or toys in general, for that matter.

He went to his room and got turtle, looking over its pale green fur and the glass beads it had for eyes. The stuffed representation was supposed to be a sea turtle, the kind with flippers instead of feet. Christoph had never seen a real one. He thought they lived on beaches in very warm places, and he wished he could go to a place like that someday. He thought it would be nice to go somewhere different, exotic, with palm trees and strange birds. Maybe there'd even be a volcano there, if he went to a tropical island like the one he imagined. He could almost conceive of keeping turtle out of the bag tonight, to sleep with him and remind him of the beautiful, strange sights of the tropics, but he knew that would be wrong and irresponsible, so he walked to the entryway, to put the stuffed animal in its rightful place.

Greta was standing by the bag, putting a doll in. She had chosen a boy doll, one of only two in her collection. She had more dolls and toys than Christoph, but she was older, and a girl besides, and he understood how she needed more stuff. He was fairly sure her boy dolls went in the bag more often, because Greta preferred the girl dolls and wanted to sleep with them or play with them right before bed. She didn't seem to take the choice or the air raids seriously enough.

Greta wrinkled her nose at him. If she'd been more cooperative and helpful earlier in the day, Christoph now saw her more usual, teasing, petulant side. "A turtle?" she said. "I never saw you put a turtle in the bag. Stuffed animals should be warm, furry, cute animals. Not a turtle."

"Animals don't have to be cute," Christoph responded, feeling himself blush. "And besides, he is. And I put him in the bag the same amount as the others. Always."

She scowled as Christoph retrieved beaver from the bag and put in turtle. "I don't think you do. I think you just feel guilty tonight so you're putting him in. But really you don't like him. I know I don't."

"Stop it! I do too! They all get a turn. You're the one who doesn't put your dolls in the bag in the right order. You keep out the ones you like, and you put in the ones you don't like! I've seen you!"

She stuck out her tongue at him. "Well, I'm putting in this silly boy doll tonight, right next to your silly turtle, so we're even."

Four hours later, Christoph was running down the street, clutching his father's big hand. The boy's jacket was draped over his pajamas, and his boots were pulled on without being tied, so he kind of hobbled and bobbed along, struggling to keep up. The air raid sirens whined above the heavy thumping of the anti-aircraft batteries, as all around them their neighbors scurried toward the shelter. There were no screams or panic, just a steady rush of disheveled, confused, and frightened people.

Christoph looked behind his father's back and saw the knapsack on his other shoulder, and beyond that, his mother pulling his sister along.

They didn't have far to go—the basement of the church across the street was the designated shelter for their block—so he didn't feel particularly scared.

He looked over his shoulder, back at their building, at exactly the moment that a four-thousand pound bomb hit the roof of a taller apartment building nearby. If the bomb had been one of the regular ordinance that the RAF used, many on the street that night would have died instantly, either buried under the falling walls after the bomb tore deep into the interior of the building and exploded, or else shredded by the shrapnel from the metal casing of the bomb itself.

This bomb, however, was designed to go off on the roof and not penetrate the floors; it was also made with an exceptionally thin metal skin, so there was almost no shrapnel. It had been built this way to blow the roofs off all the surrounding structures, so that the tiny incendiary bombs that were falling a few seconds behind it could ignite inside the buildings and cause a much worse conflagration that could not be fought by the fire crews.

The enormous shock wave did just what it was designed to do, and it also knocked all the fleeing people off their feet, slamming their faces, elbows, and knees into the pavement. Although the giant bomb did not rain down as much deadly debris as might've been expected, it did send one chunk of roof tile flying into the right side of Greta's head. The girl could only groan from the impact, though her mother let out a scream when she saw the blood gushing down the side of her daughter's face.

Christoph felt his father's hand yanked from his and saw him run to Greta. As the variously injured people in the crowd rose, real panic set in, and he felt himself shoved aside as people rushed between him and his family. He could see his father scoop Greta up and resume his run for the shelter. Christoph's mother took a step with him, still touching her daughter's face, and for a terrified moment, the boy thought he'd be left alone on the street, trampled by the crowds before more bombs fell to finish him off. It was only the briefest moment, thankfully, as his mother almost immediately turned back, lunged through the press of people, and grabbed his shoulder, pushing him after the rest of the family and toward the relative safety of the church.

They spent the night huddled in the church basement. The explosions stopped right after they arrived there, but through the narrow basement windows, Christoph saw the flames dancing all night. Greta was pressed between his weeping parents, while he leaned against the knapsack, slightly apart from them. The heat in the basement continued to increase, until he was quite sure they would all die there, baked as though they were in a black oven. He wished they had died outside where at least it was cool and the sky was clear and starry above them.

Eventually, long after dawn, the heat began to decrease. The wailing and prayers within the basement also subsided; the people just sitting there in shocked silence, punctuated by an occasional cough or moan. The place was foul with blood, sweat, and smoke, like nothing Christoph had ever imagined. Finally, someone opened the basement door and they emerged to their smoldering, burned-out neighborhood, where nothing remained of the buildings but the exterior walls.

The four-thousand pound bomb that had sent a piece of masonry smashing into Greta Hahn's head was of a type nicknamed "cookies" by the RAF crews, and the Hahns had just been subjected to a process the Allies called de-housing.

Greta did not die right away. In the weeks that followed, she suffered constantly from headaches and couldn't keep her balance. Then, while they were living in a barn outside of the city, she caught cold and died. After that, Christoph always had the nagging feeling that his parents were made more miserable by the fact that it was their daughter rather than their son who had been killed in the War. Nothing direct was ever said, of course, but it was something in how they looked at him a little quizzically, as though wondering, "Why you?"

He also heard it in how they spoke of his dead sister. They often mentioned her in some way that seemed to Christoph to betray a preference—how beautiful her blonde hair was or blue eyes or fair skin, for example, when the boy had black hair, brown eyes, and a darker complexion. He never heard anything as overt as blame or regret, but ever after, he felt only a dull ache and anguished disappointment emanating from his parents toward him. It was a wound to Christoph that was no less painful and real just because it was illogical and unverifiable.

Christoph never saw a sea turtle, except on the television after he moved to the United States, and he never went to the tropics.

But he did vow that night and every night thereafter to leave Germany.

CHAPTER 9

Friday, April 6, 2007 – The Sublunar Sphere

Christoph was at the Wishing Well for what seemed a long time that afternoon. He did not think it seemed like long enough, however, for all the evil he had done. There were all sorts of things people were guilty of—sinful urges of the flesh and deceits of the mind he could barely comprehend. Theoretically, he knew, God could forgive any of them, if the person just repented. He understood, too, how it required only the smallest sign of repentance, like the good thief on the cross. It certainly did not require separate, often bizarre acts of penance, as the papists taught.

That would be like saying the sinner could somehow make up for what he had done, when Christoph knew that one could only throw oneself on the mercy of God and trust in His grace. Yet as much as he remembered these things, when confronted with the reality that he had just hurt his grandson, all he wanted to do was punish himself for what he had done. Hurting one's own family—that was more monstrous and unforgivable than anything else he could imagine. At that moment, the idea of God being infinitely forgiving and merciful was not a comfort to Christoph, because he wanted to be punished and chastened, he wanted to feel pain like he had made his strange but wholly innocent grandson feel.

When he first began to pray that afternoon, he had thought perhaps the fact of his hurting the boy unintentionally would mitigate his feelings of guilt. It wasn't as though he had directed some ill thought or feeling toward the children. That would surely have made him more culpable. But what had happened was the fault of this horrible place, with its backwards, unknowable rules. He didn't know—he couldn't know—that thoughts and desires for nice things would manifest themselves as physical injury to the children. If he had known that was how this place worked, he wouldn't have gone near them or wished they had gingerbread.

The excuse-making only intensified his self-loathing and desire for his own punishment, even his own extinction. This place was where God had put him. That was about the only thing of which he was now certain. So he could never, ever blame this place for what he himself did. It was God's will that he be here, and Christoph would not let himself add blasphemy against God to all his other crimes, for Jesus had said that was the one sin that could never be forgiven. God knew what was best for all His creatures, even those bound for hell; He knew their rightful place and they could no more go to a different place than water could flow uphill.

So Christoph belonged here because of what he had done and what he had become, and that was what made the realization so awful and final. He now knew he had become a monster, more a citizen of hell than of earth, and anything he tried to help or fix would be destroyed and sickened, not by his intent or purpose, but just by his very presence. His existence was now a curse to others as well as to himself.

And because all this was God's judgment, and God had even graciously seen fit to inform Christoph of this decision, all he could do was thank God for his present existence, cursed and damned though it may be.

Christoph finally left the Wishing Well when he felt another presence in the park. The Enchanted Mill Forest wasn't open for the season yet, so it couldn't be any legitimate visitor. It didn't seem to be night yet, so it probably wasn't any of the hedonistic teenagers, either. Besides, this didn't feel like the energy given off by a living person, and Christoph now wondered what else he was able to detect.

While it seemed part of neither penance nor gratitude for him to patrol his former home, he had the same protective feelings of ownership and responsibility that he had had in life, so he moved toward the presence to investigate.

As Christoph passed the Three Little Pigs, the feeling of someone else nearby grew stronger, though it still lacked that urgency and edge of the fully alive; this was more like a warm glow than the flare and buzz he felt from his grandchildren. He glanced at the carefully arranged remnants of the straw house and the house of sticks as he moved past. Years and years ago, they'd had real pigs in an enclosure there, but now it was just paved over, with the bits of the houses sticking out of the macadam. There had been several displays of small animals in the Enchanted Mill Forest when he'd first worked there—Billy Goat Gruff and the Goose that Laid the Golden Egg and the White Rabbit from Alice in Wonderland—but the zoning laws had changed, forbidding livestock within the village limits.

Christoph still felt proud that at least a few city children had seen some real animals before he'd been forced to get rid of them. The pigs were usually the children's favorite, they were much cleaner and more playful than most people thought. The rabbits were actually the nastiest and dirtiest of the lot, he thought, and tended to bite tiny fingers stuck through the chicken wire, so he had gotten rid of them with the rest, even though the law had not declared them livestock. He didn't miss the rabbits, but he wished the pigs and goats were still there. They helped bring the place alive.

He neared the brick house of the third, wise Little Pig and felt that something was definitely making that structure seem more alive than it had in his previous wanderings of the park. The entity, whatever it was, must be inside there.

Christoph entered the house; it had been a very tiny room before, with the four foot high ceiling of most of the buildings. There was just enough room for people to file past the black cauldron—the wolf's feet dangling from the chimney above it while the smiling pig stood next to it. Inside, protected from the elements, it was the last of the displays that still had a working sound system, which would tell the ending of the story and play a happy jig that would end with the pig's triumphal laughter and the metallic clang of the lid being slammed down.

As he entered the brick house now, everything was different about it. Its usual furnishings were more shadowy than the other physical objects Christoph had encountered since his death. They were barely visible to him now, but almost looked like sculptures made of smoke. The interior of the brick house seemed to open up into a much more spacious and solid room than it had in "real" life.

In the center of this new, large room there was a fire burning in a brazier set into the floor. It created no smoke, but Christoph could feel something like heat emanating from it. Not so much a physical warmth, but a kind of calm and confidence, a sense that this was a place where one belonged, a place it was good to occupy. The feeling was not as invigorating as the life force of his grandchildren, but neither was it as demanding and overwhelming. All around the fire, the room was full of the kind of sleek and modern furniture that had been in vogue when his son was born—Barcelona and Eames chairs, delicate cherry-wood tables, metal and glass and plastic lamps in strange, industrial shapes that looked like they had been taken from a space ship.

It took Christoph some time to figure out where he had seen such a collection before, but then he remembered trips to the Museum of Modern Art with his wife. So many years ago, he hadn't thought of it in ages. He'd been able to appreciate such things for the craftsmanship and design that went into them, for their symmetry and balance, but he would not have considered them pretty. He went for her sake, since she preferred the MoMA to the Metropolitan, though of course she'd go there when he wanted, too.

Those were such happy times. He remembered that back then, Central Park wasn't so crowded that two young people couldn't sneak off to find a place to kiss, another thing he hadn't thought of in years. It was one of the few nice thoughts he'd had since he died, and although he found the scene mystifying, he welcomed its beauty and forgotten familiarity.

Around these furnishings, the floor, ceiling, and walls were stark white, and gave off a soothing brightness like Christoph had not experienced since coming to this grey, featureless place. There were no decorations or windows on the walls, except for a metal hatch in the wall opposite him. That seemed to be composed of iron that had thoroughly rusted to a shade far darker than was possible in the normal world. Some sort of thick sludge oozed from the seams around it, seeping down in rivulets that looked like black hair or moss growing down the wall. At least the dark excretion didn't form a puddle on the floor nor run across it, but just seemed to disappear into a crack between floor and wall. He shivered at the sight of the vague horror on the opposite wall—the same physical reaction he'd had whenever he felt himself in the presence of a new and awful, accusatory revelation in this place.

Most surprising of all, however, was the other occupant of the room, for she was neither beautiful nor familiar. On one of the modern chairs sat a young girl, dressed in furs and skins. She had her legs folded under her, with each bare foot tucked under the opposite knee. She looked to be not much taller than Nat, but older and stouter than he, perhaps ten or eleven. She had a broad face with very dark brown skin, and long, straight black hair. She appeared more gnomish and mysterious than pretty and welcoming. The girl's form was still that of a child, but something about her gave off a weary calmness that few men Christoph's age achieved, or even that they would necessarily want to. Perhaps death did that to people. She looked at him the way one would inspect something fragile and broken, that one did not wish to ruin further.

"Hello, sir," she said. Her voice had the pitch of a girl's, but with some weight and inertia to it. She gazed at him steadily and looked unsure as to whether or not he would reply.

"Hello," Christoph said. "You speak English?"

The girl considered the question. "No, not really. I don't know how I can speak to the other people I meet here. Sometimes I can't. Sometimes they don't seem to know I'm even here. But if they do know I'm present and they try to speak to me, then somehow we understand each other. It's strange."

Christoph understood how strange this place was, and her description matched up with his experience with Oswald. "Have you been here long?"

The girl considered the question again. "Do you mean, have I been dead for very long?"

He liked her precision. "Well, yes."

"I died a very long time ago. I don't even know how to say how long it's been. I can go for a very long time without meeting anyone, and when I do, I often stay and speak with them for days. And I have met thousands of people, it seems like, since I died. So it must be a very long time."

"You are an Indian?" Though he didn't think it'd make a difference to a spirit who'd died hundreds or thousands of years ago, Christoph remembered he wasn't supposed to call them that. "A Native American?"

"Well, we didn't call ourselves that, but that seems to be how you think of the people I lived with on Earth. From what I have heard from others I've met since then, we lived in this area before the people you call Indians, and before other people like you came here from other lands. Someone told me they would've called us cavemen and that sounded funny. We didn't live in caves. Sometimes we'd go down in them in the summer, because they were cool in the heat, and we'd store things there, but we never lived in them."

"And who are you, miss?"

This question again caused her to pause and consider. "Who am I? Do you mean, what is my name?"

"Well, yes."

"When I was alive in the physical world, people called me Quekulukquihill-hinotitch. But I don't think that is a name you are used to."

"No, no it isn't. I'm afraid I wouldn't know how to say it right, and I don't want to offend you."

She smiled more broadly this time, enough to see her top teeth. "Oh, don't worry about that, for it doesn't much matter now. That *was* my name, in the past. In this place, I still don't know if we have names, or if one day we will get new ones. I hope so. My old name would've meant something like *lame bird* in your language. When I was very young, I slipped into a deep ravine, and I always limped after that, so that's what they called me." She stood up and slid her right foot along the inside of her left leg till it was by her knee, then extended it forward, pointing the toes forward like a ballerina would. She sat back down. "But now—I'm not lame! So perhaps I'll get a new name, though I don't know who'll give it to me."

"Well, I should have something to call you. Shall we pick something?"

Again, she considered before answering. "Yes, that would be fine, I think. You go ahead and choose one you can say properly."

Now it was Christoph's turn to pause and consider. One doesn't go around naming people every day, so it was unfamiliar, and felt a bit presumptuous and dangerous. He tried to think of any names that meant something like bird, but "Robin" was the only one he could come up with, and it seemed so dull and American. As he looked around at the furnishings in the room, he thought again of his wife, and he remembered the name they had picked for their child, if it had been a girl. It was another thing he hadn't thought of in years, but he thought he remembered his wife saying the name meant some kind of bird in her native language, French.

"Would 'Merla' be all right?" he said finally.

The girl tried it out a couple times. The *r* and *l* right next to each other seemed to give her trouble, but Christoph knew that he had never said his *r*'s right, either—at least according to his wife. He remembered how they both used to laugh at how Americans spoke, and that would lead to them playfully teasing each other. They would each say words in German or French the other couldn't pronounce, making funny faces and breaking down with laughter.

"You people make such strange sounds, but that name will do, I think," she said finally. "And your name, sir?"

Part of him wanted to tell her Mr. Hahn, as that's what he'd usually be called by a child her age. But then, she was really hundreds or thousands of years old, apparently, so that didn't exactly make sense, either. He remembered hearing somewhere that you don't get any older than dead, and now that seemed to make more sense to him. "My name is Christoph."

She had less trouble pronouncing that than she had had with her own new name. "Well, Christoph, I am very happy to meet you."

"I'm happy to meet you, Merla, but what are we doing here? Why have you come here, right at this time?"

Another pause, this time Merla stared into the fire before answering. "That is almost as mysterious to me as how I can talk with other people here. Whenever I meet someone in this strange place, I meet them by a hearth." She gestured to the non-physical flames between them. "When I have spoken with each of them, they told me they had not seen a hearth since dying. This is true for you, I assume?"

"Yes, that is true. I have been cold and alone, and this seems better, more sheltering and comforting to me."

Merla nodded. "I am glad. That seems to be the first thing I provide. I make different people feel at home in this place, when previously they had wandered, unattached, despairing. Beyond that, it seems different for each person. I have listened, sang, and talked to people. It seems as though I've played every game and musical instrument man has invented. Sometimes I've braided women's hair, even though they no longer need to attract a mate, or I've helped men find a deep stream where giant trout lie, even though they can no longer catch and eat them. Each has felt better and happier with something different."

He appreciated her efforts, but it still didn't seem right. "I don't know how I can feel at home in hell, Merla."

"Yes, I have heard other people use that word. I still don't completely understand it. It makes no sense to me. But I know this place is not what you call hell. Whatever this place is, all the people I have met have moved on from it to somewhere else. Whether they have gone to the place you call hell, or the place you call heaven, or to something completely different, I cannot say. But this is not a place where people suffer forever—of that I am sure."

He stared at her tiny, but sturdy frame. Oddly, his first reaction to her description was not hope for himself, but confusion and fear for her. "But what about you, then, if you don't leave?"

Her smile this time was wan—not pained, exactly, but bemused, even resigned. "Oh, I have wondered that, and I have no answer. I can only do for each person as they arrive. I have not yet met the person who will help me to move on." Her smile broadened. "Perhaps it will be you. That is always a funny thought I have whenever I meet a new person—that they will be the one to help me. And even if they are not, I enjoy each of them and the things we do together. There is no suffering here, really, except what we do to the living and what they do to us."

Christoph suddenly felt cold again, as he remembered his grandchildren. "Do you know about that?"

Merla sat back and her eyes widened. "Know about what? I don't understand."

"I—I hurt my grandson right before I met you. I thought that's what you were referring to."

"Ah, I am sorry. But perhaps his pain is what called me to you, Christoph, and now you can learn to be more careful. You are barely a part of the physical world anymore. You have only the tiniest hold on it—air and smoke and vapors are almost in your grasp, but anything more solid will fall through your fingers, or you will pass through it, as if you existed in two separate worlds. Your thoughts and feelings, however, are much more penetrating and powerful than when you were alive, especially to the people you knew and loved.

"No one knows me anymore. The thoughts of anyone alive today cannot touch me, nor can mine touch them. But your thoughts and emotions can harm your family, so you must always be on your guard. You can't stop feeling, I know... but you must discipline yourself. And likewise, your family's feelings—which you could've ignored in your physical life—will now crash into you like an avalanche."

Merla gestured to one of the other chairs. "But for now, sit. In this place, you needn't always be doing something, and sometimes it is best just to sit and rest and think."

"Do you mind if I pray?" he asked, as he sat down.

"Of course not. That is an excellent thing to do here. Thank you for reminding me."

Merla put her hands on her knees, closed her eyes, and leaned her head back. Christoph assumed that was her posture for prayer, but he took up his more usual position of leaning forward with his elbows on his knees and his hands clasped in front of his forehead.

As he cleared his mind, he couldn't help but think how strange it was to be here, praying with this little pagan. God only knew what spirit or devil she prayed to, but she clearly knew the rules here better than he did, so he had to be grateful for her help and would try to overlook their differences. There was also no denying that her presence filled him with a sense of calm and belongingness, so that he could pray with a hope and confidence he had not felt for many years, even before he died.

CHAPTER 10

Friday, April 6, 2007 – Northern New Jersey

Darrah stabbed at the penne boiling in the pot. Satisfied they were done, she drained off some of the water, but made sure to leave some in the pot with the pasta. That way, when she added the can of chickarina soup to the noodles, there'd be enough for both her and Nat.

Sometimes she wanted to go with the other kids to the convenience store on Route 23 and just buy junk food and eat it, even though it was overpriced and not nutritious, or go with them to the Palisades and buy something other than practical clothes for school. Hell, maybe even something girly like mom liked.

Sometimes she wanted those things, but not too often.

Darrah let the soup heat through for a minute. She could hear the laundry tumbling around in the dryer in the basement, and she felt good about everything she'd accomplished that afternoon— mountain climbed, nosebleed stanched, laundry done, lunch made. She poured the soup into two bowls and set one in front of Nat, who was already at the kitchen table, looking at a Lego catalog that had come in the mail.

"Thanks," he said, plunging his spoon into the soup. He sounded all clogged up now. Their mother would hear that when she got home, and Darrah could do without the drama.

"You're welcome," she said as she sat down across from him. "How you feeling?"

He sniffed once. "Okay. It gets all dried and stuffed after and I can't breathe, but it doesn't hurt."

"Yeah. I'll boil some water with that minty junk in it and you can breathe the steam in, okay? That way you'll be unclogged when mom gets home."

"What about dad? He must be around somewhere."

"Yeah, but he doesn't get all weird when your nose bleeds."

"Yeah."

Darrah could tell he was a little embarrassed about the nosebleed, but he wasn't getting too wound up about it.

"Don't worry, Natty-Bo, I'll take care of it." She pointed to the catalog with her spoon. "Anything good in there?"

"I still think the Viking sets are the coolest, but kids at school talk about the new Star Wars ones."

Darrah had heard her parents talking several times, late at night, about how expensive the newest sets were. She remembered how excited her mother had sounded when she talked about finding one really big set—the kind that went for a hundred dollars when it first came out—on clearance at the Palisades. She even saw her dad kiss her mom, and her mom looked kind of pleased at the gesture. Days later, Darrah had seen the big plastic bag hidden on the top shelf of the hall closet and she'd peeked inside. It was one of the sets from the discontinued Dino Attack series.

"I hear the dinosaur ones are cool," she offered.

"Yeah? I dunno. They don't make those anymore. Some of the dinosaurs didn't look that good. But a lot of the vehicles had guns that shot real missiles and bullets, so that was cool. Maybe you're right."

Darrah finished her soup a spoonful after Nat, and put their dishes in the sink before she started washing out the pot. "Go get the mint stuff," she said to her brother. "You know—it's in the downstairs bathroom medicine cabinet."

As Nat went to get the eucalyptus oil, Darrah filled the pot with water again and put it back on to boil. She stood by the stove as she waited, enjoying the heat from the gas flame. It was pretty chilly in the house—more money-saving measures—but Darrah knew not to turn up the thermostat. She'd heard the heat running earlier, so they probably hadn't run out of heating oil, which was a good thing.

An unexpected bill for over a thousand dollars would cause more consternation and fights and accusations in the home.

Nat returned with the little brown bottle. He handed it to his sister, as she made room for him by the stove. "Come on, Nat, stand by the fire. It feels nice."

She glanced at him as they stood close to each other and waited for the water to boil. Darrah knew her brother could be a handful, but really, he didn't get as mad or disappointed as people seemed to think. People just blamed him more for it, and then they acted all weird around him, like he was a ticking bomb. You just had to be playful with him, mostly. It was usually kind of fun.

The phone rang, and Nat moved, grabbing it before Darrah could. He made a face as he handed it to her. "It's your boyfriend," he said, cackling.

Darrah stuck her tongue out at her brother as she took the receiver. "Hello?"

"Hi Darrah," said a male voice from the phone, faint and slightly static-y. The phone was older than Nat, and had to be the last one in the tri-state area that wasn't cordless. And never mind asking for a cell phone.

It was Cory, a boy from school, nearly as big, awkward, and shy as Darrah. They'd do stuff together—movies, bowling, the mall. Sometime just walks. He liked to kiss a lot, and a few minutes of that was a welcome change for her as well. So far he hadn't been too pushy about doing more than kissing, and that was nice, too.

"Hi," she said. Hearing him made her feel happy and safe, but she hated how her voice would get higher and more bubbly when she talked to him, like she was weak or stupid. She'd even run her fingers through her hair as she spoke, which she'd never do any other time. "What's up?"

"Oh, nothing," Cory replied. "I can't do anything tonight." Darrah knew he played *Magic: The Gathering* and *Guitar Hero* at his friend's house almost every Friday. "But I just wondered if you wanted to, you know, take a walk or something this afternoon."

She was quite sure that "something" involved kissing, but she liked that nearly as much as he did, so she didn't mind the implication. She liked it enough, in fact, that for a moment she even thought of leaving Nat alone and sneaking off. He was inside. He had lots of toys and books. He'd probably be fine.

She sighed. With a nosebleed as bad as he'd had, she couldn't leave him alone right now. It wouldn't be fair to him. *Dad would lose it, too, if he comes home and finds Nat alone. Besides, I'll have to get the laundry out later and put it away before Mom spots it.* There was no way to risk it.

"No, I can't," she said. "I have to watch my twerpy brother." Darrah wrinkled her nose at Nat as she said this. He scowled back at her, but when she smiled, so did he.

"Oh. Okay," Cory said. Poor kid sounded like he'd been told he had cancer in an especially bad part of the body.

Darrah was smart enough, and just vain enough, to know that most of the disappointment in his voice was because he wouldn't be kissing her this afternoon. She was also realistic enough to know that a tall, skinny boy with acne who played the trombone wouldn't give up too quickly on the possibility of kissing some other time, even if it meant having some patience. Persistence was a good thing, and it made her feel good, too—in a different way than the kissing, of course. But, oh—the combination of making him wait and keep asking, and then finally getting to the kissing part? Now that was something really worthwhile. She thought sometimes he'd cut her upper lip, he'd mash his mouth into hers so hard at times like that. It was glorious.

"Maybe tomorrow?" he added. His voice got a little higher, too—that pleading tone of his.

"Yeah. Call me tomorrow afternoon, about the same time."

"Okay." There was a short pause. "Love you."

Unlike her altered voice, Darrah didn't dislike the little giggle she gave at times like this. It felt good to have a girly gesture at something secret, intimate, and pleasant. "Me too."

He didn't sound disappointed now, but more hurt and pouty. "Can't say it?"

More giggle. "I told you, silly, twerpy is here." Nat bopped her shoulder, and Darrah gave him a shove. She laughed louder.

"Okay. My little sister is crawling around here somewhere, too. I'll call you tomorrow."

"Okay. Bye."

Darrah put the phone back and returned to the boiling water.

"How's lover-boy?" Nat teased.

"He's fine, Mr. Uber Duber. Not that it's any of your stinky bees-wax."

"Hey, that's what Opa would call me. You can't." They had always called their strange, reserved grandfather by the German nickname *Opa*. Nat gave a pouty face, but Darrah could tell he was still playing and wasn't getting seriously angry.

She held the little brown bottle over the pot. "All right, enough about the Indian guide's lover, and enough about Uber Duber Land. How much of the ancient, Indian herbal medicine do you require, oh great, white explorer?" she asked, smiling.

"I dunno. What's today?"

"Friday."

"No, I mean the number."

"Oh." Darrah had to think for a second. "The sixth. You want six drops?"

"Make it seven. One for luck."

"Good number!" Together they counted out the seven drops as the room filled with the pungent, medicinal scent.

Darrah turned the flame as low as it would go and stepped back. "Okay, you breathe that in, Natty-Bo. It's supposed to give you a nice complexion, too."

Nat took a deep breath and Darrah went to the sink to do the rest of their dishes and utensils. "That's for girls," he said, coughing from breathing in too much of the steam.

"Yeah, yeah. I know, but don't knock it. It's good for you."

As Darrah washed the dishes she could hear her brother taking in the vapors. When she was done, she walked over to him and was satisfied his breathing sounded clear. She turned the stove off and dumped the water down the drain. "Hey, open the kitchen door a sec," she said to Nat as she rinsed out the pot.

The boy opened the side door and stood there with the cold air rushing by him. "Why? It's cold out."

"I know, I know, just for a sec. We should let the smell clear out some, so Mom won't smell it when she gets home."

"Yeah, good idea."

She put the pot on the rack and hung the dishtowel on the handle of the oven door. "Now, let's go play Legos," she said as she walked over to her brother and closed the outside door.

He followed her out to the living room where his blue, plastic bin of Legos lay. "But you're a girl."

She snorted as she sat cross-legged next to the bin and tipped it over, sending blocks cascading out on to the old carpet. "So you keep telling me, Mr. Uber Duber."

"Hey—I told you to stop calling me that!"

"Okay, but stop reminding me I'm a girl. I'm not too likely to forget, you know." Darrah smiled at her brother, and gradually he relented and smiled back. Whether or not it could be characterized as goofy, she really did have the most infectious grin. "So let's build something, unless you want to go back to Uber Duber Land."

When she was very young, she'd heard her grandfather use Uber Duber as an exclamation, and she'd found the sound of it so amusing, she kept repeating it, enough so that it had caught on in the family as just a funny nickname for one another. She'd since found out the Uber Duber nickname was a little insulting—not quite all the way to calling someone a Polack, but headed in that direction.

Nat tore into the pile of rainbow-colored blocks and started arranging them by size and hue. Darrah grabbed a random handful and clicked them around in her hand like dice. "What're we building?" she asked.

"Let's build a tower. A big one. I haven't done that in a long time."

"Sounds good to me, Natty-Bo."

They started building, occasionally distracted by other interesting pieces, like wheels and axles, and one or the other would stop to build a little vehicle that would drive around the base of the building.

"Just like New York City," Darrah said as she added to the tower.

"Yeah. It reminds me of when we went there with Opa. I could tell he liked it there. I thought that was funny, 'cause he didn't usually like crowds and stuff. He'd never go to the Palisades with us, but he liked it when we'd go to New York City."

"People are funny, especially old people. He must've remembered something there that made him happy. I bet when he first moved here, the Palisades was probably just a big empty field, so he didn't like it being all different than he remembered."

"I guess. He was funny."

Nat needed a piece that was too far away for him to reach, and he stood up so that he could take a step toward it. Before he could move forward, he staggered and fell down. "Fuck!" he shrieked as he sat back up, kicking his legs and partly wrecking what they'd built so far.

Darrah could tell that being playful wasn't going to be enough this time and she'd have to ride the storm of one of his real fits. She knew immediately that he had stood up too fast and gotten dizzy. It was another physical problem he frequently had.

He'd had one of his colds that lasted longer than it should, and it had finally ended the previous week. When that happened, the infection would often settle in his ear and mess up his balance for even longer. Then he'd fall and start angrily thrashing around, as he was doing now. Like the nosebleeds, it was supposed to go away as he got older.

No longer cursing, Nat just howled incoherently as he kept kicking his feet, swinging his arms, and picking up pieces and throwing them. *Never at me*, she noticed, as she had during other tantrums—*always just around the room so they wouldn't hit anyone.*

His frenzied movements slowed and decreased, until he just pressed his fists into the carpet in front of him and panted. "I just want it all to stop! All th-this bullshit! To stop! I want it to go away!" He sounded like he was about to cry, and Darrah hoped they could avoid that. If someone saw him crying, he'd fly into a rage ten times worse than before.

Darrah gave him time to calm down and master his tears before she tried to touch him and comfort him. When she sensed he was ready, she reached out and smoothed his hair, then put her hand on his shoulder. "I know. It will stop, it will go away, I promise. And I'll help you until it does. I'm a girl. Girls are good at helping."

She could see Nat wasn't going to get more worked up right now. Instead, he was deflating, sinking into sullenness and despair. "Mom isn't. She's a girl."

Darrah felt her own anger and shame threatening to boil over. She swallowed hard. "I know. I know she hasn't been good at it, but I think she might be getting better at helping. Last week when you had a cold, she made you soup and read to you and she didn't get all worried and moody like she usually does. You even stumbled a little when you stood up that one time, and she grabbed you and laughed. She doesn't usually laugh." Darrah's optimism was about one-third actual observation of some change in her mother, one-third the innate, unrehearsed virtue of hope, and one-third wishful thinking, rationalizing, and excuse-making.

Nat seemed to want to accept his sister's evaluation—he nodded slowly and pulled himself up, sitting straight and not looking so dejected. "Yeah, maybe."

"So I'm here until mom gets better at helping. And I'm here until all this bullshit goes away."

Nat smirked a little, as eight-year-olds do when other people use bad words. "It sounds funny when you say it."

She peered down at his face until he looked up and saw her big smile again. "That's 'cause I'm a girl, silly."

"Yeah." He started picking up the blocks he'd scattered.

They spent the rest of the afternoon quietly rebuilding the tower, higher and stronger than it had been before.

CHAPTER 11

Monday, March 19, 1956 – Manhattan, New York

Christoph looked around the brightly lit room as the immigration officer went through his papers. Everything was so clean and well-kept here, much more so than back home, and infinitely more so than the boat on which he'd come over. The high counter separating him and the officer was spotless Formica, the tile floor looked to be hardly any less clean. The ceiling was covered with panels lit by fluorescent tubes, none of which were burned out. The men behind the counter looked strong, well-fed, freshly-scrubbed; more than that, they looked alert and in charge, presiding over a well-run operation of letting people into their promised land. The people on Christoph's side of the counter, by contrast, looked tired and timid.

Christoph looked again to the officer opposite him, trying not to appear nervous or over-awed, though he was both. The man and his uniform weren't too imposing, thankfully. Not like they would've had back in Germany when he was little; large, stern, and silent men, always in black or grey, always with a pistol at their hip. This man looked to be in his late thirties and his build was slight, somewhat smaller than Christoph had now grown. He did not carry a weapon, and looked more like a postman than someone people should fear or placate.

Christoph noted that Americans did not like scary, intimidating things, even in their police or government. He found that very odd, wondering how it could possibly work, but watched the smaller man with new interest.

The immigration officer looked at him. He didn't smile, but his face wasn't threatening or severe, just serious, perhaps a little cold. "It says you sailed from Bremerhaven, it lists your home as Wiesbaden, and it says you were born in Darmstadt. Care to explain that?"

"I was born in Darmstadt. We move to Wiesbaden after Darmstadt. The bombs fell on it."

"And Bremerhaven was just where you got the boat?"

"Yes sir."

"Hm-hmm. Darmstadt and Wiesbaden are in Southern Germany?"

"Yes, sir."

"Right by Bavaria?"

"Another state is Bavaria, to the east and south."

"Isn't that by Nuremberg, where the Nazis did all their stuff, all their big rallies?"

Christoph could feel himself blush at this. "Nuremberg is Bavaria in. I never go there. We do not travel so much, in Germany, sir."

"Hm-hmm. Lots of Nazis in your town?"

Christoph blushed harder and paused, making himself panic more. "I think so, sir. I was a boy, but I saw people waving the *kleine...* the, umm... little flags at parades, or hanging the big flags out windows."

"And what about you? Ever join a political party? I know you're still young, but even a young fellow, looking for work... maybe upset about how his country's being run... sometimes a young fellow can be pretty active in politics."

"No, sir. Never. I go to school, and then I hear there were better jobs in America."

"Don't change the subject." The officer's voice now had an edge to it. "We'll get to employment in a minute. You just think hard about politics. Never went to a meeting? Hung up a poster? Hand out leaflets? Lots of men do that."

"No, sir. Really."

"Didn't know any Communists? Never heard people talking about it, and thought it sounded interesting?"

"No, sir. That's in the East. The Communists are not where I was."

The man looked at Christoph more intently. "They're everywhere, son. We know that. We have to be careful, it's our way of life we're talking about. They got half of Europe, and now they got most of Asia—not that there's much important over there. They stole the bomb. Then they stole the H-bomb. God knows what else they have. It could all end any day, if we drop our guard."

Christoph made another mental note: *Americans are really scared of foreigners, especially Communists.* He shared this fear, as deeply as any religious faith, having heard all the horror stories at the end of the war, of what Russians and Poles did to Germans. He was a little surprised and disappointed that these seemingly secure, supremely confident Americans could be as shaken and frightened as he and other Germans were. If people such as these Americans were so scared, maybe there really was something to be afraid of.

The officer shook his head and gave a hint of a smile. "Well, I don't think they're going to take over because of some big, goofy German kid like you. You look like the boy who works at the German butcher shop by my house in Clifton, where my wife buys pork chops and sausage. I don't think you'd make a very good liar, kid."

"No, sir. I don't think so."

"Your English is good, though."

"Thank you, sir. We study it in the school. I know I have the work on it."

"That's good. You'll have to work hard a lot in this country."

"I know, sir."

"You filled in 'baker' as your profession. You've worked as a baker?"

"Yes, sir, for the last year. I was an apprentice baker in the school. I study it many years now."

The man frowned. "We need skilled workers, kid. I don't know how much skill it takes to bake stuff. No offense. Let's put something better in your 'secondary skills' blank, to help get this application through. You have any other skills?"

Christoph stared a moment. "I'm a very good wood carver. There was a man in our neighborhood. He showed me. I do it after school. I get good at it."

The officer smiled. "Wood carver? This is the twentieth century, son. We don't need cuckoo clocks and wooden shoes." He frowned and tapped his pen on the counter. "Tell you what. You seem like a good kid—quiet, polite, smart. So let's put down 'carpenter' instead of 'wood carver,' okay?"

"Yes, sir. Thank you."

"Do you have a job lined up already?"

"A friend wrote and told me about this place, not far from here. He said there was a new bakery—a big, modern one—and they needed lots of the workers. Hallicott Mills was the name."

The man smiled at Christoph's pronunciation, which he knew had made *Hallicott* sound like *Alley Coat*.

"All right. Now, for next of kin, you only list your mother, is that right?"

"Yes, sir. My sister was killed in the war. The bombs."

"I'm sorry. And your father?"

"I don't know, sir. When we left for Wiesbaden, we lost him. He go to look for the food and not come back. Maybe he died. But we don't know."

"That's rough." His gaze moved from Christoph to some mysterious spot on the wall. "My brother died in the war. He was younger than me, too. Never got to Germany. Died in the Ardennes, buried there. Don't know if I'll ever get to see his grave. I doubt mom and dad will. He and I were both in the infantry, just grunts. I was in the Pacific. Nearly killed on Okinawa. I hadn't even heard Sammy was killed, until I was in that hospital in Hawaii. He'd already been dead for months." He bowed his head, seeming to return from where his thoughts had taken him. He looked again at Christoph. "You see what I'm saying?"

Christoph blinked, several times. "No, sir. I'm sorry."

The man leaned forward. "I mean a lot of people bled and died so you could come here—hell, so that this place could even be here at all, for people like you to come to. That's what it means to be an American, son—it means earning all that blood, making it mean something, making it worth it, 'cause just too damned many people died for you, without them knowing it. But now *you* know it, so it's your responsibility. Are you gonna remember that when you're making your apple turnovers and wooden knick-knacks and finding some girl to make babies with?"

"Yes, sir. I will."

The officer nodded. "All right. If you do that, then you'll be a good American, and I guess I'll have done my job. I'll put this paperwork through." He extended his hand. "Welcome to America."

Christoph shook his hand, then turned from the counter and made one more mental note he'd never forget. He would never fully understand it, but it would forever be a part of his own outlook after that day. Americans were so proud of the idea of their country—not the fatherland or race or language, but the idea, the "way of life" as they always liked to say—that they were almost arrogant and vain before this idealized monument to courage and self-sacrifice. Their pride was not the smugness of feeling superior, but something much more dynamic, the driven zealousness of knowing they were right. They also felt this revelation had, in some mysterious way, been earned and paid for, but could also be revoked at any moment, perhaps in a fiery apocalypse, sent by an angry God who had withdrawn His favor.

Christoph now knew how exhilarating and emboldening it felt to hold simultaneously such certainty and fear, and it would drive many of his decisions throughout the rest of his life.

CHAPTER 12

Friday, April 6, 2007 – The Sublunar Sphere

Christoph did not pray for as long as he had on previous days. He felt a bit awkward, with the strange girl nearby. She was slightly disconcerting as well as comforting. *Perhaps I'll get more used to her with time.* He sat up and looked into the fire, thinking quietly for a while, until he noticed that she too, was looking at the fire.

The girl smiled thinly, without showing her teeth. "Was your prayer to your god enjoyable?" she asked.

Christoph wondered in what way she could be deemed the appropriate guide for him, but immediately chastised himself for questioning God's ways. If God had seen fit to use Oswald as His messenger, then He could certainly use a little prehistoric heathen. *She is just so odd, though, it is hard to answer her questions.*

"I don't think prayer should be enjoyable," he said. "It is necessary. It is a duty. We should be glad to do it, but not have fun while doing it."

Merla nodded. "That is one way to look at it, I suppose. What did you pray for?"

"I didn't ask for anything. I just thanked Him for all He has done for me."

"Ah, then you know how to pray well, I think. But we will still have to figure out, you and I, what it is you want. You must want something. That seems to be what all the people I've met here have in common: they want something, but don't know what it is. When we figure it out, then they move on to wherever they go."

Christoph shifted his gaze from Merla back to the fire. "I want to be in heaven and not here. I want not to hurt my grandchildren. My time here is done, I don't want to be here."

"All right. As I told you, I don't really understand this heaven you people talk about. How do you know this place isn't it?"

He looked back at her dark face and scowled. "One thing I'm certain of is that this place is not heaven. It's cold and grey and I feel bad all the time. You've made me feel a bit better, but not much. No offense."

Merla smiled again. As Christoph had observed when first meeting her, she was not pretty by any modern standard, but her eyes had a depth and gentleness to them that contrasted with her flat, weathered face. "It's all right," she said. "I understand what you mean. But what is this heaven place like? Why do you want to go there?"

"Well, no one knows what it's like, naturally. People talk about clouds and light, but we all know it can't be described in human language, to a human mind. It's where God lives, and God can't be described that way. I want to go there to be with God."

"I still don't understand. Whatever you mean by God, I think it means something or someone who is everywhere, all the time. He doesn't live or die, and He's not in one place. So how can He 'live' in 'heaven' as you say, and somehow be distant from you?"

"No, no, you don't understand. It's not like that." Christoph paused and wondered if the loneliness were preferable to the frustration and confusion this tiny heathen brought. "I don't know how to explain it."

"Don't get angry. I just thought it might help if you explained it. But we can talk about something else, if you like. There's no hurry. I'm sure of that."

"No, I should try harder." He would've liked to take a deep breath, but he was denied that physical comfort and reassurance. "God is everywhere, but there are many things that keep us from seeing Him. When we go to heaven, all those other things will be gone. We will finally see God without any interruption or distraction. There. That is how I would explain it."

"That would be a very nice thing, I think. Thank you for explaining it to me."

"You're welcome."

"So when you say you want to go to heaven, you mean that you want all the things that keep you from seeing God to go away. Is that right?"

"Yes, that sounds about right."

"I think that's what all the people I've met have been striving for, even if they didn't talk about God. They didn't so much have some goal they needed to achieve, but they needed to remove the obstacles that kept them here. There always seemed to be something that tied them to this place, bound them, and they were unaware of it." She paused a moment. "You weren't murdered, were you?"

Christoph couldn't gasp at this, and had to content himself with widening his eyes at her shocking question. "No. I mean, I don't think so. I don't remember my death, how exactly I died. But I can't believe anyone would do that to me. I was old. I didn't like to go to the doctor and take his horrid medicines. I probably just died in my sleep. Maybe I was sick for a short time in the hospital, but I have no memory of my last days."

"I've met a few people who were murdered. You don't seem like one of them. They were much more angry and violent. I sense you can be a very angry person, Christoph, but they were at another level. So much rage they were incoherent for what seemed like years before they could move on. So much disappointment at unfinished business, like they would've given anything to live another day, but it was taken away from them and they couldn't believe or understand how that could be, and they didn't know how to exist without that extra time, and the things they thought they would've done with it. You don't sound as though you had lots left to accomplish and were enraged by having that chance snatched away."

"No, nothing like that."

"And it is a very good thing you don't remember the moment of your death. It is another thing that keeps people here, reliving the pain and outrage. It's as though they're so shocked by it, even if it was not a bad or painful death, they can't turn away. They're mesmerized by it. I know I had trouble with that for a long time, and I'm glad you've been spared that."

"You remembered your death?"

"Oh yes, for a long time. It was a very slow, violent death." She held out her hands and looked at the backs of them, then turned them over a couple times. "Such a tiny body, but it withstood so much pain for so long before it finally broke. I suppose that's what bothered me—not that I died, but that I hadn't died sooner."

"That's terrible."

"Oh, it was. I have found people always assume the time they live in is somehow special, that the people they lived with are much more virtuous, or much more wicked, than anyone ever has been at any other time. That's just not true. When I lived, the men would fight the men of other clans. They usually wouldn't do much harm. There weren't many people back then, and lots of land, so there wasn't much to fight over. Besides, we had animals to fight and kill for food, so it didn't make sense to risk being hurt by going out to kill other people.

"But sometimes people aren't just interested in food, or even in killing. Two young men found me alone, gathering nuts and berries too far from our village. So they took me. They raped me, of course, over and over. I knew to expect that. Then they seemed to enjoy just hurting and degrading me in all different ways. They tried lots of different things, with sticks and knives and fire and other things. They decided to keep me in the woods, so they wouldn't have to share me with others back in their village. Maybe they also feared my village attacking theirs, if I was found with them. So they kept me tied up in the woods, so they could rape and cut and burn me, for days and days.

"And then, when I got so thin and sick from fever, because I'd been sleeping outside and rolling in my own filth, so that I was too grotesque for them to stomach the idea of raping me anymore, *then* they bashed my head in with a stone. My family finally found my body, and then they did attack the other village and many more people died. I remember hearing people from my clan telling stories for years and years after, how my blood soaked into the ground, and that's why the dirt is so red around here."

Christoph just stared at her, speechless. Odd as ever, she picked that moment to grin broadly. "That story doesn't make any sense though, does it?" She even laughed then, a noise that sounded almost blasphemous to Christoph. It battered his ears like the crash of shattering glass would. "I remember when I was alive, the dirt here was red then, too, so the legend makes no sense! But people love a good, bloody story, don't they?"

"I suppose so," Christoph said quietly. "Is that why you are here, why you haven't moved on, because you were murdered?"

Merla turned serious again and nodded. "You know, I thought that for a long time. But as I realized I was no longer angry, and I saw how much angrier other people were, who then moved on, I didn't see how that could be what was holding me back." She shook her head. "No, it must be something else, because I haven't been attached to that misery in a long time. I can describe it now to you with no feeling whatsoever. I can laugh at it, because it doesn't hurt me. I don't even remember the hurt. So there must be some other reason that I'm still here, but I have plenty of time to figure it out."

Christoph turned from her and focused on the fire. It was impossible for him to understand or empathize with Merla, someone who could laugh at the horrors she just described. He supposed that wasn't part of the arrangement here. She wasn't there to teach him anything about herself.

He finally looked up at the rusty, leaking hatch. "What is that?" he asked.

"I have no idea. Do you want to open it? You can try if you want."

"No. I don't want to go near it. It's awful. Why don't you open it?"

She shrugged. "Because I feel no need to. I don't have the fear of it that you seem to, I feel nothing toward it. It'd be like asking me to breathe: I just don't anymore. If you have some strong feeling toward it, then it must have something to do with you. That may be something we find out, eventually."

Christoph gestured to the rest of the room. "What about the other things? Don't they seem strange to you, all these pieces of modern furniture? Why is it decorated like this, if you're here?"

She smiled; it seemed less offensive now that they had changed subjects, though it still didn't make Christoph want to share in her strange sense of mirth. "Oh, that's something I've noticed with other people who have been through here. Some of the things in the room we both can see, and some appear differently to each of us. I'm guessing you see things you're familiar with?"

"Yes, I do."

"Well, I see things I knew and loved and felt comfortable with. Deer and bear skins. Drinking gourds and willow baskets. Sleeping cushions stuffed with alfalfa that remind me of summer. Nuts and honeycombs in clay jars. What do you see?"

"I see a room that reminds me of my wife. She died a long time ago, and she liked this place. It feels good to be back."

"Good! Those are the kinds of thoughts you should have here, memories of the good things of the past. Memories you had forgotten. I am very glad to be in the room that makes you feel that way. Enjoy it with me."

Christoph's wife Rachel had been as young and foolish as he, and they had gone about discovering this new country and its many wondrous sights, like this room in the MoMA. She didn't mind his modest jobs at the bakery and the Enchanted Mill Forest, though the latter meant he wasn't free every weekend. It was all so simple, a circumscribed, undemanding existence. In that sense, the room he was in now wasn't just like the one at MoMA, it was a good representation of what his whole life had been, before Rachel died and things became complicated and painful.

"I wish I'd come here more, when she was alive," he said.

It surprised him, how quickly Merla got up. She was already halfway around the fire, coming toward him. "Stop that, Christoph," she said quite loudly. "That is not how you should think. I warned you about it before."

"But it was so nice. Why didn't I come here more? And with my son and with his children, too. We only went once in a while, and we should've gone more. I wanted to, but they were too busy, so much of the time. It wasn't right. We wasted our time, squandered it."

Even though the Hahn's home was on the other side of the park, Christoph again felt the explosion of pain from Nat; not like such a wave as before, but more like an arrow that flew unerring through the trees, and which he could sense coming before it hit him. When it did, it was as though someone were pressing a very hot needle into his ear. He grabbed the side of his head and fell over from the chair he was sitting on, crying out in pain. He expected to feel blood coursing between his fingers, though he knew that was no longer possible. When he looked up, the room was spinning and he felt sick all over, like his brain were a wet towel someone was wringing out.

Christoph felt a new sensation as Merla started kicking him in the ribs. Oddly, it barely hurt at all. A slight pressure, not really a blow. "I said stop it, you foolish man!" he heard her shouting now. She fell on him, hitting him in the head with her fists. That hurt more than the kicking. "Stop it, do you hear? I'm going to hit you till you stop hurting them this time!"

The more Merla's beating focused his attention on her, the less Christoph's head hurt inside, until he could actually think straight and keep his balance. As he did, he put his hands up to defend himself, and Merla slowly relented.

"Stop! Stop!" Christoph shouted. "I'm done. I'm all right now."

She stepped back as he pulled himself back into his chair. "Those are the kinds of thoughts I told you to beware of," she said. "You have to be more careful."

He rubbed his face with his hands and shook his head. "I don't understand. You told me to enjoy the memories, and I was, but then it started hurting."

"Yes! It started hurting because you weren't remembering and enjoying the past! Regret is the enemy here, Christoph. You can remember and love the past. You can smile or cry at it. You can feel its hurt, even, if that is now what you need to learn from. You can feel guilt, so long as that guilt is just your own and not blame you put on others.

"But what you must *not* do—ever—is wish to change anything in the past. That longing is so overpowering that it consumes and even destroys living people who feel it. And for someone who has died, their spiritual power is just too strong for them to indulge in such desires. You must be on your guard, because I may not have the strength to stop you again, if your family's energy feeds off yours and drags you both down into despair. Do you understand?"

"I'm trying to, Merla," he said. "Really, I am trying to understand. I'm not trying to hurt my family or cause you any trouble. It's just so frightening, and so different from the life I led. I'm sorry. I need your help."

"I know. And I want to help. I enjoy it, even. So let me help you." She extended her hand to Christoph. "Come. Let's walk through this forest of yours. I take it that it meant something to you, that it gave you some pleasure?"

He took her small hand. It felt like bark, it was so rough. He stood up. "Yes. It gave me great pleasure. It made other people happy, too."

"Good." She started leading Christoph by the hand, out the door of the building. "Then show it to me. We will enjoy it while it's still light. And please make sure to only think of the people it made happy, all right? Not the ones it might've made happy or the ones it didn't make happy enough."

"Yes, I'll make very sure to do that."

"You'll learn. It's hard for everyone at first. We will find the obstacles blocking your way to this thing you call God. First let's see what made you happy. I think that is part of the way we must find, too."

Though it was still grey and featureless as they moved down the path, Christoph thought perhaps some of the buildings in the Enchanted Mill Forest looked somewhat brighter than before.

CHAPTER 13

Friday, April 6, 2007 – Northern New Jersey

After tossing the bag of trash into the dumpster in the parking lot, Ben doubled back for a look around the Enchanted Mill Forest. If the kids weren't around there, he'd head back to the house and see what they were up to. It was a nice enough spring day, despite the cold and clouds. They'd be fine. In the meantime, he'd see what else needed fixing, so he could get started on that tomorrow.

Humpty Dumpty looked fine as ever. Ironically, he was always in good shape. *Too high up for people to mess with*, Ben guessed. Also, right by the entrance, so people probably still worried someone at the ticket counter was watching them, and they wouldn't go grabbing and pulling and scratching him, like they did so many other figures in the park. Humpty usually just needed a wipe down from bird shit, and today he was even free of that.

Rapunzel's hair could use some touching up with yellow paint; when the color faded, the white of the plaster showing through looked worse than if she had dark roots. She had a little overhang above her balcony that partly protected her face, and Ben noticed her cheeks had a remarkably lifelike, rosy glow. Painting her had been one of the last things his father had puttered around with last fall. Ben was not the most loving son in the world, but even he got a lump in his throat at the memory, and paused to wipe his right eye. He'd do the best he could with her hair tomorrow.

Ben looked around at the little buildings and the trees, wondering for the millionth time why his father had been so obsessed with the place. It wasn't like he'd been into kid stuff otherwise. He always seemed rather uncomfortable around his grandkids, and he'd avoided the visitors' children as much as possible. Never mind that he hadn't been the best father, not be a long shot. Ben reminded himself—as he had many times, as far back as he could remember—how hard it must've been on the old man, raising a kid alone, after his young wife died. That had to be rough, and even he had to cut his father some slack. No, even though Ben could have the natural, visceral reaction of any adult whose parent had regularly beaten him as a child, he knew rationally that his father had had a hard time of it, and was not entirely to blame for his shortcomings. Not that blame was the only thing he had to consider; whether or not anyone was to blame for the scars, they still hurt and had never completely healed.

Ben had seen photos of his mother—black and white ones, they were so old—and she looked so young, blonde, and pretty. Way too young for any man to be prepared for her death. It was twentieth century America, and a man wouldn't have expected his wife to die in childbirth. That was something from the old days. And then to have to raise a kid on his own? It had been the sixties, and most men didn't expect to have to change diapers and warm bottles on their own. Some couldn't do it, even with their wives' help. Those that did have to go it alone, most of them would have had their mothers or siblings to help out.

All Christoph had were some older women from the Congregationalist church who were willing to watch his son so he could go to work; Ben remembered they'd been just as liberal with the backs of their hands as his father ever was, so it wasn't like the old man was the only one who enjoyed smacking kids around.

Remembering the church ladies and their unchristian ways made Ben think of Holy Book Land. Now there was an obsession he could understand his old man indulging, back in the early 70s when the land was cheap and the Enchanted Mill Forest was doing relatively well. A chance to recreate all those scenes of the various atrocities committed by an angry God. How could anyone so afraid of a predestined, supposedly richly-deserved hellfire resist such an opportunity? The walls of Jericho tumbling down, Sodom and Gomorrah being blasted to rubble, Lot's wife turned to a pillar of salt, terrified people hammering their fists on the side of the ark, forever refused entry to be among the elect who'd be saved.

What amazing and appalling tableaux his father had created in plaster and wood and concrete. They'd hardly been balanced out by the New Testament scenes, either. Jesus was depicted as relatively calm at the Sermon on the Mount and the Feeding of the Multitudes, of course, but he sure looked ready to go all Old Testament on the people at the exorcisms and the Cleansing of the Temple, never mind how hideous Lazarus looked, like something from a zombie movie. The whip-cracking and screams that played over hidden loudspeakers at the Cleansing were an especially nice, if ironic, touch for the Prince of Peace, Ben thought as he shook his head at the memory.

His father could even take a fairly mild or upbeat tale and transform it into something numinously terrifying. Ben remembered the terrible whale from the story of Jonah. It wasn't until he studied *Moby-Dick* in college, that he understood the figure he'd helped his father build years before. Between Melville's implacable Leviathan sent by an inscrutable and amoral God on the one hand, and the fairly tame "big fish" that the Biblical God had used to save the people of Nineveh on the other, the whale in Holy Book Land much more clearly resembled the former. The similarity to Melville's monster was all the more uncanny, because his father had never read the novel. Ben asked his father about it, and received confirmation of what he had suspected; no, his father had not read the novel described by its author as a "wicked book."

Ben knew that the Jonah figure—meticulously carved by his father from the softest, lightest pine they had cut down to make room for the park—had much the same effect on him as the oak cross in the little chapel. He couldn't take his eyes from it. Jonah was rendered much more deliberately ugly than the cross, which was so sensually pretty throughout its form, but they both shared the same quality of being awful; quite literally, they filled him with awe.

Unlike the cross, however, which his father hated for reasons Ben could never fathom, he knew the old man loved the Jonah statue. He considered it his best carving of a human figure, and with good reason. The detail and emotion were not just palpable, they were overwhelming. For one of the few times in their adult lives, the two men were in complete agreement that the Jonah statue should survive the general destruction visited on Holy Book Land when they sold that part of the property.

Ben made his way through the park, noting where paint had chipped, plaster had cracked, or shingles had blown off in winter storms, heading to where he knew the prophet formerly known as Jonah was now disguised. He entered the castle of the wicked, jealous Queen from Snow White. The Queen was one of the last figures Ben's father had carved for the park, and his artistry and skill matched that of any of his best pieces, including Jonah. He'd created her from a walnut tree they'd made sure to cut down before leaving Holy Book Land to the mall-builders. Ben's father had said its timber would be exquisite, the darker color of its wood fit for a Queen such as this.

For a figure done late in his life, he had perhaps softened the Queen's blatant malice, just a little, but he had captured her awful beauty nonetheless; anyone who looked upon her would be hard-pressed to agree with the magic mirror's evaluation when they saw Snow White further down the trail. The girl was pretty in a way that made you feel happy. The Queen was beautiful in a way that made you want to die. Or kill. And with that kind of beauty, Ben's father had rendered the Queen the most powerful, awesome figure in the park, now that the terrible whale had been abandoned to destruction.

With some skillful use of forced perspective, the Queen looked about seven feet tall, towering over visitors, looking down on them with condescension and pride, freezing them with the threat of her unknown powers and unknowable intent. Ben looked upon her and felt cold, as he always did in this display; cold and alone, small and useless. Like every other time he came here, it thrilled him in its wondrous, irrational way.

Kneeling before the Evil Queen, there was Jonah, transformed into the hapless woodsman, tasked with killing the Queen's rival, Snow White. The contrast between the statues of the Queen and her subject was striking, in the color of the woods used, as well as in the figures' postures and expressions. Jonah's former piety now seemed like the woodsman's perfect abjection and despair before this higher power. The whole composition was brilliant. No one would ever suspect that the woodsman figure had once been someone else, that he had once cried out to a merciful God instead of to his fearsome Queen. Perhaps the artist had captured their similar attitudes toward their tasks, as both men begged their terrible masters to relent and not force them to do what they did not want to.

Ben could not stay in the Queen's presence for long, before he had to emerge into the air that now seemed much less cold than her bottomless heart and limitless mind. He needed to warm up. The thought of Darrah's patient love and Nat's sometimes frantic need made him quicken his pace toward home.

CHAPTER 14

Friday, May 31, 1957 – Northern New Jersey

The Hallicott Mills Bakery closed early this afternoon, and Christoph Hahn was glad to emerge from the hot confines of the building into a sunny, breezy spring day.

The day before had been Memorial Day, and with the factory closed completely, he'd gone on a lovely picnic with Rachel, the French girl who worked in the bakery office. He was glad she'd spoken to him, for he was sure he'd never have had the nerve to start a conversation with a woman as beautiful as she. Small-framed, with dimpled cheeks, upturned nose, and golden hair, her brown eyes were several shades darker than his. That was maybe the most striking feature of her looks, the contrast of such large, dark-colored eyes with such bright blonde hair.

It had embarrassed him to ask her out, when he didn't have a car, but so far their dates had been the best times he'd spent in the United States. They'd go to the movies or picnics; on the weekends they'd take longer trips by bus to the City. They'd even tried bowling, though neither of them knew how to, and it had been hilarious. In fact, laughing was the thing he most remembered about their times together.

Rachel can be moody, though, he thought as he left the bakery. That made her laughter all the more enjoyable by contrast. It also made it hard to make plans, and always threatened to bring him disappointment and hurt. Although he thought they'd had a wonderful time the day before, she hadn't wanted to make a date for the weekend. She frequently did that, or went to the other extreme and called him out of the blue, wanting to go out at the last minute. It was all exciting and spontaneous, of course, but could be somewhat maddening, too, especially to someone like Christoph, who appreciated order, organization, and predictability. When he'd sat with her at lunch today, she'd been sullen and uncommunicative, and he knew not to push her.

He would probably be on his own this evening, but felt optimistic that perhaps she'd call tomorrow with some plan to go do something enjoyable and unexpected.

Christoph looked across the road to where work had begun on some new park connected to the bakery. It was supposed to be good advertising for the bakery, luring people out here to visit the park and take a tour of Hallicott Mills. Although he liked the theme of the park—German fairy tales he knew from his childhood—he also thought it sounded a bit silly and impractical, building something so children and their parents could look at scenes from story books. But he'd noticed how Americans liked to have fun in as many ways as possible, and couldn't get over how many playgrounds, carnivals, bowling alleys, theaters, restaurants, drive-ins, golf courses, tennis courts, and swimming pools he'd seen in the area.

Hallicott Mills was kind of out in the sticks, as the expression was; the density of amusements only got thicker as you moved east toward New York City. He'd even heard of more exciting diversions in Atlantic City, with the beach, gambling and shows, but that would have to wait. You didn't ask a girl on an overnight trip, and although he was smitten with Rachel, proposing marriage was not conceivable to him, not yet. He blushed to think that it might be one day, and not that far in the future.

Christoph waited by the side of Route 23 as an enormous Plymouth Fury cruised by, the windows rolled down. He saw a young woman with huge sunglasses and a bright yellow scarf tied around her head in the passenger seat. The car itself was pristine; two-tone paint job—ivory on top, turquoise on the bottom—with the line separating the two colors sloping just slightly downward, from the front of the car to the back. The roof sloped down to the trunk in an even more graceful curve, while the sides of the car slanted up to form two huge fins at the back. These enclosed the large, triangle-shaped taillights.

As the car pulled slowly away from Christoph, he thought how the lights looked like the eyes of the carved Jack-o-Lanterns he'd seen for the first time last October; they didn't have Halloween in Germany. They also didn't have cars like that. A car with fins? A car in bright colors, like a child's toy? A car that seemed built not for speed or practicality, but only for the pleasure of how good it looked? Christoph smiled as the creation drifted out of sight, shaking his head at its beauty, which seemed to him both undeniable and absurd.

He followed the sounds of hammering to the farthest edge of the parking lot. Under the trees, he saw some men finishing the walls of a small building. He recognized his friend Jacob, the one who had come over from Germany before him and recommended he join him in Hallicott Mills. A year older and having been there longer, Jacob was already a foreman at the company, where they'd given him some responsibility in the building of this new project.

"Christoph! I'm glad you came to see what we're working on!" Jacob waved to him.

"Hello, Jacob," he said. On the ground were several wooden toolboxes of hammers, awls, screwdrivers, files, and chisels, along with many small cardboard boxes of nails and screws. Christoph eyed their contents with interest and felt a plan forming.

"What do you think?"

Christoph turned to consider the building. It looked sturdy enough, and had the whimsical, faux medieval look that it was supposed to. It was scaled small, down to a child's size, so he bent down to look in the windows. *The decorations are much less satisfactory,* he thought. They'd filled it with some toy furniture and figures, all of them made out of plastic, cardboard, or metal. The pieces were of different scales and didn't match. It was a tacky hodgepodge and didn't look at all imaginative, playful, or fanciful.

Christoph stepped back and looked over the outside again. "The building looks great," he said as vaguely as possible, as his plan became more definite.

Jacob frowned and clapped his friend on the back. "Christoph! You don't like the decorations, do you?"

He turned to his friend, smiling, but shook his head as he did so. "They're plastic. Cheap-looking. *Schrecklich.*" He looked around at the trees and the other partially-constructed buildings. "You want this place to look nice, to make people think they're in a fairy tale, yes?"

"Well, yes, but it's not like the company wants to spend much on it. They just want me to throw some stuff together, to get people going through the bakery and buying the cakes and cookies."

"I know, I know. People have been talking about it for months. Fine." He put his arm around the smaller man's shoulders, to lead him away and talk. Christoph wasn't sure why he felt so expansive this afternoon. Maybe it was a byproduct of how good he felt about Rachel. Or maybe it was the sight of all those woodworking tools and the memories they gave him of when he had learned to use them skillfully, in a way that would fill others with wonder and awe. Whatever it was, he felt a strange urge to hatch a plan with his friend, to convince him to do something different and bold. "That's no reason not to take pride in your work. You don't want to just make a pile of *scheisse* here by the side of the road, do you?"

"No, no, of course not. I just mean, we have limits."

Christoph nodded as he gripped his friend closer and led him further away. "Oh, *natürlich.* I understand. It's good to have limits, I think. It makes you ... um ... oh, what's the word? *Findiger?*"

"More resourceful."

"Yes, yes, exactly. You say you don't have much *gelt* to work with here? But you want to make some pretty decorations, things people will appreciate? Things they'll remember, and want to come back to see again? And I think your boss will like that, too, if you're resourceful and get things done. Am I right?"

"Yes, of course."

"Well, you remember Herr Zimmermann?"

"Sure. He could make anything out of wood. Helped a lot after the war, making us all furniture and things from the scraps that were lying around."

"Yes. Very resourceful. And I loved to go and help him after school. It didn't seem like work, it was so enjoyable to make things from stuff that would be thrown away. And mama and I could use the money I made from working with him. I loved the work and I got good at it, Jacob."

"I know, I'd see the little figures you carved for the smaller children. They were very nice."

Christoph gestured to the trees around them. "You're going to have to cut down a lot of these, to make room, right? You probably have a pile of the ones you've cut down already, somewhere?"

"Yes, further down, behind that hill."

"Well, get them off the ground, so they don't stay damp and rot, and that's all I'll need." He stopped his friend. "Look at them. A lot of pines. I'm surprised, this close to the sea, and not in the mountains. Must be some reason they grow here. But pine is soft, easy to carve. I could use it for the figures that go inside, protected from the weather. I could make you anything you want. Oh, and I could use it for the little pieces of furniture, too, more pretty and real looking than anything you could buy in a store. And look." Christoph bent down and grabbed something off the ground. He held out his hand, and in his palm there were several small nuts, broken shells, and the little caps that had been on the nuts. "Look. Oh, what is it in English? *Eicheln*?"

"Um, wait, I know it... *acorns*."

"Yes." Christoph looked up at the tree the nuts had fallen from. "Oaks. Some of those here, too. Very hard wood. Difficult to work with, but the things I build would last. Ah, and over here." He took several quick steps and picked up something else from the ground. Jacob caught up with his friend, who was holding a large, black and cracked orb, nearly as big as an apple. Christoph stuck his thumbs into one of the cracks and pulled the husk apart, digging out the small, white nut from the center. "Oh! I thought it was a walnut, but it's one of these kind. We don't have them in Germany. I don't know the name, but I've seen them around, and I think it's from another kind of hardwood tree. There are probably some walnut trees here, too, if we kept looking."

Christoph put the nut in Jacob's palm, then folded the other man's fingers into a fist around the nut. Christoph gave him a big grin and Jacob couldn't help but smile as his big, overly-enthusiastic friend took him by the shoulders and shook him a little.

"You see?" Christoph beamed. "I have everything I need right here! So stop buying cheap, plastic *scheisse* and let me make some real things. Things we can be proud of. What do you say?"

"I like it, Christoph, I like this idea of yours. But when will you do all this work? You're moving up in the bakery, and that's what you're trained for, what you went to school for. You shouldn't give that up. I don't even know if this park will last or what will happen to it."

"Just talk to your boss. Tell him you have an idea for how to make this place... what's it going to be called again?"

"The Enchanted Mill Forest. We'll get the sign up soon and open any day now."

"A good name. Well, tell him you have an idea for how to make the Enchanted Mill Forest much better, and it will hardly cost a thing. I can do the carving after work and on the weekends, and if your boss likes how the pieces look, then maybe you can get him to take me off the line one day a week, and I'll work on the park that day. Can you do that?"

"That's a great idea. I'll do that on Monday. I think it'll work out very nicely."

"I think so, too."

After saying goodbye, Christoph walked back across the parking lot and east on Route 23, toward his apartment in the small downtown of Hallicott Mills. He could not believe his good luck. He hadn't touched a woodworking tool in over a year, and now he realized how his hands ached to hold them again.

Nor could he get over how the whole plan had come to him on the spot, like a vision or an inspiration. He smiled at the idea that Rachel must be making him more spontaneous and less predictable, and he thought how, if he heard from her tonight or tomorrow, it would be the best weekend he'd spent in America.

CHAPTER 15

Friday, April 6, 2007 – The Sublunar Sphere

Christoph vividly remembered that conversation with Jacob as he moved through the park with Merla. In fact, after showing her other scenes like Goldilocks and the Three Bears and Little Red Riding Hood, Christoph led her to the exact spot where he had volunteered to help with the Enchanted Mill Forest, so he could better recall that first thrill of being able to make something beautiful and lasting, something people would remember and come back to years later.

"Here," he said as they stopped by the shadowy outline of the first scene he'd ever worked on in the Enchanted Mill Forest. "These are the first figures I carved here."

Merla looked over the scene with some care, seeming to move through the building's walls to examine each statue more closely. "What are they?" she asked.

"See the girl? The larger figure? Oh, I wish we could see them more clearly. It's so hard to show you when they look so hazy, like they're out of focus."

Merla's voice was firm. "Christoph, you promised not to wish for things. I don't think regretting the limitations of our current forms will cause us any trouble, but you should still be more careful. One thought leads to another, then another, and sometimes you can't stop in time."

"Yes, all right." Again, he would've liked to be able to take a deep breath to start over, but had to content himself with pointing to the girl figure. "There, the larger one is Snow White."

Merla drifted about the tiny room to stand in front of Snow White, who was a bit taller than she. Christoph tried to hide his smile, as the dark, squat figure of Merla could not help but look like a large toad before the dainty Snow White. "She's so pale."

"Yes. She's Snow White, of course."

Merla gave a sort of grunt. Christoph didn't know how exactly she could do that, and he hoped he'd learn; it would be nice to be able to express himself again with such physical gestures and sounds. "I've noticed for some time now how you people like such pale skin. It looks painful to me, like something too delicate to be in the sun. Or maybe something that's dead already and has been bleached by the sun. I don't like it."

The little savage was certainly candid, he had to give her that. But then, people had often said that Christoph was unable to lie, so perhaps it was a good thing in her, too. She could be more polite about it, though.

"No, you don't understand. It's for purity. She's like snow, or milk, or wool; she's pure and simple and natural. She cannot lie or hurt others. There is nothing ordinary or sick or blemished about her. I used the palest wood I could find for her, and I carved the most delicate, feminine features. I was working quickly, because I wanted to show the people who owned the park what good work I could do, how fast I could finish the job, but I still got her to look just right. Do you see?"

"Yes, Christoph, I see the fine work you did. It is a very beautiful figure, except for the color." She turned to consider the Seven Dwarves. "Who are these little men? Their color is more right, but they look even stranger than she, with their stubby legs and big heads."

"They're the Seven Dwarves in the story. They help Snow White."

"What does she need help with?" Merla looked around the scene. "The pale woman is by the stove, so she's preparing food? And there's a basket by her. Are those tools for making clothes in the basket?" She looked at the long, low table Christoph had made fifty years before. "There are seven little bowls on the table, and seven little hats on the backs of seven little chairs. So does she do all the work here? I don't see how the strange little men are helping.

They're carrying those bigger tools, the pointy ones, but I don't know what they're for."

"They're picks. The dwarves use them to work in the mine, and Snow White makes their food. And yes, those are long needles in her basket. They are used to knit and make clothes."

"All right. So she makes them food and clothes. I still don't understand what she gets from the little men. I could understand if they hunted for food."

It wasn't as frustrating as trying to explain God to her, but it was rapidly getting close to that previous experience. "Well, I'm sure they get food, too, but usually people remember them for the mine. It's just part of the story. And mostly, they help Snow White by letting her hide in their house, deep in the woods, because the Evil Queen wants to kill Snow White."

"Oh. Why does she want to do that? You said Snow White can't hurt anyone. So why does this woman want to kill her?"

"Because she's evil, and because she's jealous. Snow White is the most beautiful woman in the land, and that makes the Queen so jealous that she wants to kill Snow White, so no one will be more beautiful than she."

"That is odd. I knew many jealous women when I was alive, but never have I heard of something like that."

"You said yourself, sometimes people are not just interested in food, or even in killing, but just in hurting others. Jealousy is like that. It just makes us want to hurt someone, even if that doesn't get us anything."

Merla turned from the wooden statues and moved back out to be next to Christoph. She looked at him quite intently and nodded. "You are right again, Christoph. That explains it very well. Thank you."

"You're welcome. Come." He moved away from the Seven Dwarves' house and down the trail toward the Evil Queen's castle. He could still feel the lingering cold there, as Ben had left the building shortly before. But the chill was quickly dissipating, driven off by the heat Christoph always felt from the two figures there. He'd felt it when he was alive, just a little, and now that he was dead, it was much more palpable. Not like the electric vitality of his grandchildren, or the comforting centeredness of Merla. It was more like the vague, slightly painful warmth you got when you rubbed your face or arms really hard; the heat of friction and conflict, spinning forever between the ruler and the subject.

"Perhaps I should've showed you this before Snow White, as it's earlier in the story," he said as they drew near. "But I wanted to show it to you last, for it's my favorite piece. And it's one of the last scenes I created. I think it's my best work."

They moved into the castle and the figures of the Queen and the woodsman got as clear and focused as they could to the vision of dead people. Merla seemed so struck by them that she stopped before getting closer. "Oh, my, Christoph. This is an amazing work. Tell me what the people are doing here."

"That is the Evil Queen. She is telling the poor woodsman that he must take Snow White out into the forest and kill her. He doesn't want to, but he can't refuse his Queen's power. When he is out in the woods, he can't bear to do it, so he lets Snow White go, thinking she'll probably be killed by animals anyway, but at least it's out of his hands. For now, he's caught here, always begging the Evil Queen not to make him do what he cannot. And she is always commanding, never letting him go."

Merla considered the two figures as closely as she had Snow White and the Seven Dwarves. "The man here, he's pale like Snow White, but he looks so different."

"Yes." Christoph pointed above the door. "The narrow windows let in a little light, through some red glass. It brings out his look of fear, I think."

"It does. And his face... you can feel the pain and guilt he's feeling."

"And the Queen? It's a different wood, much darker. Perhaps you like it better."

"Oh, yes. She's so beautiful. The eyes and mouth are so sensuous and realistic. And yet I feel frightened before her, just as you intended."

"Do you feel warm at all, in front of her? It's always been an odd feeling I've had in this room."

"Perhaps, a little. But not really in a good way, I think. More like a fever I'd like to be rid of. I don't mean to put down your work. It's just so... overwhelming."

Christoph nodded. "No, I understand. I don't know exactly how I feel about it, either, but I know it's my most powerful work, the kind of thing that would last."

They contemplated the figures a moment longer, before Merla again took Christoph's hand. "Let's go, Christoph. It will be dark soon. We can sit by the fire and think and pray more till daylight."

They moved back through the park, passing some more fairy tales that Christoph explained; Hansel and Gretel, Jack and Jill, Little Miss Muffet, Little Red Riding Hood, and others.

Merla stopped at one point. "These stories, Christoph, they remind me of some we had when I was alive, stories about naughty children being killed or eaten, or of wicked people who wanted to hurt others, but were killed by their own evil plans. So I understand them, I think. But I know we also had other tales, stories about how the world or our people came to be, stories about gods and spirits and how they help run the world. Do you people have those stories, too? And did you put them here, in your forest, for people to see?"

Christoph frowned. This would be hard to explain, like her questions about God and heaven. "Yes, we have stories like that." He was going to add, 'But ours are true,' though he decided against it. "We have them in a big book called the Bible, except they're all about the One God. And I did make some of the stories from the Bible into scenes here in the park."

"Oh. Did you show some of them to me today? I thought the poor woodsman looked like he was praying, and I wondered if it was a scene about your God and your religion. But then you explained it was part of that strange Snow White story."

Christoph could not imagine trying to go into all the details of how he and his son had incorporated some of the figures and buildings from Holy Book Land into what remained of the Enchanted Mill Forest, so he decided to pass over it. "No. I built them in a separate park. But people didn't seem to like them as much."

"That's odd. I wonder why? When I was alive, people liked all kinds of stories, silly ones and serious ones, ones about the gods and the great ancestors, and ones about animals and insects. We liked them all."

"Yes, it was strange. I don't know why it was that way. But people didn't come to see the scenes from those stories, so we took them down."

"Oh. I'm so sorry. You must've put a lot of work into them. It must've hurt you, to tear them down."

"Yes, but it had to be done. We kept the stories people liked, and that's what matters."

Merla smiled more broadly than ever before. "Oh my, now you have reminded me not to show regret, but to be glad for what's happened. You learn so quickly! I fear you won't be with me long, if you keep this up!"

This time her smile didn't seem inappropriate at all to Christoph, and he joined her. Perhaps he could understand and empathize with her, after a fashion. She was making a noble effort to do so for him. "Thank you, Merla. I'm sorry I said before that I wanted to leave here and get away from you, and that you don't make me feel much better. You've been very kind, you do make me feel better, and I do appreciate it."

"Of course. I know you do. And I want you to move on, too, when the time comes. I'm pleased at your progress."

They had reached the house of the third Little Pig, and sat down in the chairs they had occupied before, on either side of the fire. "Thank you very much for showing me the things you built," Merla said after a few moments. "But it makes me wonder. What will happen to the park, now that you've died? Is that perhaps what is bothering you, making you stay connected to this place? Are you worried about it, and about all the beautiful things you made?"

Christoph paused to consider this. "Maybe, if I thought about what would happen in the far future. But for right now, my son and his family own the park, and they're taking care of it." He thought again of keeping a secret from Merla, like the details of where the woodsman statue had come from, but this time he decided to be more forthcoming. "I don't know how to say this, but my son and

I weren't always close. Sometimes he didn't seem to like me very much, and he certainly never agreed with me about many things. But he did always like the Enchanted Mill Forest, and he's always taken very good care of it."

"That's good. I wondered, because you said you worked here, and others owned the park, so I didn't understand."

"Oh, yes, when it first opened, I just worked here, and at the bakery that used to be across the road. For years, my friend Jacob and I would save all we could. We worked very hard, both of us, here and at the bakery. So when the company wanted to sell the park, we were able to buy it. And eventually, Jacob moved to Florida with his wife, and he sold me his half. At a bargain, too. He was a good friend."

"A friend is one of the most wonderful things a person can have. You were very lucky. And a son who helps you in your life work, and takes care of what you've done, even if he doesn't always agree with you on other things. That is something to be glad for, too."

"Yes, I suppose it is."

Christoph stared at the fire and for the first time he could remember, he felt like praying to God for his son - not to thank God for Ben's limited virtues, or his hard work; not to beg God to please keep him from hell, or to please bring him back to the church; not to ask God to punish or discipline him for all his waywardness and backsliding - but just to thank God for the boy, for his very existence. He really didn't know what it would feel like to pray for such a thing, but he decided to try it this evening.

CHAPTER 16

Friday, April 6, 2007 – Northern New Jersey

"Hey you two!" Ben called out as he came through the door.

"Hi Dad!" Darrah and Nat replied, at the same time, from their place at the foot of their Lego tower. It had grown to where it was almost as high as the back of the sofa.

"There you are!" Ben said as he kicked off his boots. "I wondered where you two were."

"We were outside before, but then we came in," Darrah said. She could almost feel Nat tense up, even from a few feet away, as though he wasn't sure whether she'd keep her silence about his earlier episodes. He ought to know better by now.

Ben sat on the sofa near Nat. "Where'd you go, Natty-Bo? See anything?"

"To the top of the big hill," Nat said. "I got there first. Saw some birds."

"Ah, I was down on the other side of the park. You two have lunch?"

"Yeah. Darrah made some soup," Nat said. "It was good."

"Of course it was good. Darrah's good at making stuff." Ben smiled at his daughter, then he picked up some Lego blocks to play with, snapping them together and pulling them apart. "I see you're both good at making towers. It's really tall, like in New York City. We should go there again. We haven't been in a while. Gosh, I think your grandfather was with us the last time we went. We should go back."

"Mmm-hmm," Nat said. Darrah could see he was tensing up again. "Don't talk about Opa."

Darrah and her father exchanged looks. "Oh, okay," Ben said. "I didn't know you were still sad about him. We all are."

Darrah thought this was something of an exaggeration on her father's part – especially as to the feelings of the older members of the family – but she knew there were some things one just had to say, whether or not they were entirely true.

"Not sad," Nat said, focusing on looking for a certain block in the pile. "But just don't talk about him, okay?"

"Sure thing, Nat," their father said with a quizzical glance at Darrah.

"So, what were you doing, Dad?" Darrah asked, taking one of the little vehicles she had made, and wheeling it around the base of the tower.

Ben turned back to the blocks in his hands, snapping and unsnapping them. "Oh, I had to fix that hole in the fence the teenagers made, and then clean out the little chapel. Then I just went around, seeing what needs some touch-up paint and what not. I checked up on the Evil Queen from Snow White. I always like looking at that scene."

"She looks mean," Nat said. "I don't like her. And the woodsman looks silly. He oughta chop her up with an ax, but he looks all stupid instead."

Now Ben raised his eyebrows at his son, though since he was sitting behind Nat, the boy couldn't see him. "Wow, Nat, you'd make it a different story."

"Yeah, the woodsman would chop her up, then he and the Seven Dwarves could go fight a dragon. There oughta be a dragon in the story, as the bad guy, instead of the Queen. Girls can't be bad guys."

"What if it were a girl dragon?" Darrah asked. She looked at her brother sideways, and although he kept building and didn't look up, she could feel him relax a little. He didn't take much to defuse. It wasn't his fault if he felt tense and anxious around their parents.

Nat thought just a moment about the new scenario. "I guess that'd be okay. Then they'd have to destroy all her eggs before they hatched, and they'd get all the goo from the eggs all over the place, and it'd burn like acid, so that'd be cool."

Ben shook his head. "What do you think, Darrah?"

"I don't think there needs to be a dragon in the story," she said as she nudged her brother with her foot. He pushed it away, but she could see he was giving a little smile as he did so.

Ben laughed out loud at that. "Oh, I know that," he said. "I meant, what do you think of the scene of the Evil Queen? I remember how the woodsman used to scare you when he was in his other place in the old park."

"I think he looks better now. It was the whale I didn't like. The Queen is so pretty. I love how... she was carved." She'd nearly said who carved it, but had caught herself at the last moment. "It's still kinda creepy, and I can't look at it for very long."

"Yeah, I know what you mean. I can't look at it for long, either. But I hadn't looked at it in a long time. Funny, how sometimes you want to go back and visit something like that, and see if it has the same effect on you."

They sat for a minute, with the clicking of the blocks the only sound in the room. Then their father dropped his blocks back into the pile and stood up. "You want to help me with dinner?" he said to Darrah as he stepped around the tower and roughed up her hair.

"Sure, Dad," she said, following him into the kitchen.

"What's for dinner?" Nat called after them.

"Don't know, Natty-Bo," Ben replied, pausing in the doorway to the kitchen. "Brussel sprouts? Spinach?"

"Yuck!"

"Well, you're probably in luck – I don't think we have either of those."

"Good!"

"Maybe meatloaf?"

"With mashed potatoes?"

"Nope. No potatoes. I'll have to scrounge up some rice or noodles."

"Okay."

"And broccoli. I know your mother bought broccoli."

There was a pause, and Darrah watched Nat put a block at the top of his tower. "Yeah, broccoli's not too bad," he said.

"You two hoodlums watch TV this afternoon?"

"No, not a bit," Darrah replied.

"Okay," their father said. "You can watch some while you're building, Natty-Bo. How's that sound?"

"That's good." Nat picked up the remote from the coffee table and flipped on their old television. It took a couple seconds for the little dot to get big and fill the screen. Darrah hadn't seen a television as small at any of her friends' houses in years. She hadn't seen one without a cable box in years, either.

Darrah and her father went into the kitchen and let the door close behind them. Her dad turned to face her, putting his big hands on Darrah's shoulders and squeezing as he looked in her eyes. "You want to talk while we make dinner, or is this one of your secrets that you think you got under control and you don't need help with?" His voice was gentle. Exactly like Nat, he could be pretty nice most of the time. You just had to handle him right, too. Darrah wondered why her mom never seemed to get that.

"No, we can talk." She paused. "I don't mean to keep secrets. I'm sorry."

He gave her a smile. His was always much more tentative than hers. "Don't be. You handle him great. I know that. And I know... I know you handle everything great around here. I know it's hard. So I'm the one who should be sorry."

Ben put his big arms around Darrah and hugged her tightly. It was a good embrace, one that didn't just say he loved her, but that he was big and strong and could help. She let herself relax some and feel how nice it was to have someone to rely on, thinking that being needed was way overrated. She wanted more of this feeling; every day, and not just when Nat acted up, and from her mom as well. Being held so strongly, even that last part of what she desired didn't seem so impossible.

Her dad moved back to hold her at arm's length. "Better? We can make dinner and talk?" he asked.

"Sure."

"Why don't you start the rice and the broccoli, and I'll make the meatloaf?" Ben said as he opened the fridge and started handing her things. "If we don't have rice, see if we have some pasta somewhere.

And when you cut the stalks off the broccoli, be sure to keep the bottoms. I can make broth out of them after dinner."

"Okay, Dad."

They worked together for a minute in silence, Darrah getting the steaming basket and two pots while her father turned on the oven and started chopping an onion. He threw away the papery skin, then set the outermost white layer to the side of the cutting board. "So, what's up with not talking about your Opa?" he started, talking quietly. The television sounded loud enough that Nat probably wouldn't hear them.

Darrah put water in the pot with the basket. "I don't know, really. We just had a couple weird things happen today, and the second time, it was right when we were talking about Opa, so I think Nat thinks they're connected."

"Mmm-hmm. Okay. What weird things?" Ben put the bits of onion in a metal mixing bowl and started adding the other ingredients.

Darrah set the pot for the broccoli on the stove. "When we climbed the hill, he got a nosebleed. A really bad one. I haven't seen that much blood in a long time. Mom would've had a kitten and not talked to us for days."

Even at a distance, she could feel her dad tense up, just as palpably as she had sensed Nat in the living room. "You cleaned everything up?" he asked.

"Yeah, it's all in the dryer. I put spot remover on his coat sleeve, and it's red anyway, so it should be okay."

He relaxed. "Thanks, kiddo. You're the best." Ben poured some ketchup on top of the hamburger meat and bread crumbs. "But you shouldn't get him all worked up, going up that hill. He gets them worse when he's over-exerting. You got to take it easy with him."

Darrah measured the water into the other pot before setting it on the stove. "But he was having fun, Dad. I don't mind cleaning it up, if he's at least had a good time. It's better than scrapping with him, trying to keep him from doing stuff. That never works."

Ben sighed. "Yeah. You're right." He opened the egg carton and there was only one inside. "Oh, shoot, there's only one egg." He paused, then shrugged. "Oh, well." He cracked it into the mixing bowl. "Less for you."

"Hey!" She'd moved next to him at the counter, and she shoved her shoulder against her father's. He pretended to be knocked to the side and they laughed.

"But I don't get what's so weird," Ben continued. "He's had nosebleeds plenty before. And I don't get what this has to do with your grandfather."

Darrah cut the broccoli, piling the stems off to the side. "I don't know if Nat noticed," she said with her voice lower than before, "but right before his nose started bleeding, there was this weird smell. I was trying to figure out what it was when I heard him shout and saw the blood."

"Smell? Like what? Gas? Something burning?"

She frowned. "Sort of burning. Not like smoke, but it was a burning sensation when you smelt it, you know? Not strong, but you could tell it was there. Spice – that's what it was like. Like when you smell pepper or some spice like that."

"Up on the hill? There's nothing around there that should smell like that."

"I know. I thought of the Chinese restaurant, but it wasn't like the smell from there. It was more like baking than frying type spices. But something was wrong with it, so it didn't smell nice or tasty, but kind of – I don't know, almost like it was toxic or spoiled. Or just wrong, like the spices weren't mixed right and they were causing some reaction. I don't know. I'm not explaining it right. But it was weird how there was a strange smell right before Nat got such a bad nosebleed."

Darrah's father had finished mixing the meatloaf ingredients and he now formed it into a greasy, pink blob in a baking pan. "Well, that's a little weird, I guess. The bakery has been closed forever, and when it was open – well, the smell was nice, not something nasty like you're saying. Heck, better than nice, it was amazing. But, either way, I certainly can't explain what happened." He opened the oven door and put the meatloaf in. "But you said there were two weird things. What was the other one?"

Darrah dumped the broccoli tops into the steaming basket and put the lid on the pot. "When we were building with Legos, Nat stood up too fast, and he got dizzy and fell down. But I guess what was weird about it, was that we'd just been talking about Opa – we were even saying how the tower looked like New York City, and we'd gone there with him, the same way you talked about that. So I guess when Nat heard you saying the same thing I'd said right before he fell over, he got scared and wanted you to stop talking about it. I know it doesn't make sense, but I guess that's how he was thinking about it."

Her father measured a cup of rice, dumped it in the boiling water in the other pot, and put the cover on. "Oh, things that frighten us don't have to make sense," he said as he turned down the heat on both burners as low as they would go. He stepped away from the oven and leaned his back against the counter, next to Darrah. "That makes about as much sense as a lot of fears. You get hurt right when someone's talking about something, then the next time somebody talks about that same thing, you tense up and expect to get hurt again. The idea is not that far out there."

Darrah leaned against her dad a little, craving some of the reassurance she'd felt when he held her. "I guess not. It sounds weird, but it made me wonder about what happens when a person dies. I mean, no one knows, right?"

"Nope. That's why we never told you something about them going somewhere, or being asleep, or whatever, because no one knows for sure, so we just left it at that. I guess it would've been easier to make something up, but it was one thing your mother and I agreed on, not to tell you something we didn't think was true."

"Well, it made me wonder if there was, I don't know, some lingering effect from the dead person. Not exactly a haunting. I don't want you to think I'm acting all strange and stuff."

Ben put his arm around his daughter and hugged her from the side. "Don't worry about that. I already think you're strange."

"Dad!" Darrah turned and smacked his shoulder, but she didn't stop him when he pulled her close again.

"Don't pay attention to me, princess. Try to describe what you're talking about."

"I don't know. Like they have some effect on us, even after they're gone. Live people can hurt you or make you happy, and maybe a dead person still has some of that power. Or maybe it's just the memory of them. Even if it were just the memory, it could still be really strong, strong enough to make you sick and stuff, the way they used to say people would die of a broken heart."

"That's true. That doesn't sound weird at all. I don't want to say something mean about him, but your grandfather... well, he could make me feel kind of bad when I was a kid. And I still feel that way now, when I look at all the stuff he made. Even though the carvings are so beautiful, they make me sad or angry sometimes. So I know what you mean."

"I'm sorry you feel that way, Dad."

Ben took his arm from around her and went over to turn off the broccoli and pull the steamer basket out. He dumped the water out, then returned the broccoli to the pot and covered it back up. "It's okay," he said as he worked. "And, um, I'm sorry if your mom and I make you feel sad sometimes. I don't mean to." He didn't add it immediately, but after a moment he said, "She doesn't mean to, either."

Darrah nodded. "I know. It's been better lately."

She heard the front door open and close, then her mother's voice. "Hi, Nat!" she could hear her mother call out. "Where is everyone?"

They couldn't hear Nat's reply, then Ruth came into the kitchen. "Hey, you two!" she said.

Darrah thought, as she often did, how pretty her mom was, and her smile certainly improved her looks. "Hey Mom!"

"Hey there, Missy."

"Hey, you," Ben said as he stepped over to kiss his wife. She didn't even turn her head, like she usually did, Darrah noticed, but let him kiss her on the lips.

It wasn't exactly a tight clinch, but no teenager could resist noting and mocking her parents for it. "You two want to be alone?" Darrah said as she opened the cutlery drawer.

"Darrah!" her mom said, but she was laughing. She had a nice laugh, too – not big and horsy like Darrah's, but not a girlish giggle, either. It was full, but kind of balanced and measured.

"I'm teasing, I'm teasing!" Darrah said as she raised her hands to defend herself from her mom's playful swats to her shoulders and butt.

"Better be!" Ruth said as she composed herself, leaning back against her husband. "You three have a good day?"

Ben put his arms around his wife from behind and held her loosely. "Yeah, I think it was pretty good."

"Good," her mother said. "But are you sure Nat's okay? He sounded a little stuffed up. God, I was so glad I hadn't seen any blood in a while. I think I'd have a fit if I did."

Darrah didn't need to feel anyone else tense up, as her own insides snapped taut. She looked her mother right in the eyes and shook her head.

"No, he was fine all day," Darrah said.

She knew she had the right tone and had raised her eyebrows and lowered the corners of her mouth just right. Unlike some teens, Darrah didn't exactly enjoy lying to her mother, but she had gotten good at it. She thought of lying as a kind of tool; it just had to be used sparingly so it didn't wear out, or wear out its user.

"That's good. Well, I got a lot of writing done today, and I think I won't go in tomorrow. I need to do some food shopping, and I can clean up around here. That'll be nicer than that cold, empty office."

"Nobody around there today?" Ben said, and squeezed her a little tighter.

Ruth looked down. "Nobody special."

"Mmm-hmm." Darrah thought her dad's tone just then had a bit of a hurt, sour edge to it; she'd heard it before, but this time it didn't seem like it would flare up into a fight, at least. They were more in their "simmering" mode, though even that seemed to have dissipated a bit, so that there could be glimpses of something like affection and playfulness between them.

Darrah went out with the plates and flatware. They didn't have a separate dining room; the table was just at one end of the living room. "What are you all laughing at?" Nat called from the sofa.

Darrah set the stack down on the table. "Nothing," she said. "Just being silly. How you doing?"

"Good."

Darrah set the four chipped plates at their spots around the old table, flanking them with the mismatched forks and knives. Her grandfather had made the dining table, as he had most of their furniture. Though it was a beautiful piece, made from rich, dark cherry, it was now something like forty years old, and thoroughly banged-up. Stepping back to consider it, Darrah thought it wouldn't be right to cover up such glowing, gorgeous wood, but it could do with some sprucing up. She decided a runner for it would make a good Mother's Day gift – either a frilly one, with lace and stuff, or a colorful one, with a flowered pattern. Mom always liked girly and flowery things, and Darrah kind of liked looking at them in the store.

The thought pleased her quite a bit as she straightened the flatware, but then she remembered she'd better get the laundry out of the dryer before her mother spotted it, and she trotted off to the basement in her usual rush.

CHAPTER 17

Friday, April 6, 2007 – The Sublunar Sphere

Praying for Ben was even harder than Christoph had expected. He didn't know what, exactly, to say or think, and just kept fumbling around with the same words in his mind. It was so hard to keep bad thoughts from coming in, too – thoughts about how disobedient or ungrateful or faithless Ben was – at least when he had those thoughts, he could beg God to rid him of them, so that gave him something definite for which to pray. Further, the damned inconvenience of not having a regular, physical body with which to breathe and sway and shift continued to plague him and make his prayers not flow as they should. The beginning of that evening was very arduous for Christoph Hahn, as prayer had long been his main source of solace, both before and after he died, so if it came with difficulty and confusion as it did now, he felt even more lost and alone.

Little by little, however, the right feeling began to fill Christoph. He could just feel grateful. For some reason, after a while, the negative thoughts were the ones that slipped away. He felt an irresistible warmth and attraction toward the better thoughts of his son; his success in school, his physical strength and health, his hard work, his strange, unpredictable wonder at various things, especially the things Christoph had made in the Enchanted Mill Forest. He felt more at peace than at any other time since he had died.

As peaceful and grateful as he felt, there was nonetheless one distracting figure who kept creeping into his thoughts, threatening to derail his prayers and plunge him back into frustration and despair. Christoph couldn't help but think about his son's wife. The urge to think of her was so strong, her presence so palpable, that he felt quite certain she must've come home. It was probably about that time of day.

Christoph's feelings for her had always been negative. She was certainly pretty enough, and that was always a good thing in a woman. And very feminine-looking, too – not like so many women you saw nowadays. But as far as Christoph was concerned, Ruth's virtues more or less ended at her physical appearance. She was too assertive and meddling, and over the years Christoph had attributed several bad events to his daughter-in-law's influence, blaming her for turning Ben away from the faith, and for persuading them to sell Holy Book Land.

He had attributed these personal setbacks to her so frequently and for so long that he had convinced himself the causation had some basis in reality. He had long since trained himself to ignore the fact that Ben had stopped going to church his senior year of high school, and had been vehemently against it long before that. He was also quite practiced at overlooking how Ruth had never shown any encouragement for selling Holy Book Land, and had even gone out of her way to help with the salvage of some of the pieces from there. Oddly, Christoph did not blame her for her constant bickering with her husband; he knew how difficult his son could be, so he suspected any marital difficulties were mostly Ben's fault, though she probably bore some blame for bringing out the worst in him.

Although his previous thoughts about his daughter-in-law had always been as hostile and distorted as all this, tonight Christoph's state of mind was purer. He had reached that kind of focus in prayer that absorbs and inverts even negative, erroneous thoughts, so he was able to take this one bad intrusion, and turn it into something hopeful and positive. Rather than curse Ruth, or wish she'd never been born or had never met Ben, Christoph thanked God for her giving him such beautiful grandchildren. He again felt embarrassed he'd been so critical of them earlier, especially Darrah, and his guilt for hurting Nat burned more intensely than before. He begged God to forgive him for that.

For a moment he forgot the things he blamed Ruth for, and instead prayed to God that she and her husband would learn to live better and more peaceably together. Christoph even considered that perhaps he'd been a source of some tension and conflict in their home, so he thanked God for taking him out of there, and doing so in such a gentle, painless way that he didn't even remember his passing. Thanking God for his own death felt comforting to Christoph, and was a measure of his focused and grateful he was.

Then Christoph felt another overwhelming assault, at once alike yet different from the other two that terrible day. It was neither the explosive blast that had knocked him over on the hill, nor the red-hot piercing that had violated him here in this room earlier. Instead, it felt as though a truckload of wet cement had been dumped on him. The damp and cold were as painful and disorienting as the enormous weight bearing down on him. It wasn't as though the weight were just on top of him, either. It felt as though it had penetrated and become a part of him, as though he were now a dead, wet lump, incapable of either heat or movement or thought. He tried to open his eyes, but it felt like they were sewn shut with freezing cold, steel wires.

Christoph collapsed from his chair to the floor with a wet slap that sounded like a pile of soaked laundry had been flung on to a concrete slab. It didn't feel as though he'd been pushed or thrown there, however, but more like the floor had pulled him down to itself, his damp inertia drawn down to its proper place. Nor did this pulling feeling decrease, once he was face down on the ground. He couldn't move any part of himself, the downward attraction was so strong. He even had the oddest fancy that he was being absorbed into the ground; not just like quicksand, but like he was becoming part of the earth. He could almost feel the cold grit of the blood-colored clay easing in between the strands of his elements, the way sand would fill up a sieve if you pushed it down into a sandbox.

Christoph couldn't feel fear or pain at this point, he had become so dull, lethargic, and discouraged. How could he be frightened of becoming part of the floor, if he already felt like part of it? It must be where he belonged, so why fight it?

A pressing on his shoulder announced that Merla hadn't given up, however. When she spoke, it sounded distant and bubbly, though it still had her peculiar insistence and intensity. "Come on, Christoph." Her voice sounded as though she was straining at something, though again the pressure he felt was barely noticeable. "We have to get you turned toward the fire. Something's happened. Spirits in the sky! How did you get so heavy?! Roll over, you! Come on!"

There was a pause, then Merla's voice sounded closer, like she was lying on top of him and putting her mouth close to his ear. "Listen, you strange little man. I've met people who've believed all sorts of things, or nothing at all. But I've never met anyone who wanted to be underground, rather than above it. You're sinking into the ground for some reason, and you're as cold as a puddle of muddy slush. I'm going to try again to roll you toward the fire and warm you up, but you've got to push as hard as you can. You have to help. You have to do it for yourself. I can't do everything for you. Get ready to push."

There was the pressure again on his shoulder, and Christoph tried to push with what little strength and concentration he could muster. "That's it," he could hear again from a distance. "You budged a little. Let me kick this bear skin away, so I can plant my feet better. Now!"

With a sort of sucking, wet pop - like when you pull a stick out of the mud - Christoph felt himself partially freed. He rolled on to his back, and the momentum was enough to carry him over on to his left side, facing the fire. He could barely feel it when Merla flung the wool rug over him. He felt it more when she pressed herself up against his back and threw her thick, corky little arms around his shoulders and neck. He felt her hand rubbing his eyes, like she was scraping off something that had caked on to them. Now he could open them just a little.

"Stare into the fire, Christoph," she said, again close to his ear. "I don't know what's happened to you, but you've got to fight it. I'm sure your God is under the floor, too, but I don't think that's where you'll see Him best, since that's what you say you want. So stare into the fire. Let it warm you. Know that I'm here and I'll help you. It's what I've been put here to do. Fight whatever was pulling you down and freezing you."

Slowly Christoph could open his eyes more, until the fire was not just an orange glow, but he could see the individual flames dancing. He could move his right arm a bit, too, and open his mouth. He tried to speak, but it was more of a wheeze.

"Don't move," Merla said. "Just look and listen and think. Concentrate. Your mind and heart will revive you, if you work them as fully as you can. The hearth is centeredness, rest, belonging. The ground is also rest and solidity, but it can be deadening, brutal, and nameless. Something must've happened to shake you loose from the hearth and thrust you down to the ground. Something made you feel deader than you are. Don't move, let your strength come back to you. But tell me what you felt."

"Like I was dead... stuff," Christoph whispered. "Just stuff. Not a person, not even an animal. Wet, cold stuff. I couldn't move or fight it, because it felt like that was what I really was, what I was supposed to be, and there was no point in doing anything to try and change it. It was my fate, my being. I felt like I didn't exist. Like I'd never existed."

"Yes, that's what I thought. I told you that your family's thoughts and feelings would affect and possibly hurt you, just as yours have done to them. That must've been what happened. You must learn to weather it, Christoph. Only your own emotions and thoughts are under your control, and they can withstand even the most terrible assault. Do you know who disturbed you this way?"

"My daughter-in-law."

"You didn't sleep with her, did you?" The fact that her response came without the least pause made it all the more shocking.

Christoph tried to sit up at that outrageous remark, but the effort made him feel like an enormous door had slammed into him and pinned him between itself and the doorjamb. "*Mein Gott!* How can you say such a thing, you little monster? Of course not!"

Merla kept holding him. Her voice was never gentle, exactly, but now it was soft and matter of fact. "It wasn't an accusation, Christoph. Just like when I asked if you'd been murdered. I've seen many dead people through the years. When a man says his daughter-in-law has revealed something about himself that makes him feel dead inside, I have to think of similar cases I've seen before."

"You've known men who did such things?"

"Oh, I wish with all my heart that that was the worst I'd heard of men doing. After all this time, I don't know that I'd blink if you had done that. Or worse. I know I wouldn't blush at the thought, even if I still had that ability."

"Well, I didn't do that, so stop talking about it."

"All right. What would she know about you, then?"

"I don't know. My mind's not clear about what happened, exactly."

"It will come to you."

"I never liked her. I'm sure she did something bad, to hurt me. This is her fault, somehow. Why did she always do things to hurt me and break up my family?"

Merla's voice was no longer soft, though it was still matter of fact. "Christoph, I've warned you before. Blame is as bad as regret here. You will not think that way, or the next time I'll help shove you through the floor myself. Do you understand me?"

Christoph mastered his anger and felt himself relax somewhat. "Yes. I'm sorry. I'll try harder."

He stared at the flames, but their heat still felt weak, distant, and unreachable. It was hard not to hold on to his dislike and distaste for his daughter-in-law, because so much of the rest of his memories seemed to have been sucked out of him, and that petty little hate was the only thing that felt like it could warm and illuminate the dark emptiness inside him.

CHAPTER 18

Friday, April 6, 2007 – Northern New Jersey

Ruth looked at her plate and thought how meatloaf was a most reliable thing. So was rice. Broccoli was a bit less satisfying, and still not up there with steak or tiramisu – those kinds of foods that are either so orgasmically good you can't stop eating them, and you just keep on going 'til you feel sick, or else they are so wretchedly bad you can't eat them again for months. Either way, the encounter is always a threat of something unpleasant.

A plate of meatloaf, rice, and broccoli wasn't a bit like that. Ruth pushed the side of her fork through a piece of the ground beef concoction, got some rice on to the fork as well, stabbed a small broccoli floret, then raised the mixture to her mouth. Not delicious, but warm and wet, a little grainy and chewy. As it should be. As always.

"Hmm, good," she said. "A little crumbly." Ruth leaned a little toward her husband, who was sitting next to her.

"Yeah, we only had one egg," Ben said.

"Oh. I'll get some tomorrow at the supermarket. Sales end on Saturday."

Ruth looked at Nat, who always sat at the head of the table. He'd already eaten all his broccoli – he was one of those people who ate all of the things he liked least on his plate first. Ruth stared at him until he looked up and noticed.

"What?" he said, looking a little defensive.

Ruth smiled. "You must really like broccoli."

"No, I just eat it first to get rid of it. You know that."

She kept smiling as she returned to her own dinner. "Oh, so you don't like it."

"It's okay. I don't mind it."

"You have to learn to like lots of different things."

It was her standard admonition to eat vegetables, but she still tensed a little on the inside when she said it. A few years ago, Ben would've made a double entendre about how she'd be the one to know about liking lots of different things. It'd be just vague enough that he could get away with saying it in front of the kids, but he'd give it just the right caustic tone to get his message across. And if she weren't in the mood for his passive-aggressive bullshit, then she'd say something nasty back, and off they'd go. No make-up sex, either, on those nights – just one of them sleeping on the couch. She'd noticed, however, that he didn't say those things so much anymore, and he didn't tonight. If a big, blunt block like him could change, then she could make some effort, too.

"I do. I eat most stuff," Nat responded.

"Yeah, you're not so bad, I suppose. I guess we can keep him, huh?"

Ruth gave her husband a nudge. Lately, she had noticed that whenever she saw that dolt Peter, it would make her want to be more playful and affectionate to her family. Every time she saw that walking advertisement for chastity, she'd get this idea that it would somehow prove her superiority, if her family life were now better than his. She could even increase the enjoyment of her gloating, by imagining Peter slinking home to his dumpy wife – she'd been bony when Ruth first met her, and now after two kids she'd gone to the other extreme and was a huge, flabby mess of a woman. Hell, he probably couldn't even get it up for his wife anymore, not that the poor woman was missing much. Deep down, Ruth knew it was all a silly and slightly nasty daydream she had in her car on the way home from work, but she still liked how it made her feel.

"Keep him? Did we get an offer from someone to take him off our hands?" Ben played along.

"Maybe some carnies will come through in the summer and we can get rid of him then," Darrah added. "He could be like Wolf Boy or Dog Boy or something. He's always out in the woods anyway."

Ruth saw her daughter grin at her and then at Nat; she had always been able to keep him happy and under control, even when she was a lot younger. She thought how much harder it would be if Darrah were less patient and helpful, and besides feeling superior to Peter for that blessing, she felt a little humble and grateful. As she examined her daughter, she also noticed Darrah needed some new clothes. She should go shopping with her next week.

"Hey, stop!" Nat said, but he was smiling and laughing.

Ruth pointed at him with her fork. "And why are you at the head of the table, anyway, little mister?" She squeezed Ben's shoulder with her other hand. "This is the big, strong man of the house. He ought to be at the head of the table!" Again, a few years ago, that comment would've been guaranteed to elicit some remark about how she would know all about men. He probably wouldn't have gone as far as making a play on the word "head," but my God, he'd come close a few times, even in front of the kids or in public. She didn't deserve that kind of embarrassment, even if she had been stupid and immature, needing too much to be desired and in control. It was a nice evening, now that he refrained from such bullshit.

"Yeah!" Ben joined in. "Move aside, squirt!"

"You put my chair here, when I was little!" Nat objected. "You can have your dumb spot back if you want!"

Ben laughed as he got up and cleared his place. He put his hand on Nat's shoulder as he walked by and playfully pushed him back down into his chair. "No, no, you keep your spot, chief. You've earned it, I figure."

Everyone cleared their dishes and flatware out to the kitchen, where Ben started filling the sink with hot, soapy water.

"Is there anything for dessert?" Nat asked as he dropped his knife and fork into the rising suds.

"Don't know," his father replied. "I can't think of anything. Check the freezer."

Ruth was close to the fridge, so she rummaged in the freezer and came out with an ice cream carton. "There's a little ice cream left," she said as she looked inside the container.

"What flavor?" asked Nat.

"Well, it was a box of vanilla, chocolate, and strawberry, but now there's just a little vanilla and strawberry."

"I want the strawberry," said Nat.

"Don't you share with your sister?" Ruth asked.

"Yeah. Do you want some strawberry, Darrah?"

Darrah was standing in the doorway to the dining area. "No, you go ahead, Nat. I'll just take some of the vanilla that's left."

Ruth scooped the ice cream into two bowls, working hard to stifle the thought that vanilla suited a plain girl like Darrah perfectly. That was a terrible thing to think, especially when the girl was just being nice and polite, but she couldn't help it. As she handed Darrah her bowl, she considered her daughter more closely. Gawky, gangling body, with nothing in proportion – but who the hell did have a nice figure at that age?

Ruth remembered she'd been flat as a board, and my God, the acne she'd had in middle and high school. Darrah always had such nice skin, and she had a lot of other assets, too. She'd inherited her mother's hair and eyes, which Ruth knew were both especially beautiful. The girl was already an inch taller than her mother, and with that height, she'd have incredible legs when she got older. Her neck was nice and long, too, she just needed to wear longer, dangling earrings to accent it better. *In general, the girl just needed a little sprucing up*, Ruth thought. They'd definitely have to go shopping next week.

The kids went back out to the dining table to eat their ice cream, as Ruth got the dishtowel off the oven handle and went to help her husband with the dishes.

"Everything good at work?" he asked. There was another question that until recently would've been one more shit-bomb thrown at her, to which she would have responded in kind. But now it was just an everyday question, the kind people ask when they're doing the dishes.

Ruth took a plate from the rack next to the sink and started drying it. "Oh, you know college administration. There's nothing too bad going on right now, no one's all pissy about some slight they think they got or some new bullshit policy. We have to overhaul the departmental website, so that'll be a major pain in the ass. Same shit, different day." She might've added, "No one's banging anyone else in the department," to a different conversation partner. She had always liked cursing, ever since high school. She wouldn't normally drop the F-bomb though, she'd think it to herself, and she wouldn't curse in front of the kids. But otherwise she liked the feeling it gave her, naughty and in control.

Ben put one of the pots on the rack. "Yeah. Well, no one can tell me if I'll have any classes for the fall. Probably be at the last minute, as usual. Or, they'll tell me they're a go, then pull them at the last minute. It'd fucking kill them to be a little considerate. Like two grand is going to break the university's fucking budget, if the fucking class has twenty kids in it, instead of twenty-five."

His cursing always included the F-bomb, and seemed to Ruth to have more of an edge to it than hers. Hers felt like it was letting off steam, his seemed to indicate just how much anger still remained. At least it wasn't directed at her. She knew the job and money worries were hard on him, but it wasn't her fault.

"Hey, did you start going through your father's stuff?" she asked, partly to change the subject, partly because she'd been thinking about it.

"What? Oh, no, not really. I just don't feel like it yet. It's all in his room over the garage, so it's not in the way or anything, at least."

"Mmm-hmm." Ruth took the pot and put it back on the stove. She was about to propose a strange idea, and although she didn't think it would have any effect on her husband, it was still a very odd thought, so she didn't rush right into it. "I hope you don't mind, but I was looking at those two photo albums of his."

Ben shook his head. "No, that's fine. What'd you see?"

"Well, the smaller one has pictures of you when you were little, and pictures of your mom and dad together. And the really big one has much older pictures, from when he was a kid, with his sister and their parents. Did he ever show you any other photos, or are those all there is?"

Ben frowned as he put another plate on the rack. "No, that's all that I know about. He didn't have the big album when I was really little. His aunt sent it when my grandmother died."

"Well, this is going to sound weird, but up until his sister died, there are a lot of photos of the family. All different seasons and holidays, arranged chronologically. Very organized. Then there are just a few pictures of your dad and his mom and aunt."

"Well, I guess they were distraught over his sister, and then over his father missing, too. Probably back then, women didn't take pictures as much as men did, either."

Ruth put a dish in the cupboard. "That's true. I know when I was little, my dad was in charge of the camera and my mom didn't touch it. So I can understand that. But what's weird, is that there are no pictures of your dad as a baby. There are pictures of his sister, all the way back to her birth, but his start when he's a toddler. He looks like he's about two years old in the first picture they have of him."

"Yeah, that's a little weird, I guess. Was there something going on at the time that would've kept them from taking pictures? The invasions of Austria and Czechoslovakia were right around then, weren't they? Were there shortages or something?"

"Yes, but like I said, they had pictures from all during the war. And, what's stranger, is that they had pictures of his sister at the time when he would've been a baby. But no pictures of him. So they were taking pictures in 1937 and 1938, just not of him."

Ben put a glass on the rack. "That's getting weirder, definitely. But what are you thinking about it for?"

"I'm wondering if he was adopted. He looks so different from them in the pictures, too. They're very blonde and Germanic looking, and his hair's so dark."

That made Ben stop and look up from the dishwater. "Really?" he said, looking at his wife. "Wow. That is a really strange thought. I guess back then they would've kept it more hidden, because he sure never mentioned anything about it." He went back to fishing around in the sudsy water for more things. "You know, he did always complain his parents liked his sister better - that they wouldn't have been as sad if he had been the one to be killed. He'd say that sometimes, if he was trying to guilt me into something. Like he knew it was hard for me not to have a mother, but at least my father loved me, while his parents liked his sister better and wished he'd been the one to die, so I should be grateful for what I had. Those kinds of things. Always trying to make me feel bad, or feel sorry for him."

"It would make sense. I mean, I'm sure he exaggerated it, but it would've been hard, to see your biological child die while the child you adopted survived. It'd be hard to hide your feelings, no matter how much you reminded yourself you should love them both equally."

"Yeah, it's hard to hide your feelings, even around kids."

Ruth took the glass from the rack, wiping it as she stepped to the cupboard where it went. "Well, I'd noticed that about the photos a few days ago, and it intrigued me, then I was talking to a colleague in the history department, and she was telling me about her research on the Holocaust." Ruth still put a little extra emphasis on *she* and *her* when she talked about conversations with other professors. "She's written some articles and now she's working on a book about Christian families that secretly adopted Jewish babies and raised them, so they'd escape the Nazis. Sometimes they'd say the kid was from a relative in another city or state. They'd have forged papers if they were really careful. Sometimes it worked."

Ben had the larger pot out of the suds and was now rinsing it. "You're saying you think my father was Jewish?"

"Maybe he was born Jewish. My colleague said the Nazis defined anyone with three Jewish grandparents as a Jew. It didn't matter if the person ever practiced the religion at all. Even if their parents were completely secular and assimilated, it was considered a racial thing. I know he didn't live as one or believe in it. I know this sounds funny, but was he circumcised?"

Ben chuckled as he put the broccoli stalks and onion peel into the big pot and filled it with cold water. "Now there's a question I never thought I'd have to answer. Well, come to think of it - yes, he was."

"Not very common back then, for non-Jews."

Ben put the pot on a low flame and turned back to the sink, searching for the last few things at the bottom. "He could've had it done later in life. A lot of men get infections, so they have it done."

"True, but still. It's another piece of evidence that makes you wonder."

"Oh, you got me wondering, that's for sure. And I guess it'd make his parents' reaction to his sister's death more understandable - that they'd gone and saved this kid they thought of as a foreigner, a stranger, an alien from a different race, but they couldn't save their own flesh and blood. That'd make anyone feel guilty and conflicted." He shook his head. "Still, it is pretty funny, since the old guy hated Jews so much."

"It's not like they're born with the genetic information that they're Jewish and they're not supposed to believe Nazi propaganda. If he was raised in a regular German household, he would've heard all that growing up and believed it. And he was no worse than a lot of men from his generation, even here in the United States. He was always polite to everyone and just kept to himself."

Ben got out the last of the flatware from the bottom of the sink. "Ruth, there was like an unholy trinity for him – Communists, Jews, and Catholics – in that order, up from the bottom. Sometimes Jews and Catholics would swap places. Communists had a lock on first place, Satan's number one cabana boys, right on the shores of the lake of fire."

Ruth started drying the knives and forks and putting them in the drawer. "I don't think he was as bad as you make out."

"Well, it's a wild thought, that's for sure, that he might've been Jewish. I can't think of anything that would disprove it, and it makes sense of some things." Ben turned to check on the broccoli, and saw Darrah standing in the doorway. "Oh hi, princess."

Ruth saw Darrah's look change instantly from shocked to guilty. "Sorry," her daughter stammered. "Nat went to see what's on TV, and I was bringing in the bowls. It's okay if he watches some TV, isn't it? I told him he could." She was talking too fast, as children always do when they're caught at something.

Ben took the bowls from his daughter. "Oh, sure, I think so. Right, hun?"

Ruth closed the cutlery drawer and turned to face them. "Oh, it's fine. What isn't fine is you standing there eavesdropping, Darrah."

Darrah came all the way into the kitchen and let the door close behind her. "I'm sorry. I came in right when you said Opa hated Jews, and it just made me stop for a second to listen. And then you said he was a Jew. Do you really think so?"

Ben washed the bowls and put them on the rack. "You mother's convinced me it's possible, but I guess we'll never know. Funny thing is, if he were here, he'd be so upset just by the suggestion that I doubt we could talk about it. Poor guy would've blown a gasket to find out he was one of the hated ones who was dragging the world down into oblivion, a member of the Chosen People and not the Master Race."

Ruth thought Ben could be so unnecessarily cruel about his dad; and it wasn't right to talk that way in front of Darrah. She'd always gotten along with her grandfather and she should be able to have those memories without them being tainted like that.

"Ben, he wasn't a Nazi," Ruth said. "He was just a kid when it happened, and he grew up to be a little scared of foreigners. That happens to people who grow up during a war. He wasn't so bad."

"Yeah, whatever. I'm going to go read some. I have to write a book review. Put another useless line on my useless c.v." He was back to his old mood, and it wasn't any prettier than it had been before. He stepped past Darrah and left the kitchen.

Ruth stared after him, then turned toward her daughter. "I think your father's too hard on your Opa. He was always nice to you, wasn't he?"

"Yeah. He was a little strange. But he was nice."

Ruth took a step toward her daughter. "Please don't believe all the bad things people think about one another," she said very softly. "Not about your Opa, and not about... not about anyone else, either. Please. People don't always mean to hurt other people, but it just happens."

"I know, Mom."

Ruth looked into Darrah's eyes for a moment; if anything, they were an even prettier shade than hers, and so bright and sparkling. Most people never had eyes as clear and innocent as that, and they sure didn't have them after their twenties. She and Ben shouldn't have done so much to tarnish beauty like that with their foolishness and selfishness.

"You always liked the things he made around here," Ruth said. "I know that made him happy."

"Oh, I love the stuff he carved. He made such beautiful things."

"Yes, he did." She brushed Darrah's hair from her face with the back of her hand. Ruth seldom touched her, now that Darrah was bigger, but right now she was overcome with the need to. "You're the only beautiful thing I ever made. I was thinking that when I looked at you across the table." Well, maybe not when she looked at her before, but it was definitely what she was thinking now.

Darrah smiled; not her big grin, but something much more shy and vulnerable, with her eyes cast down. "Thanks, Mom."

"We'll go do something special next week, okay? Just you and me. We can leave those gross, nasty boys at home or drop them off at the zoo where they belong."

Now Darrah's smile was its usual size. "That'd be nice, Mom."

"Okay, now go keep an eye on your brother while I finish up in here. Maybe we'll pop a movie in the VCR later and watch it together."

Darrah left the kitchen as Ruth took the two bowls off the rack and put them in the cupboard, then hung the dishtowel on the handle of the oven door. She reached into the sink of water to pull the plug. Then she remained for some time, looking into the black hole that had just drunk all the hot, soapy water with a final, loud slurp. It would be such a nice little hole, if you could just pour all your filth and shame down it and not have to worry about the son of a bitch backing up and vomiting it all back on to the floor. Or worse – you had to worry that it'd swallow you up, and leave nothing but the bad stuff behind. You'd think someone could make the damn thing work better.

"Fuck, I got to get my shit together," Ruth muttered as she turned off the light and left the kitchen.

CHAPTER 19
Friday, April 6, 2007 – The Sublunar Sphere

Christoph had finally warmed to the point where he could move and get back up in the chair he'd fallen from. It was one of the wide Barcelona chairs, so Merla sat next to him. It was odd, how she snuggled next to him. It wasn't like a child would. Even though she was centuries old, it wasn't like an adult would, either. *And thank God for that*, Christoph thought. Everything was strange enough here without that confusion.

No, the feeling of her was more like a cat – a big, dark cat made of coarse wood and straw, comfortable in the way that old, hard, rough things sometimes are. She'd wrapped him in the wool blanket as well. He wondered if it looked like a bear skin to her, but didn't bother asking. His head still hurt too much, and was too focused on his own pain and emptiness, to worry much about such things.

"Do you know more about what hurt you before?" she asked.

"I think so, yes," Christoph said.

"You may tell me, when you're ready."

Christoph pulled the blanket tighter around himself. "Well, I got this overwhelming sense that I don't belong, that I never belonged, that I'm not who I think I am. I still can't describe it completely. It was like I was a stranger, looking at my life as though it were someone else living it."

"You moved to this country, didn't you? So you are a stranger, in a way. It's a feeling you're used to."

"Yes, but not like this. Not like the way I feel, when people celebrate Memorial Day or the Fourth of July, and it makes me feel like I don't belong here. Those are American holidays, by the way."

"Yes, thank you for explaining them."

"Not like that. You're right. I was used to that feeling for many years. And homesickness, too. But that's what made this so awful. It was like feeling the worst homesickness I could imagine, and then knowing that the place I was longing for wasn't mine, either, like I didn't belong here or there, and I was totally alone and lost."

"That must be terrible. I am sorry for you. I will help you find your way."

"Thank you. I'm sorry I got angry at you before, when you said... what you suggested about my son's wife."

"Don't worry. As I told you, I've seen so much, I'm not shocked by such things, but I understand when other people do. You have just left the world of appearances and lies, so you still think according to its rules. The rule there is not to talk about unpleasant things. But we will. I know it will upset you. I hope you are prepared."

"I'm trying."

"So you felt like this land was not yours, but the land you came from was also not yours? What was the name of it?"

"Germany."

Merla tried saying it a couple times, but she kept putting the emphasis on the penultimate syllable and it sounded funny, so she gave up.

"All right, go on, I'm sorry," she finally said.

"Well, yes, I felt like nowhere was my home. But it was more than just the countries. I started getting all these memories of my childhood, of my family."

"Bad memories? Did your parents hit you? Hurt you?"

"No, not like that. I mean... it's difficult. I had an older sister. When I was very little, I always thought she got more attention. She had more toys and clothes. Everything I had was shabby, worn out, broken, given to us by cousins. Her stuff was always new. My parents doted on her, helped her with schoolwork, gave her birthday parties. I started remembering all those things. I remembered what happened after she died. There was a big war, and she died. And I remembered how, after that, my parents became even more distant from me. It was like they blamed me for it, and they wished it had been me that had died. Later, my father was gone, too. They said he was probably killed, but I'm not even sure he was. I sometimes think he just wandered off, to be away from me and the responsibility of taking care of me. I hadn't thought of all those painful memories in a long time, and tonight they came back, so strong and evil."

Merla shifted next to him, again giving him that feeling of being simultaneously disconcerted and comforted. "All right," she said. "But you'd thought these things before, yes? What happened to you earlier – when I thought I was going to lose you to the underground – that seemed as though it was some new and more terrible revelation, something you'd never felt before."

The realization became even more concrete to Christoph, as he tried to put it into words, and he could feel himself collapsing again, losing all strength.

Merla threw her arm across his chest and pulled him up. "Stay with me, Christoph," she said loudly, right in his face. "Look into the fire and keep talking. You were doing fine. I won't let you perish. But we can't just forget about what happened. You have to say it."

Christoph blinked and tried to focus. It would be so much easier just to slip away. Merla was right, this had to be done. "Yes, I had thought before about how my parents liked my sister better. But tonight, I could suddenly see clearly why they felt that way. It occurred to me that I might be adopted. I had never thought that before. My parents weren't really my parents. That's why they did what they did. It made perfect, awful sense."

Merla kept her hand on his shoulder. "They raised you. They were your parents. When I lived, parents often died and others raised their children. It is nothing that you should let annihilate you."

"Yes, I know, and I suppose I could be comforted by that, but there was more to it, something even worse. I thought that they might have adopted me because I was a Jew."

"I'm sorry, that word I don't understand."

"It means I was from another race. I wasn't a German, but a Jew."

"I still don't understand. Your skin was the same color as theirs, wasn't it? Otherwise how could they raise you without you knowing you were different?"

Explaining things to her was always so difficult, and usually ended up being embarrassing as well. "Yes, of course we had the same skin color. I didn't say I was from another continent."

"So you were from another country?"

"Not exactly. Jews are a religious sect, but it's not just that. They're also a race, but back then they didn't have a country. They lived in other countries, like Germany."

"I don't really understand this, but all right. You were from a different clan, let's say, than the people who adopted you. I still don't know what's upsetting you."

"Well, the Jews have another religion, too, and one I don't believe in."

"Then don't believe what they believe. You don't, do you? I mean, whatever it is that they believe that you find so upsetting. You weren't suddenly forced to change your beliefs when you found this out, were you?"

"No, of course not, but it's not as simple as that. Being a Jew isn't just belief, you can't get rid of it as easily as that. And it's worse, because, well... during the war, the Germans killed a lot of Jews. Not all Germans, I know, but some bad ones killed many Jews. Not just in fighting, but they murdered them, usually in terrible ways, with poison. So my real parents must've given me to my adoptive parents to hide me and keep me alive. Then my real parents must've been killed with all the other Jews. I feel now like I don't belong to either race."

"That's a horrible story, what happened to those people, but you survived because two sets of parents loved you and took care of you. I know it must be difficult, to discover all this now, but it shouldn't leave you with the feeling of worthlessness and non-existence that you had before. Someone should only feel that way only if he's done something monstrous and ugly, not just for who his parents were."

"I can't help it. It's everything I was raised to believe in, yanked away from me. What could be worse than to find out you're a different person, and everything you believed was just tricks and lies? I'm not who or what I thought I was. I don't know what to believe."

They sat for a moment in silence. Merla started again after a while. "Christoph, I promised to help you and I will. But this is something I think you will have to figure out on your own, at least to start. I cannot understand what these different races and religions are, or what they mean to you, so I can't help you yet. I see it has cast you adrift. It has separated you from centeredness and belonging, emptied you of your self-worth. Those feelings will come back, but it may take time. Until then it will be difficult and painful for you."

"May I go outside? I think I'd like to be alone now."

Merla squeezed his shoulder. "Outside? At night? I doubt that is a good idea. I have little strength, away from the hearth. You'd be alone and vulnerable to more bad thoughts and feelings. I don't think you could withstand them."

"I don't think there's anything worse that could be revealed about me. There's certainly nothing that would surprise and depress me more."

"I have little power to stop you. You must do what you think best. But remember... everything you do here can really only hurt you. Your family may feel momentary discomfort from what you do, but for you, the effects are permanent. Please be careful."

Christoph got up and moved toward the door. "I'll try. Thank you for your help."

The night seemed to him exceptionally cold and dark, but he wanted to be in the shadows, concealed from everyone in his shame and confusion.

CHAPTER 20

Friday, April 6, 2007 – Limen of the Sublunar Sphere and Northern New Jersey

The grey rabbit hopped into the little chapel in the Enchanted Mill Forest, pausing at the doorway to survey the interior. Her eyes weren't of much use in this enclosed space; she could see the cross on the far wall more clearly than the pews which were right next to her. Her hearing and smell were much better attuned to her surroundings. There was no sound except the slight breeze as it moved the branches outside. There were lots of human smells, but not the scent of their actual presence. These were the leftover smells they scattered all over, wherever they went – the rank odors of their weird, gross bodies, the sour and sweet smells of their strange foodstuffs.

The big creatures seemed to favor this place, and she'd often found human food here. Their food would sometimes hurt after it was eaten, and it tasted both rancid and cloying. This time of year, though, food was scarce. New plants were just starting to sprout and she needed to find whatever she could.

Three hops took her halfway down the center aisle. The moonlight came in through the yellow windows and made it reasonably light for the middle of the night. Everything was now equally hazy to her, since she was in the center of the room. The smells were too diffuse; there might not be any actual food here tonight, but just the lingering scent of it. There was one sour odor to the right that seemed more distinct, however.

The rabbit hopped the rest of the way to the front, then took smaller steps to the source of the smell, sniffing all the way. She angled toward a long-necked, brown bottle under the pew. It was far too close for her to see it distinctly, just a darker blob in the general fog. She kept inching toward it until she could put her mouth on the bottle's opening. The glass was smooth and cold, nasty and unnatural – definitely human. The odor of some sickening human food was strong on it, but there was nothing for her to taste.

Christoph had disliked rabbits when he was alive. They were dirty, foul creatures, eating their own shit. Promiscuous and vile, as well. Unclean animals if ever there were any. Pigs were far better. He'd read somewhere that pigs were really rather intelligent, and their hearts were the most similar to human ones. An animal with an almost human heart – there's a clean, noble beast. A rabbit's heart was a little, wriggly lump like a chicken's. Those stupid birds ate their own shit, too. Leave all such absurd, grotesque creatures to their own shit and depravity.

If Christoph had disliked rabbits when alive, now that he was dead, he had no need to limit or control his feelings. Now there were no children who wanted to cuddle the little vermin, so that he'd have to keep a hutch of them for the amusement of silly, irresponsible children. Now he could hate the creatures without restraint. He hated filth and disorder. He hated secrets and lies. He hated things that sneak around at night, or wriggle through tunnels like furry worms with fangs, eating the things that hard-working, honest, decent people have planted for themselves.

Who had allowed this abomination into the little building he had put up to honor his God? For that matter, who had allowed so much disorder and chaos into the world, in general? Everything just turned to shit, all the time. Nothing got better, things only got worse, sicker, more twisted and sinful. A man lives his life, trying to be a good person, trying to believe the right things and please God, just to find out everything was a lie, a façade to hide something dark and primitive and wrong.

Even once the hideous deformity was uncovered, it couldn't be fixed or atoned for. How could it? What the hell did it mean to be a Jew, if he'd never read their books or spoken their language or worshipped in their mysterious synagogues with their secret rites? Even worse, he knew if this had been revealed earlier, when he was still a child, his own people would've tried to kill him. His own people! He could've cried out that no, he was one of them, a good German, he wasn't really this horrible monster, and it wouldn't have mattered. So if his own people wouldn't want him and would try to kill him, then what was he?

Nothing.

There was the aching, galling mystery of his birthright: he owned nothing, he was nobody, and no one wanted him.

Christoph couldn't rid himself of his shame. He certainly couldn't rid the world of all its suffering and evil. But if he were alive, at least he could rid himself of this beady-eyed little pestilence, mocking him in the church he had built with his own hands. Now he even lacked the ability to defend himself against that, and so the impotent rage in him grew and flared beyond any limits it had ever had before.

The room got suddenly warmer. At first, the heat was pleasant to the rabbit, but then she felt and heard the brown bottle begin to tremble. She took two hops away from it before it exploded like a glass grenade, the jagged bits of glass tearing into her body in a hundred different spots. The blast pattern was like that of a shaped charge, all the glass flying directly at the rabbit, and not just exploding outward in all directions from the bottle. The shrapnel shredded the animal's body, splattering wet chunks onto the wall in an irregular, oblong splotch about two feet wide and a foot high.

The hot mortality steamed in the cold night air, a few thin wisps snaking as far up as the old oak cross. Christoph, however, was utterly focused on the bright, ragged stain itself. For a moment he could not see his shame, but only the awful beauty of the blood.

PART TWO

CHAPTER 21

Saturday, April 7, 2007 – Northern New Jersey

Nat finished the wet heap of supermarket brand Cheerios, then drank up the sweet, gritty sludge from the bottom of the bowl. On channel seven, the Power Rangers had just finished fighting the bad guys, so he flipped it over to channel five. After sitting through a few commercials, he saw it was an episode of the Teenage Mutant Ninja Turtles that he'd already watched three times, so he turned the television off. He'd seen the ads for the TMNT movie, but it looked stupid. *300* looked like it was cool, but his dad hadn't taken him to see that.

The Lego tower was still there. Nat admired it for a minute, then arranged the vehicles they'd made into a neat row at the base. Those were the cars of the people who worked in the tower, along with the delivery trucks for what they made there. He wasn't sure what they made, probably robots and stuff—maybe the delivery trucks were even driven by robots, that'd be really cool. He figured the people who worked in the tower were there mostly just to make sure everything ran right and the robots didn't get out of control. If they did, the people would have a self-destruct button to blow the whole place up, so the robots didn't take over and destroy the world, like in *Terminator 3*.

Nat made an exploding sound, and shook the base of the tower a little, but was careful to leave it standing. It looked too cool to knock down now, and Darrah didn't always want to build with him so much anymore, so it'd be better to leave it up. Sometimes she'd want to go off with her dumb boyfriend, instead of building. That was especially stupid of her, he thought, because she was really good at building, for a girl.

Nat's mom came into the living room, her head tilted to one side, threading an earring into her left earlobe. "Hi Nat," she said, smiling.

"Hey, Mom."

"Your dad already went out?"

"Yeah, he just went out to do some repairs. He said it was supposed to rain later, so he'd come in during the afternoon."

"Oh, okay." She primped her hair in the mirror by the door, then doubled back into the living room to get her purse from the end table. "I'm going to go to the supermarket. You want anything special?"

"Can you get real Cheerios? Maybe even the Honey Nut ones?"

"Damn it, I was going to go to Super Stop and Shop, but I think those are on sale at Shop Rite. I didn't want to go to two stores." Though it took her a minute to calm down from that minor setback, she managed it with some obvious effort. "Well, okay. I'd have to swing back around on 23 anyway, so it's not that far out of the way."

Nat decided to go all out. "And some dessert."

"Not so much sweets, little mister." Having gotten control of her frustration, she was obviously trying to be more accommodating. She smiled again. "You always eat your vegetables, so I guess it's okay."

"Thanks, Mom."

"Oh, it's no big deal. I just heard the water turn off, so your sister must be out of the shower. Go get dressed, then see if she wants to go outside, otherwise stay in the house. Don't go traipsing off by yourself. I'll be back before too long. You two behave!"

"Yes, Mom."

She went out the door as Nat returned to his little vehicles. Maybe the robots wouldn't get out of control and they could keep on making them in the tower. That'd be almost as cool as if they did go berserk and everything had to be blown up.

He went upstairs and followed the sound of the blow dryer to the bathroom. The door was ajar and he banged on it to open it further. It smelled a little girlish in there, but not like when Mom was in there, that was like a girl explosion then.

Darrah was in her old plaid bathrobe, drying her hair. The mirror was steamed up, except for a face-sized oval. She turned toward the partly open door. "Hi, Natty-Bo," she said, then pointed the dryer at him with a laugh, blowing his hair around.

Nat put his hands up in front of his face. "Hey!" he said. Darrah turned back to the mirror, again aiming the dryer at her hair. "Mom just went to the store, and Dad's outside somewhere. You want to go up to Opa's room and see what's there?"

Darrah turned off the blow dryer and scowled at him. "Why do you want to do that? I don't think Mom and Dad would be too keen on that."

Nat shrugged. "I don't know. He used to have cool stuff sometimes, old tools and things. We haven't been up there since before he died. It'd just be something different to do. We won't stay long."

Darrah put the dryer back on the vanity. "Well, okay. But just for a little while. Go get dressed."

Nat went to his room and got changed into jeans, sneakers, and a Pokemon sweat shirt that was a little small for him, leaving his Spider Man pajamas balled up on his bed. He left his bedroom, and had just made it to the living room, when he heard Darrah start down the stairs. She got dressed really quick for a girl, he'd noticed, not like their mom who always took forever.

"You going without a jacket?" she asked. She had on a flannel shirt over a t-shirt, with jeans and her pink sneakers.

"I don't know. Isn't it warmer today?"

"I guess," she said. "Wait up a sec." She disappeared into the kitchen for just a minute, then reemerged. She smiled at him. "We can always come back in and get it if you want. Let's go."

Under the mirror in the foyer, there was a wooden rack made by their grandfather, with four little hooks to hold key rings; a gnome playing a flute looked down on the hooks from the right side. Darrah grabbed one of the rings and they headed out the front door. They went around to the side, where they climbed up the stairs to their grandfather's apartment, where she unlocked the door and they slid inside.

It was dark and a little musty in there. To the left was a small bathroom, to the right, a closet, with the rest of the apartment opening up in front of them as one big room. They stepped into that area, going through the little kitchenette part first. The curtains were drawn, but Nat could see better, now that his eyes had adjusted to the dim light. He made for the big desk his grandfather had made decades before. The wood was scarred and oily, full of the same mystery and durability as its maker.

Nat turned on the old goose-neck lamp that sat on the desk. There were two photo albums lying near the front of the desktop. He remembered his mother said she was going to go look at some things here last week, maybe she'd been looking at those. Nearer the back of the desk stood a metal cabinet of tiny drawers. Opa had shown him this before, so Nat knew the drawers were full of various nuts and bolts, screws and nails, pins and needles, springs and tacks. Some even had the tiny pieces of clocks and watches in them, gears much smaller than a dime, with teeth so small you could barely see them, springs and wires that looked like eyelashes.

Stacked up next to the cabinet of drawers there were six old cardboard cigar boxes, filled with broken shoe laces, bits of string, wooden spools that had once been wrapped in thread, snapped rubber bands, used razor blades, dried-out pens, tiny nubs of pencils, and bottle caps from brands of soda and beer that were no longer made. Only the latter were of any interest, with their strange names in faded ink on bent metal; Horlacher, Krueger, Koehler, Rondo, Lotta Cola, and Cornell Root Beer. Opa had never thrown anything away, whether he was better or worse than Nat's parents in that respect, depended on how one evaluated such pack-rattishness.

Darrah drifted over to look at the book shelves to the left, as Nat opened a few of the tiny drawers and fingered the cold cascades of metal inside them. A boy doll about a foot tall leaned on the side of the cabinet of drawers opposite the cigar boxes. He was dressed in black and white striped coveralls, and at his feet was a very faded, threadbare stuffed animal that was supposed to be a sea turtle. Nat reverently patted both of them, just barely touching their fragile surfaces, careful neither to profane nor damage them. They didn't look as happy as Humpty Dumpty, but Nat knew they were just as brave and just as undefeated after all these years.

Darrah set a small jewelry box on the desk. It was made of very dark wood, with tiny indentations carved in the surface, into which had been inlaid hundreds of bits of porcelain and glass in elaborate, leaf-shaped patterns. Even though it was girl-stuff, Nat admired the craftsmanship that had gone into it, running his fingers lightly over the top.

"I haven't seen this before," Darrah said. "He had it up on one of the higher shelves."

"Do you think it was our grandmother's?"

"Well, it doesn't look like Opa's, and I don't think he had a girlfriend, silly."

"Of course not. He was married to our grandmother." Although some things his father had said when he was little confused him on the matter, Nat was fairly certain that someone couldn't have a spouse, plus a boyfriend or girlfriend. Grownups were often confusing and complicated and did all sorts of things they weren't supposed to. *Mom and Dad were like that, but I'm pretty sure Opa wasn't.* "What would we have called her, again, if she were alive?"

"Oh, he told us once. What was it? Oma. That was it."

"Yeah. That would've been nice. Go ahead and open it."

"I'm kind of scared to. It must be private, since he kept it hidden away." Darrah was nice about not going into other people's things. She never went into his room without permission. Sometimes she'd get perfume or makeup out of their mother's stuff in their parents' bedroom, but that was different. Grownups made all the rules, they shouldn't get privacy, too.

"It's okay, I think," he offered. "It probably just made him sad to look at it, so he put it up there."

"Well, okay. But don't touch anything."

"I won't. It's girl stuff anyway."

Darrah opened the lid. The box was lined with black velvet on the inside. There were just a few pieces of jewelry in it; a plain, thin wedding band, a string of small pearls, a silver comb - the kind ladies put their hair up with, a few dangly earrings. Darrah held up one of those. It had a gold hook and setting, with two long triangles of what looked like tortoise shell hanging down. The light shone through the blotches of yellow and brown in the shell, so they glowed warmly.

"These are pretty. I think Opa said she had blonde hair. The brown and gold must've looked so nice on her."

"I guess."

Darrah put the earring back and closed the box. Nat watched her set it back on the high shelf. "Okay, little wolf boy, I think we've seen enough. Let's go climb one of the smaller hills."

Nat headed toward the door. "Okay. Maybe up to the little church?"

As Nat started down the steps, Darrah locked up after them. "Yeah, that sounds good," she said.

About two-thirds of the way down, Nat felt a wave of dizziness and nausea. He gripped the railing tighter and cursed inwardly. He'd forgotten all about the stuff yesterday. So much pain and embarrassment all the time. He didn't want it anymore. Like he'd said, he felt like there was always some shit happening to him, and he wanted it to stop. All he could do right now, though, was stand there and sway and hope he didn't go crashing down the stairs.

But as she had promised, Darrah was there. She stepped on to the same step Nat was standing on and held him gently but firmly by the shoulders. "You dizzy there, great white hunter?"

Nat closed his eyes and waited for it to pass. "Yeah, just a little."

"It's okay. I've got you."

It passed in just a moment, less than ten seconds, and Nat nodded. Darrah slipped first one hand, then the other, from his shoulders, and he started back down.

"It's okay," he said. "It was funny. I felt dizzy as I thought about going up to the church."

Darrah walked alongside him. "We don't have to go there. We can go somewhere else, or go see what Dad's doing."

"No. It's just a little hill. I'll be okay. I'm not a sissy."

"Never said you were, tough guy." Darrah punched his shoulder, then laughed and ran on ahead.

Nat gave chase down the trail. He still felt like maybe they shouldn't go there, but he didn't want to appear weak or scared. Besides, with Darrah around, he knew he'd be all right.

CHAPTER 22

Saturday, April 7, 2007 – The Sublunar Sphere

For the rest of the night, Christoph remained mesmerized by the blood he had shed. It was not until the gore had cooled and thickened into a sheen of fur-encrusted tar, and the light glinting off it was no longer from the moon, but from the rising sun, that his longing gaze began to make him feel a little uneasy and embarrassed. It wasn't guilt, exactly. He did not feel like praying to be forgiven for that act of violence, but he was embarrassed at the mess he'd made, and the thought that Ben would stumble on it and have to clean it up. Still, Christoph had cleaned up enough messes over the years, this hardly seemed exceptional. Besides, Ben always seemed so glad to tidy up after the teenagers' debauchery, he surely couldn't complain about this minor incident.

As the sun rose, Christoph drifted back to the house where he had left Merla. One of the Eames chairs was turned so it faced away from him as he moved into the room. He assumed Merla was sitting there, as he didn't see her anywhere else in the room.

"Merla?" Christoph said tentatively. He hadn't been afraid in this place since meeting her, but now that he didn't see her, he realized how frightened he still was, and how much he'd come to rely on her. He was so relieved when the chair slowly turned and he saw that Merla was sitting there.

Relief was not what he felt when he saw she was holding a large, grey rabbit on her lap.

Merla's small hand petted the creature's head, pushing back its long ears. The animal's expressionless eyes made Christoph feel cold, but Merla's burning, dark eyes froze him completely. "You look surprised," she said in a measured, icy tone. "You didn't expect to see the victim of your wickedness, I suppose."

Christoph sat in his usual chair, on the opposite side of the fire from Merla and her new companion. "It's only an animal," he muttered, looking down at the floor.

"Yes! You should be glad it's only that! Do you really think I'd sit here and talk to you if you'd hurt a person? Tell me. Is that what you think? That I'm supposed to forgive any terrible thing you do? And still help you, when you show no sign of deserving or appreciating it?"

"No, no. I don't think that." He still didn't feel guilty, but his embarrassment had definitely increased to shame. Merla had been very generous and patient with him, and he'd let her down.

"Good! You shouldn't. Pain is pain, Christoph. We can think more than the animals can. We have more control of ourselves and more responsibility. But there is little difference in our capacity to burn and bleed, to feel flesh tear and rip, bone snap and shatter. And not just the physical sensation of it, but also the monstrous injustice of it. I think they can even feel that as keenly as we do."

"I'm sorry. I didn't think..."

"No! That's exactly it! I'm beginning to see that is the problem with you, you don't think. I told you to be careful of what you thought. I reminded you. I even hit you. And you wander off and think something so violent that it kills this little creature? What if you come close to some person and think something horrible? What then?"

"I don't know. I don't think I know how to control it."

"Then you'd best be learning to quickly, my friend. I have met evil spirits, like you are becoming. I never went near them; they're too terrifying and there's no one capable of redeeming them, so all we can do is ignore them. Is that what you want to be? You want to live under a bridge and whisper to hopeless people that they have nothing to live for, so you can watch them throw themselves off and die? Or maybe you want to live among the rocks by the shore, and hide the sounds of the waves crashing, so ships don't know how close they are, and they crash and sink and the passengers drown? Or now that you people are so arrogant and greedy that you fly through the air, I have even heard there are evil spirits on your sky vehicles. What were they called? Gremlins, that was it. They pull apart the machinery so the plane crashes and everyone dies. Is that what you want to be? Some evil, pathetic wraith that people hate and curse? You want to be a monster that feeds on pain and despair?"

"No," he whispered.

"And remember this, you foolish man. As much damage as you can do, none of it is anything compared to how you hurt yourself with this rage and spite. This poor thing suffered for just an instant, but you will prolong your suffering here for who knows how long, because of how you've acted. And if you do something worse? I said I have no power away from the hearth, but here I am far stronger than you, and I will beat you and kick you and throw you out of here the next time you do something so stupid and wicked. Then you can live outside in the dark and cold, and I hope you do sink down into the earth where such wickedness as yours can at least be hidden from decent people. Now do you understand me this time?"

"Yes."

Merla let the rabbit jump down. It took a couple hops, then stopped under one of the chairs, closer to the fire. "You could try to pray to your God," Merla said, a little calmer and not as angry sounding as before.

Christoph tried. He still didn't think that killing the creature was so bad, but Merla was definitely right about the rage that had motivated him. That was something sinful and should be atoned for, so he asked God to forgive and heal that.

The two of them remained there for some time, until Christoph got the strangest and most unexpectedly pleasant feeling. It was like sunshine, combined with being near someone you love and riding a bicycle on a warm day. It filled him with a sense of well-being like he did not think possible anymore; it was even stronger and more fulfilling than he could remember such a feeling when he was alive.

He didn't even notice when he stood up, the feeling distracted him so much. Merla had risen as well, and was eyeing him. "Are you going to behave?" she said.

"What? Oh, yes. I just had the nicest memory. I thought of my wife, and one of her birthdays. I gave her these earrings. They weren't really expensive or anything. We didn't have much money. But they were very pretty, I thought. And they matched her hair and eyes so perfectly. I hadn't remembered in so long how exquisite the combination was, and suddenly I remembered it all so vividly, it was like she was alive again, and I could feel and smell her again. It was glorious."

Merla nodded, though he noticed she still sidled her way between him and the doorway. "One of your family must've remembered her."

"No, she died when my son was born. None of them ever met her."

"They must've thought something about her. Perhaps they saw a picture."

"Perhaps. There were some pictures of her in my room. It was funny, but it felt like my granddaughter was connected, somehow, like she was the one thinking it. She seems very... oh, how do you say it? Self-conscious about how she looks, and I think she notices how pretty other women are." Christoph thought about that a moment and frowned. "She shouldn't be so self-conscious, though. She looks just like her mother, and they're both very pretty. I should've told her so."

"Yes, you should have," Merla said matter-of-factly. "But at least you realize it now. She must be quite wise in her own way, if she knows how to remember and celebrate the past without regret."

"Oh, yes, she's a very bright girl, very observant, and very kind to her brother when he's sick or hurt."

"Good. Perhaps there is hope for you yet, if you have such a wise and compassionate family member. She will be a help to you as you learn how to navigate this new existence."

Christoph suddenly felt sick inside, completely weak, disoriented, and spinning. He closed his eyes, trying to keep his balance.

"Oh, no," he said, barely keeping himself upright. "They're going to go to the church."

When he opened his eyes a little, Merla was right in front of him. "Don't even think of trying to stop them." Her lips barely moved, and he could see her fists clenched at her sides.

"But, they'll see everything, all the blood." Christoph had almost regained enough balance to try to take a step past Merla.

"So they'll see the horror you inflicted on something? You should've thought of that before you did it. Are you scared they'll think something bad, and it might cause you some pain? So what? You deserve it. Perhaps it will encourage you to think more next time. Or are you afraid they'll remember how you disliked rabbits. Oh yes, I know about that, too. Animals know when someone hates them, and I could sense that feeling from the poor, little one you slaughtered. Who knows, perhaps your granddaughter is astute enough even to figure out you had something to do with it. Maybe that's why you're so frightened."

"No, I have to stop them."

Christoph then made the mistake of putting his hand on Merla's shoulder, to push her out of the way. He didn't know where all her strength came from now, but when she hit him in the stomach with her fist, it felt like the bumper of a truck going fifty miles an hour. She followed it with another blow from her other hand that sent him staggering back even more.

Her fists were again at her sides. "You will stay here," she said in a voice as soft and heavy as lead.

Christoph didn't think he said "No" out loud. Perhaps his mouth opened a little, or he made a slight motion, and that was what set her off again. Either way, she let out a roar that sounded something like a buffalo, but in a lower register, more like an avalanche. Then she smashed her shoulder into him, driving him all the way back to the opposite wall, until his back slammed into the hideous, leaking metal hatch. The force of the blow was bad enough, but the freezing cold of the metal was excruciating, like he'd been shoved into a vat of liquid nitrogen. The pain made him scream in agony, and Merla finally relented, stepping back and letting him move away from the burning cold metal. He could've sworn his own cry of pain was echoed from somewhere behind the wall.

"Now will you stay here?" she said.

Christoph nodded.

Merla pointed to his chair. "Sit," she said. "I'll sit next to you and warm you, and I'll keep you company. And whatever pain you feel from what they discover about your crime, I will help you cope with it. You must learn to trust and rely on people. I think that is your other problem, besides not thinking enough before you act."

She sat next to him, and the rabbit hopped back into her lap. Then they waited. All Christoph could feel was dread at what might happen next.

CHAPTER 23

Saturday, April 7, 2007 – Northern New Jersey

Darrah hoped the short episode on the stairs would be the only one today, but feared it wouldn't be. She had the usual assortment of paper towels and Kleenex in her pockets, and she'd even grabbed some of those little wet naps in foil packages that you get at fast food restaurants. She figured they were pretty well covered, if there were more problems. She slowed down and looked back at Nat, chugging along, looking so intent.

Darrah turned and let him catch up, grabbing him by the shoulders. They tussled a little bit, her laughing as he got a couple bops in on her shoulder before they wound down. He was out of breath, but smiling, his eyes kind of smoldering, like they often did.

They started walking again, passing the Gingerbread Man (who could not be caught), and across a rickety bridge under which lived a troll, the ugly kind with a big nose and ears and a club. The three Billy Goats Gruff were there by the bridge, too. You could still pull a cord and ring a large bell there, to try to scare away the troll and make the bridge safe.

Past the bridge, the trail forked and they followed the path up to the little chapel their father had cleaned up the day before. Even on a cloudy day like this, the golden light inside the building always looked enchanting to Darrah. She also shared her father's confused, ambivalent fascination with the cross there. She always stared at it, each time finding new details in its grain and curves; the tiniest swirls and variations in color that would nearly hypnotize her with their complexity, but take a step back, and the whole figure would appear astonishingly simple, almost plain.

Darrah had never heard her grandfather say anything about the cross, but she'd never seen him look at it the way she and her dad did, either. She'd asked Nat his opinion before, but thought to check again. He seldom changed his evaluations of people or things, but often he'd add some nuance.

"What do you think of the cross in the church, the way it looks?" she asked about halfway up the hill.

"It's okay, I guess. I like it better when the carving looks like something, like a person or animal or something. That's just a shape. You and Dad always look at it funny."

"Yeah, I don't know why. I just always thought there was something about it, like the decorations on a cathedral or a castle... little touches that weren't there to do anything for the building, but made it more beautiful, almost made it come alive."

"I guess. I always wanted to wrap it in barb wire and swing it around like a mace. It's about the right size. That'd be cool."

"Nat, I don't think it's supposed to be a weapon. Opa wouldn't like to hear you say that."

"Why not? The real one was for killing people. And he never liked it anyway. He told me so sometimes, that he thought it was ugly and he'd made it wrong."

"Really? That's weird."

"Well, he did. He was a little weird, I guess. But people don't always have to agree with you and Dad, you know."

"No, I didn't say they did. I just think it's interesting he felt that way."

They had reached the doorway into the church and Darrah could see the splatter on the far wall. It had dried to a wine-dark, almost black stain. At first she didn't know what it was, thinking there might be a leak that had discolored the wall, or even maybe a burn mark. When she realized it looked like blood, she gasped and shot her arm out to stop Nat.

"Shit," she said without thinking.

Nat pushed past her arm and they both walked toward the scene. "I wanna see," he said. He seemed so fascinated by the sight that he didn't pause to chastise her for cursing, or even to laugh at it.

"Don't touch anything."

"I won't, I won't. Just calm down."

They got close enough to see it was definitely blood, but beyond that, Darrah couldn't tell what it was. It had chunks and flecks in it, as well as the dried gore holding it together. "It's gross," she said. "I don't know what happened to make this."

Nat's foot touched the neck of a broken beer bottle. That part was still relatively intact and he picked it up to show to his sister. "Broken bottle," he said. "Somebody got cut with it maybe."

"Careful with that," she said, then went back to inspecting the mess on the wall. "Yeah, there's some broken glass on the floor here too. Tiny pieces. But it's not just that someone got cut, it looks like they ripped up an animal and smeared it here. It looks like a squirrel or rabbit." Darrah paused as she got a moment of complete clarity amidst all the surprise and confusion. "Hey, didn't Opa hate rabbits?"

She looked to Nat, who had moved closer to the wall to examine it. He seemed thoroughly engrossed by the sight. "Yeah, he told me that too," he said, without taking his eyes off the small tableau of carnage and cruelty. "He called them dirty. Or he used a different word. It sounded funny. What was it?"

"Unclean?"

"Yeah, that was it. Funny word."

Darrah turned back to the shredded bunny. "But this is so sick and gross. Why would anyone do this?"

"It's wrong. Animals shouldn't suffer, only people."

"What?" His strange judgment hadn't really registered with Darrah, she was so overwhelmed by this new problem and horror. "Yeah, I guess. But Dad's going to have a cow. He always says the kids don't do much harm, and now they go and do something sick and twisted like this. And shit, he hates to call the damn cops." Darrah didn't like to swear nearly as much as her mother, but she figured this situation definitely called for it. It's hard to say "shoot" and "darn" when someone's been slaughtering animals in the middle of the night right by your house. That's scary enough to make you forget your manners. It's even worse when you know they're probably kids you see at school, and now they turn out to be sick fucks who torture animals and who knows what else.

"And people should only suffer when they want to," she heard Nat say, though again she wasn't focused enough on him, but had moved on to worrying what their parents' reaction would be to all this.

Nat gave her much more to worry about when he placed the back of his right hand on the wall above the butchered rabbit, just below the cross, then drove the jagged point of the beer bottle's neck into his palm.

CHAPTER 24
Saturday, April 7, 2007 – The Sublunar Sphere

All Christoph could do was wait and dread what was about to happen, and without any idea what it would be or how it would hurt. This realm he occupied now was full of so many pains one never knew in the earthly life; weightlessness and too much weight, along with heat and cold that were on the inside rather than the outside. Or maybe one knew them on Earth in a different way, for so much of this place seemed familiar, only more intense; the hopelessness and meaninglessness, but also the euphoria of remembering happiness and beauty. For such a grey, dim place, it was awfully overwhelming much of the time. That combination of blandness with the anticipation of something unbelievably painful made the waiting even more unbearable.

If Christoph had been ashamed by Merla discovering and judging what he had done, he was much more so, when he felt the first crackle of his grandchildren's fear and shock. They had no reason to see such a thing as he had made. It was his fault they were looking upon it, and for that he was overcome with guilt. Christoph closed his eyes and prayed as hard as he could for forgiveness for what he now felt was unforgivable. He prayed, too, that they might leave that horror behind as quickly as possible: since his mind was clear of selfishness for a moment, he even asked for this for their sakes, and not his own, out of concern for their feelings, and not fear of further pain to himself.

Merla leaned closer, seeming to sense he was caught up in some experience of his grandchildren. "It's all right, Christoph," she said quietly, in her more gentle voice. "Children can be the most forgiving, as well as the bravest. They will get through this, better than you can imagine. Trust them, as you pray for them."

The children's fear subsided slightly, into a steady buzz of wonder. For a moment, Christoph hoped they were done and would leave the church, but then his mind reeled from a cacophony of images thrust into it. He was sure it was Nat, because it was such a jumble of disparate thoughts, the way the boy always constructed one of his stories from parts of many different tales: a bird that had flown into a window and now lay dying on the ground; tiny black ants swarming out of the mouth and eyes of a dead squirrel; Ben alone, his face illuminated with the glow of the television, crying very quietly; Ruth's face very close to the boy's, her beautiful green eyes overflowing with tears, asking if he was okay, and how could he do this to her. Christoph had no idea how to put them together, since they didn't hold the same connections for him as they did for the boy, though he had a growing sense that to their originator, the pictures made complete and terrible sense, forming a perfectly clear lens of anguish.

Then Christoph felt the pain in his right hand, as sharp and sweet as any martyr's torment, as searing and erotic as any betrayal.

CHAPTER 25

Saturday, April 7, 2007 – Northern New Jersey

"Nat! Fuck!" he heard Darrah scream next to him. He felt her big right hand clamp on to his left hand and squeeze. He struggled for a second, to keep the glass inside his flesh, feel it rip and burn so wondrously.

At that moment, he remembered seeing chicken eggs in an incubator at the zoo, watching just the tips of their tiny beaks poking out of the holes they had made. Then you could see them tear the shells apart, bit by bit, 'til they'd broken down the wall that was keeping them back, keeping them from being born. For some reason, he imagined the glass was the bird's beak, and he was breaking down a similar barrier in his brittle, imprisoning flesh.

Darrah got her other hand on his, and forced her body against his, pinning him to the wall as she continued to squeeze and wrench his left hand. She was so much bigger and stronger, he had to drop the glass. As soon as he did, she flung his left hand down.

"Jesus!" she shrieked as the blood gushed out onto both of them and she fumbled in her pocket. She came up with the bundle of paper towels and slammed it into Nat's palm, still pinning his right hand to the wall.

They stood there a moment, panting, Darrah holding him tight against the wall. Her head was bowed and he couldn't see her face, but it sounded like she was sniffling. She turned her head and there were tears all down her cheeks.

"Why'd you do that?" The words were choked out of her.

"I don't know," Nat said quietly, looking into her eyes. "Why are you crying?"

Her eyebrows lowered, the way Mom's did when she saw him sick, but Darrah didn't look angry; she looked sad, crushed, totally spent. "Because you hurt yourself!"

"I'm sorry. I didn't mean to. I mean... I meant to do it. But I didn't mean to hurt you. Please don't cry."

Nat could feel her relax a little. She sniffled, then rubbed her eyes on her sleeve. Her face was really red and her hair was all tousled. The tears were still flowing. He shouldn't have hurt her like that.

She looked at him, still holding his right hand against the wall. "Nat, are you okay? If I let go, are you going to try to hurt yourself again?"

"No. I won't. Really. Please stop crying." He could feel the tears welling up in his own eyes. That usually made him really mad, but this time it didn't. The tears felt good. He wanted to cry, to show her how sorry he was.

"I can't!" Her voice cracked, and it was angrier than before, as she tightened her grip on his hand. "How am I supposed to? I've always taken care of you. I keep mom and dad happy, too, as happy as I can. Keep them from fighting, or picking on you. How do you think that feels, having to do that, all the time? And then to think you're going to hurt yourself, maybe really badly? That's just too much. It's more than I can stand. I can't take it anymore. I just can't."

"I'm sorry, I'm sorry, I'm sorry," he chanted, lightly stomping his foot in time to his begging. "Please don't hate me."

They were both sobbing now. The feeling was remarkably similar to when he'd dug the glass into his hand; it hurt like hell, even as it felt liberating, like it was transforming him. He wanted it to stop *and* never stop, both at the same time.

Darrah kept Nat's right hand pressed against the wall, but she bent down a little and slipped her right arm around her brother and pulled him to her. She smelled good. Girly, but leafy and woodsy, too. She'd hang her shirts up to dry, not put them in the dryer, so they smelled like the harsh soap and the trees outside, not all flowery like the dryer sheets. She held him tight. Everything about her was so strong, even though she was a girl. He couldn't believe she'd really cry, and he couldn't believe he'd done that to her. He'd never felt guilt like this before.

"Nat, I couldn't hate you," she whispered. "It doesn't matter what you do, I could never hate you. I love you. That's why I got so frightened. Promise you won't do anything like that again."

He held her tighter to himself with his left arm. "I promise. I'm so sorry."

Darrah pulled away and looked at his hand. She sniffled again, dragging her shirt sleeve back and forth under her nose. "But this is serious, Nat," she said. "You might've done some real damage. Move your fingers."

Nat moved all the fingers and thumb of his right hand. It didn't hurt, either.

"All right, that's good," Darrah said. "I guess that means you didn't cut a tendon. I think that's what they're called. There's still a ton of blood. I'm going to take my hand off, and you have to keep the pressure on with your other hand, okay?"

"Okay."

Darrah did as she said, and Nat pressed his left hand on to the blood-soaked paper towels.

"I'm going to wrap it up with my shirt," Darrah said as she took off her flannel shirt.

"But you'll be cold. And you'll ruin your shirt."

Darrah took his hand and wound the shirt around it. "It's okay," she said, even smiling at him a little. When she was done, his hand looked like a big bundle at the end of his arm. She pressed it to his stomach. "All right, hold that tight and let's go. We'll find Dad and clean you up. We'll tell him there was some broken glass in here and you got cut, okay? I'll tell him about the rabbit later, one thing at a time. And we'll just have to hope Mom isn't home yet."

Nat nodded and his sister hustled him back to the house. Darrah peeked around the corner, then turned back to Nat and shook her head.

"No car," she whispered as she led him to the door.

"Good."

"Dad?" she called out as they entered.

No answer.

Darrah took her brother to the small bathroom downstairs. She worked quickly and skillfully, unwrapping his hand over the sink, balling up all the bloody stuff and hiding it under the sink. The dried blood on his palm cracked a little when she peeled off the paper towels. The clotted blood plugging up the hole in the middle of his hand held fast though, so only a tiny bit of blood welled up through the new fissure in the scab, bright crimson flowing out of the darker, sticky layer.

She got some warm water flowing from the faucet, and held Nat's hand under it, carefully cleaning the blood from around the puncture, without reopening the wound. It felt good.

"It doesn't look as deep as I thought," she said as she got the gauze and tape from the medicine cabinet and started taping up her his hand. "I'm going to make the dressing as small as possible, so it doesn't look so bad when Mom and Dad see it. You've got to be careful not to bend or move it around much, or it'll start bleeding again."

"Okay."

She bent down close to his face. "Nat, I know you're sorry, and I believe you when you say you won't do it again," she said, very softly but firmly, as she looked into his eyes. *Hers are always so pretty*, he thought. He knew their mom's were the same color, and wondered why they never looked so pretty to him; maybe he'd try to look at them again, and see them differently. "But you have to tell me why you did it. You really freaked me out and I need to know what's going on."

Nat looked away for a second, then back at his sister. "I don't know, exactly. Please don't get sad again, or yell, or cry." His voice had the pleading tone again, but he didn't feel like he was going to weep again. Not unless she did.

She kept staring at him. "No, I'm not going to yell or cry, but try to think what made you do it. What were you thinking, as you did it? What were you trying to accomplish?"

He shook his head. "Nothing. I wasn't doing it like that, like a plan or something. I just saw all the blood, and how much that animal must've hurt, and I wanted to hurt, too. I don't know. Almost like, so it wouldn't be alone, so there'd be more suffering to kind of keep it company and balance out what it went through, make it less wrong, what had happened to it. It doesn't make sense, I know."

She kept her eyes on his and nodded, as she gently folded his fingers back on his palm. "All right," she said in her silky, sweet voice. "I can sort of understand that. You feel stuff too much, Natty-Bo. You got to take it down a notch. How about next time you think of how I feel and not do something like that again?"

"I know. I'll think of you, Darrah."

"Thanks."

They heard the door open, and quickly made their exit to the living room. "Oh, hi, you two," their father said as he closed the door.

He had that annoyed, distracted tone of his. That could be good, because he wouldn't notice so much what they'd been up to. Or it could be bad, because if he did notice, he'd get even more upset than usual. And never mind what their mom would be like; she'd been in a good mood when she left, so that was a good sign.

"Hi Dad," Nat and his sister said. Nat could hear their tone was too quiet and lacked any enthusiasm.

Their father went into the kitchen and didn't notice them at all. Nat looked to his sister, and she motioned for him to stay put while she began the process of breaking the news to the unpredictable adults. She walked to the kitchen doorway and stood there with the door open.

"Um, Dad?" she began.

"Yeah, what?"

"We were out in the woods, and we went in the little church, and there was some broken glass there, and Nat kind of cut his hand a little."

"What? I just cleaned that fuckin' place up!" Dad used the F-bomb a lot, for any little thing, so you had to go by his tone to tell how angry he really was. This sounded like about a six or seven; mostly it was an exasperated tone, rather than an enraged one, like the new problem was taking his mind away from something else that he wanted to concentrate on, and which was upsetting him more than this present problem.

"Sorry. I got him all taken care of. He's fine now."

Their father shoved past Darrah, halfway into the living room, and glared at Nat. "What the hell you doing, messing with broken glass, kid?"

"I'm sorry," Nat said. "I just went to pick it up and it cut me a little."

"Well, be more careful. And now we all have to hope your mother doesn't go ape-shit. Thanks a lot, kid."

"I'm sorry," Nat repeated. His father made him feel scared and like he was going to cry again. "She'll be okay. She was in a really good mood this morning."

Ben turned back to the kitchen. "Well, let's hope you're right."

"How'd the repairs go?" Darrah asked, trying to change the subject. *She's always so good at these conversations. She has good strategies,* Nat thought.

"What? Oh, fine," their father replied. "I did some. Then I went up to your grandfather's room to look around."

Nat felt his stomach tighten. Maybe they'd disturbed something, and that was what he was upset about, though he would've accused them right away, if that were the case. At least he usually came out and said things and didn't stew over them like their mother.

Darrah shot her brother a look. "Oh, did you find anything interesting?" she asked. Unlike her previous, unenthusiastic tone, now she had the right tone of casual curiosity and innocence.

"No, no. Just some old papers. Nothing. Don't you two have something to do? I'll make you lunch later. But right now, go find something to do."

"Yes, Dad," Darrah said and let the door close.

She walked over to her brother. "You better play in your room," she whispered. "He might come out of the kitchen and it's better if we're not right here in the living room. I'll get the stuff from under the bathroom sink and toss it in the dumpster. Now scoot."

"Should I take my tower to my room?" he asked. "I don't want it getting broken."

"Oh, sure. Go ahead. I'll bring up the blue bin and the other pieces in a second."

Nat could just barely carry the huge construction, with his left hand under the base and his injured hand holding the body of the tower, to keep it from snapping in the middle. He trudged up the stairs, taking it to safety.

CHAPTER 26
Saturday, April 7, 2007 – The Sublunar Sphere

The pain was as intense as any injury Christoph had ever felt, living or dead. At the same time, however, it didn't make him cry out long for it to stop. It just hammered him with steady inexorability and need, as satisfying as it was painful. He lifted his hand to his face, expecting to see it covered with blood, for the feeling was also sticky and wet, like dipping your hand into hot wax.

But there was no blood, of course. His hand appeared as whole and healthy as it had years ago, only it felt as though it were being crushed in a vise of freezing iron, while molten glass flowed within the fibers where his blood should be. None of that bothered Christoph in the least; indeed, he wondered how he'd ever managed being without this sensation.

"What is it, Christoph?" Merla asked. "I think your grandchildren have found something else."

"My grandson is feeling some horrible pain, the worst of his life. And yet, in some way I don't understand, it doesn't hurt him. He doesn't enjoy it, but he doesn't just endure it. It is a part of him. It even fulfills him, if that makes sense."

"It does," Merla said, with a tone almost of admiration, but also of concern. "Your grandchildren have learned a great and awful truth. How old did you say they are?"

"Darrah, my granddaughter, is fifteen; my grandson Nat is eight."

"The girl child is old enough. She is a woman. She is ready for such knowledge. But the boy is far too young. If he holds on to this truth for too long, or too strongly, it will sicken and twist him. Life is about suffering; it is not about wanting to suffer."

Christoph felt the pain subside somewhat. "I think it's all right," he said. "I can sense Darrah is helping him."

"Good. Put your confidence in her. She seems to know a great deal."

"She does. I don't understand what happened."

"Your grandson has learned some of the truth of suffering—its injustice, its inevitability, its necessity. It is a powerful truth, but is not meant for one so young as he."

Christoph bowed his head. "I'm sorry I made him learn that."

"As you should be. Not just sorry, ashamed. But again, there is nothing to be gained and a great deal to be risked by indulging in regret now." She waited a moment. "Can you sense if the danger has passed for them?"

Christoph tried to concentrate. The feeling was not the same as before. "It's different. They both feel some pain, but now it's not at all physical. That part is over. Before, it was a pain that felt good. Now, it feels like a kind of happiness that hurts. Does that make sense?"

"Of course it does, you silly, ignorant man. What kind of happiness always hurts?"

Christoph had never much liked riddles, though he remembered that Darrah always did, laughing in her big, awkward way at them. She liked those little slips of paper in the funny cookies from the Chinese restaurant for that reason, too. He thought they were silly. He'd always liked the story of Rumpelstiltskin, because the awful little dwarf was defeated after he proposed such a terrible, evil guessing game. Riddles were like that, just guessing for no reason, when the answer should be given in clear, reasonable statements of fact. It made sense, that Merla would be given to such trickery, since she always tormented him, even as she helped or solved any problem. Christoph reminded himself, however, that this was his fate, given by his God both for his own good, and because of his wickedness. He had to go along with it and benefit from it, however he was meant to.

Christoph shook his head. "I'm sorry. I don't know."

"And you are so quick about some things. It is strange." She stared at him a moment, as though to draw the answer out of him, but nothing came. "Tell me, then. They are close, the two of them?"

"Oh yes, very. They spend a lot of time together."

"And still you don't know? Tell me how you think they feel for one another. What is your word for it?"

"Well, they love each other, of course, the way brothers and sisters are supposed to."

"Exactly. Love."

"Oh." He considered that a moment, and was quite convinced again of the uselessness of riddles. "I see."

"Perhaps you do, though it seems to come to you only slowly right now. But you can at least be glad they see so clearly. You have told me something about her, that she's very responsible and observant, and that she's self-conscious. What else?"

Christoph thought about Darrah. There were so many details, and it seemed nearly impossible to him to know which were important. "She's quiet. She loves to be outside, but she's learned to be very resourceful around the house, cooking and such. I wish I'd shown her more about baking. I should've. She even asked me to a few times."

"Christoph, we've been over that. Stop."

He blinked and caught himself. "Oh, yes, that's right. Let's see. She's very good at predicting how people will behave. She seems to know what they want, and what's bothering them. It's good, because... well, to be honest, her parents often argue, and she's good at keeping the situation from getting worse, at making them and her brother feel better, and stopping them from getting more angry."

Merla nodded. "Those are all excellent qualities. She will be a very strong woman and mother, I think. Is she married?"

Christoph scowled. Not quite as scandalous as her question about Ruth, but he must have been getting used to Merla, for he didn't feel particularly shocked this time. "No, no, she's far too young for that."

"Your customs change so fast. It seems like it was quite recently that I met a dead girl who was married at that age." Merla shrugged. "I suppose it's easier to keep up with the changes when you're still alive. Being dead makes it more difficult." She thought about that for a while. "Tell me about your grandson. I haven't heard as much about him, until this happened."

"He's sickly. Nothing major, but lots of minor illnesses. And he gets so angry, so often. I really think they don't discipline him enough. He needs to be more controlled, restrained."

"Perhaps his being sick all the time makes him frustrated and angry, and it is not discipline he needs. Perhaps your granddaughter already knows this."

Christoph had never really considered that possibility. Children needed discipline, the Bible said so. If anything, being sick or weak made it more imperative. He would most certainly avoid mentioning how he'd raised Ben, if that was how this little pagan felt about child rearing.

"She is very gentle with him," he said. "It's her way of dealing with him, and it works for her." That was as much as he'd concede.

"Yes, I'm sure she is. What else about him?"

"He likes to tell stories, strange stories where all sorts of silly, unbelievable things happen. Not even like fairy tales, where there's usually a moral, but just weird things happening for no reason, all out of order and confused. They're usually very violent, too."

"I see. They sound like a remarkable pair, Christoph. Hearing about them and what they've been through gives me more hope. It should make you proud and hopeful as well. We will need their help."

They sat in silence for quite a while, until Christoph had another strange feeling. Not painful, thankfully.

"There's someone else nearby," he said.

"Your son? Or daughter-in-law?" Merla asked.

"No. I always feel him as a cold blank, and he's been around all day. My daughter-in-law left and is not here."

"A stranger?"

"It's vague right now. Someone I've met in passing, but didn't pay any attention to. Someone I had nothing really in common with, so it feels almost as blank as my son, just not as cold."

Merla let the rabbit jump down again, as she herself got up and stood before him.

"Christoph, it is my duty to be honest with you," she said. "I don't really know how I know that, but I can always tell when I have to inform someone of something, even if I don't agree with it. So I'm going to tell you this, even though I would hide it from you if I could. I kept you here before, to keep you from hurting your grandchildren. I hope you've learned from that."

"Yes, of course," he said. "I have."

"All right. I'd keep you here again, if it had anything to do with your family, as you have no right to harm or even interfere with them, and they have much more right to be here than you do. It is their home now, more than it is yours. But a spirit always has a right to defend his home against outsiders or intruders. The instinct is just too strong to disobey or deny, even in death. There is nothing I can do to stop you from investigating this new presence here, though I fear what you will do. You have been very foolish, stubborn, and violent. I'm afraid you'll do something evil and destructive. All I can do is warn you and tell you again to be careful."

Christoph himself was conflicted as to what to do. If it were night, he'd probably stay with Merla. He still feared the teenagers' nocturnal escapades – if anything, much more so – since he now knew that his disgust and anger might hurt someone, and such harm would only end up reflecting back on him in the end, even if it were their fault. But in the daylight? Probably just a meter reader or someone like that. He'd just watch the person for a minute, and then he'd leave. If it were a prankster or someone snooping around with no good reason... well, it might be fun to scare him off. Christoph thought he could manage it.

The thing with the rabbit had just been his uncontrolled rage, after all the pain and disappointment of what had been revealed to him. He hadn't known what he was doing, though deep down, he still felt the little pest deserved it. But if he really focused and concentrated, he thought he could do something more subtle and amusing to a human intruder; a cold draft, a chill up their spine, maybe even a little howl that would sound like it *might* just be the wind, but the person would be convinced it wasn't. That would be an entertaining challenge, really. The person might even be a burglar, someone trying to hurt his family, in which case he could do something to protect them. That couldn't be a bad thing that would do harm to him. Why would the rules allow him to protect his home, if it wasn't something he was supposed to do? He would have to go out and investigate, he decided.

"I'll go, and I'll be careful," he said as he got up.

Merla and the rabbit sat back in her chair on the other side of the room. The girl petted the animal again as she watched him blankly.

"See that you are, Christoph, or you will know real anger from me," she said.

Though her wrath was certainly nothing to be trifled with, Christoph felt un-chastened and uninhibited as he glided through the door and out into the dim daylight. Now he had a mission that would be satisfying, one way or another. After feeling so completely useless and worthless, it was good to have a purpose, especially one that might hurt someone who was more deserving of pain than he.

The feeling he was getting from the other side of the park had grown stronger, and taken on an edge of need and urgency that he found particularly noxious. He could almost taste it, like drinking a glass of cheap, bad wine while standing next to a pile of burning trash. It was fleshly, wet, and gross. While the feeling was persistent and nagging, it was weak, much weaker than he was, now that he knew what he was capable of. It would be positively exhilarating to freeze that rising, animal hunger. Freeze it and shatter it into a million jagged pieces. As he drew nearer to the source of the disturbance, he completely forgot Merla's warnings, and was overcome with the desire for there to be more blood than there had been the previous night. It would be a far better expiation or atonement, if the sacrifice were larger and more deserving of the suffering and annihilation he now longed to wreak upon it.

CHAPTER 27

Saturday, April 7, 2007 – Northern New Jersey

After she'd gotten rid of the bloody paper towels and shirt, Darrah crept back into the house; she'd suddenly remembered Cory was supposed to call any minute now. She was pretty sure he wouldn't be late with the phone call, either, since it had to do with possibly getting a chance to kiss her some more. She wanted to get out of the house, too. She thought Nat would be fine, but now her dad was acting strange and angry, so she just wanted to be alone with someone who wouldn't make any demands on her... well, no demands beyond listening and kissing.

She'd have to get her dad more calmed down, even though she was also going to have to tell him about the rabbit smeared all over the chapel wall. If she could deal with him, inform him of the bad news, and talk to Cory on the phone with a little privacy, then she would really have earned some mouth-to-mouth recreation. She supposed that maybe, like making Cory wait and beg a little, it made it better if she had to work for it, too.

Darrah slowly opened the door to the kitchen. Her dad was just staring out the window.

"Dad?" she said quietly as she stepped halfway into the room.

He didn't turn toward her. "What is it, Darrah?"

It was always good to lead with an apology. A real one, too, not one that moved on to "but" and then turned out not to be an apology at all, but more blame that just set the other person off worse. That's how her parents usually went round and round, without stopping, just flinging more shit at each other.

"I'm sorry I upset you before." She was, too. She thought he acted all weird and mopey too much of the time, but she knew how difficult her mom could be, never mind his job and the money stuff.

Her father sighed. "No, no," he said. "You didn't. I was upset about something else. You didn't do anything wrong." He finally turned toward her and drew himself up straighter. He had the inner strength, she thought; he just forgot too easily that he did. "You want some lunch?"

"I bet Nat would like some, but could I wait until later?" A risky request, as he might get upset about having to make two batches of something, or dirty two pots, but he seemed contrite at the moment, so it was best to catch him in the right mood. Besides, she needed to move on to the other bad news as quickly as possible. "I need to talk to you some more first."

He'd taken the frying pan off the stove, and stopped in the middle of the kitchen, holding it at waist height. "What is it now? More problems with Nat?"

"No, no, he's fine now. I sent him up to his room to play and he should be fine for a while. It's just, when we found the broken glass in the church, we also found something else."

Ben set the frying pan on the counter, then leaned against the counter himself, gripping the side of it. Darrah thought this would be the tricky part; once he heard about the actual weirdness, he'd probably be scared and worried, but not angry. Until then, though, he might lose it.

"Well, what was it? Out with it, Darrah. I'm just not in the mood for waiting and guessing." He sounded tired and drained, more than anything else.

"It was gross. Someone had killed a rabbit or squirrel in there. I think they used the broken bottle. It was awful."

He finally turned and stared at her. All anger was gone from his face and he just looked shocked. "What? Somebody killed an animal? That's terrible... I was just in there yesterday. It must've happened last night."

"I guess."

Her father frowned. "Maybe it was a coyote or a fox. There've been a lot more of them around lately."

Given that something had reduced the creature to little more than a greasy spot, Darrah didn't think a coyote sounded too likely. "I don't know, Dad, it was pretty ripped up," she said.

"I don't know what a coyote victim looks like, Darrah." He paused. "Well, I'll go check it out later and clean it up. Was Nat upset by seeing it?"

Darrah knew that "upset" didn't quite capture it. It was getting more difficult not to lie outright.

"No, he's a boy. I think he was kind of fascinated by the blood and guts." *That wasn't too far off the mark.*

"Yeah, they're into that at that age. He'll be okay." Her dad looked more carefully and attentively at her. "What about you? You okay?"

"Yeah, it was gross, but I'm okay. But Dad... Cory's supposed to call soon. Can he come over for a while? We'll just take a walk. We won't get in any trouble."

Ben raised his eyebrows at his daughter. "After all that excitement, you want to see your little boyfriend?"

"Dad! You sound like Nat. I'd just like a few minutes to myself, a few minutes of peace and quiet, with a friend."

"Mmm-hmm. Peace and quiet? You sure that's what that little emo-boy has in mind?"

Her father turned to get some stuff from the fridge as he gave her a slightly mocking smile. They'd had a few talks about Cory, since he was her first sort-of boyfriend. Dad liked to tease about it, but she knew he thought Cory was okay. He got good grades and read books like *Frankenstein* and *J.B.* even if they weren't assigned in school; her mom and dad both liked that. So did she.

"Dad!" Darrah swatted his shoulder. "He's not emo. He doesn't dress all in black and talk about cutting himself all the time." She did have to admit too many of his clothes were from Hot Topic, but it wasn't like all of them. Most were from Target, just like everybody else's.

Ben set bread, cheese slices, and butter on the counter. "Yeah, well, he does have pretty long hair, but I guess he's not so bad." He turned toward Darrah. "And I don't really care how the kid dresses. I just want... you know... you to be careful. Don't get in trouble or get your feelings hurt. I don't want you to be all messed up over some kid who doesn't care about you or deserve you." He paused. "There are enough people in this house acting all hurt and crappy all the time. I want you at least to be happy."

"I know, Dad. I'm careful. So is it okay if he comes over for a little while?"

"Yeah, I guess. I don't know what your mother will say when she gets home, but I suppose we'll just deal with that when the time comes. Oh, and don't tell her about the dead rabbit. I'll clean that up, and we'll hope that it was a coyote, unless it happens again."

"Okay, Dad." The phone rang right then. "Oh, that must be him!" Up went her voice again. Not so much, in front of her dad, but still enough to be embarrassing.

Darrah answered it. "Hi. Yeah, wait a second," she said as she stepped out of the kitchen with the receiver and let the door close on the cord. It wasn't real privacy, but it made it feel not quite so weird, like talking right in front of her dad. At least he was out of sight.

"So, can we take a walk?" Cory sounded better than yesterday, more confident. He could even have a cute little swagger at school, around his friends or the other kids in band, especially if she were around. That was nice, but it was nice to hear his plaintive tone, too.

"I don't know, it's supposed to rain this afternoon." Darrah didn't care about the rain, and she was pretty sure he could hear the playfulness in her voice, but it was part of the negotiation, even a rather fun part.

"Well, until it rains? Just a little while? I really want to see you." Yeah, that was the right tone, a little whine with a dash of need and a definite hint of desire.

"Well... okay." She lowered her voice. "I missed you, too. Lots."

"Good. I'll be right over."

Darrah went back into the kitchen to hang up the phone. Her father was buttering bread for grilled cheese sandwiches. Nat always liked those.

"So, emo-boy on his way over?" her dad asked.

She smacked his shoulder again. "I don't know any emo-boys, for your information. But yes, my friend Cory is coming over. It'll take him a few minutes on his bike."

"Well, the little hoodlum will be driving soon enough and giving me grey hairs, and so will you."

"I know. You want some help with those?"

"Sure. Thanks. Why don't you cook two for me and Nat, while I make some others. That way there'll be some ready to cook, for when your mom gets home, and for you and your little friend."

"Okay." She rolled her eyes. "He's not my 'little friend,' either."

"Hey, you didn't like 'emo-boy' or 'boyfriend.' I bet Nat already called him 'lover-boy,' didn't he?"

"Yes, he did. And how'd you know?"

"I told him to. I said it would make you mad."

Darrah laughed and slapped her dad one more time on his shoulder, before she took the pan, turned on the flame, and assembled the two sandwiches on top of the metal as it heated. The two of them talked about trivial stuff as they worked; how school was and where they might go on vacation in the summer and when it would warm up finally. Just regular talk. It felt good.

The doorbell rang right as the two grilled cheese sandwiches looked about right, so Darrah turned off the flame and bounded to the front door. Cory was on the stoop, wearing black jeans, with a *My Chemical Romance* t-shirt under an unbuttoned, grey work shirt from a gas station; the name patch on the left breast said "Rich." He must've gotten that at Goodwill. His brown eyes looked slightly wet, probably from riding over here in the wind. It made them sparkle nicely, Darrah thought. She didn't hear Nat coming down the stairs or her father exiting the kitchen, so she risked a little peck on the cheek as she let Cory in. Then she took his hand and led him back to the kitchen.

Ben was sliding the two sandwiches on to plates as they walked in. "Hi, Cory," he said.

"Hello Mr. Hahn."

"Excuse me," her dad said as he made toward the door to the dining area.

The two teenagers stepped back into the living room as Ben put the two plates on the table. "Would you call your brother, Darrah?" he asked as he went back into the kitchen.

"Natty-Bo! Lunch!" Darrah shouted.

She ran her hand through Cory's black hair, as he risked a little squeeze of her butt. She pushed his hand away and giggled.

Nat came crashing down the stairs about the same time Ben came out of the kitchen with two glasses of water.

"Hey," Nat said as he made for his spot.

"Hey, kid," Cory said.

Darrah started nudging Cory toward the front door. "We'll just go take a walk in the woods. We won't stay out long."

"See that you don't," her dad said as he sat next to Nat. "Oh, and Cory... I was thinking of cleaning my gun collection later and then going out to look for some coyote that's been sniffing around here way too much lately. You know what I mean?"

Darrah laughed and rolled her eyes as she pushed Cory the rest of the way to the door. "You don't have any guns, Dad," she said as she grabbed a denim jacket from the coat closet. "Stop saying silly stuff!"

"Don't need 'em for small varmints. Right, Nat?"

"No, you use an axe, or your bare hands," Nat chimed in. "Saves bullets."

As she put on her jacket, Darrah looked back and saw her brother squeezing his grilled cheese sandwich so his fingers sank into the bread and the cheese ran out the sides. She laughed again, shaking her head as she and Cory went out the front door.

She took Cory's hand and stole glances at him as they walked. "Your dad's funny," he said.

"Yeah, but he's kinda nice. I like it when he teases." She looked sideways at him and bit her lower lip. "You don't mind it when he does, do you?"

"No, no, he's fine. My dad doesn't joke around, so I'm not used to it. I can see why you'd like it. It's fun."

He'd actually told Darrah his father's bad behavior was a bit worse than just not kidding around enough. Too much drinking and hitting, was more like it. She slipped her hand from Cory's and slid it under the gas station shirt till it rested on his right hip. She tried to lean her head on his shoulder, but she was a little too tall for that. *Oh well. It still feels nice.* She hoped he liked it too.

They walked that way past the various childish displays. She knew other kids made fun of her for living there with her parents, but Darrah still liked the place. It was good to feel silly and safe, and think there were no problems in your life bigger than a wolf in the forest, a witch in her candy house, or a troll under a bridge. Even in their home, right inside the Enchanted Mill Forest, there were always so many more mundane and complicated and intractable problems. And people like Cory had even worse things hanging over them, or simmering hidden under the surface. It made her happy and proud her grandfather had made this place. She hoped they could keep it going.

They ended up at Snow White and the Seven Dwarves. Darrah was glad. It was nice and private in the Evil Queen's castle, and that made it really good for kissing, but there was just no way; it was way too dark and creepy in there for that. She smiled and blushed to think that if she had a Goth boyfriend, that'd be the first place he'd want to go to do it. That and the church, like the older kids. That wasn't right, though. Darrah really liked the feeling of sneaking around and being a little naughty, but stuff like that was wrong. It was going too far, like being bad just for the sake of being bad.

Right now, Darrah craved kissing more than she ever remembered wanting it, or wanting anything else, for that matter. She wanted so badly to be needed that it hurt. She didn't want to be needed just because she could fix or take care of something. She didn't want to be responsible or smart or careful or generous. She just wanted to be needed for herself, even just for her body. She longed to be a physical and emotional presence that someone else needed in order to survive, that he needed to soak up like a drug or he'd die.

She tightened her grip on Cory's hip just the tiniest bit, but she was quite certain it was enough to communicate to him the confused wave of love and lust that was surging up from her thighs and cascading down from her heart. He turned her and pressed her up against one of the thick wooden beams that held up the awning in front of the Seven Dwarves' home, as he mashed his lips into hers, so rough and eager he banged her head into the post a little, though she barely noticed. She closed her eyes and her ears rang as she opened her mouth for him. Both his hands immediately went to her butt, as she ran one arm around his neck and the other around his waist to pull him to her.

The initial release of their lips touching calmed Darrah for just an instant, before the burning hunger redoubled when his tongue found hers. After a moment, that gave way to the most luxurious ecstasy of letting her tongue snake around his in a long, slow dance that she wanted never to end.

As she basked in that feeling, she could detach enough to think through the other mechanics of the act; how her head should be tilted back, but she was too darn tall for that. He'd probably be able to get his tongue in better that way and it'd feel better for him. She felt a little twinge of fear and jealousy that he might like another girl better for that reason, might look at shorter girls and want them instead of her. *Screw that.* If that's what she was afraid of, then she should just make sure she kissed better than anyone else. She squeezed him tighter, letting her one hand drift down to his skinny butt, and kissed back even harder, her tongue moving furiously around his. There was no way anyone's kissing would ever feel better than this did right now.

As tall as she was, the other resulting difficulty – if you could call it that – was the hard lump that would be pressed into the stomach of a smaller girl in the same clinch, was instead grinding right into the front of Darrah's jeans. God knew it felt good right there, but him getting so turned on always made things more difficult. She loved having that power over him, of course, but it was awkward and often led to a fight.

He broke the kiss off to suck on her neck. Like when their lips first touched, it was always a jolt of intense, animal energy when she felt the flesh of her neck roughly drawn between his teeth. Darrah gasped, but also moved her hands to his hips and pushed a little, so he wasn't humping against her so insistently.

She giggled and squirmed. "No hickeys, come on," she whispered. "I can't walk in with my neck all purple!"

"Sorry," Cory said as he came up for air and they kissed again, this time softer and slower, mostly working their lips in and out and not stabbing with their tongues so much. He kept kneading her butt with one hand, though not as roughly as before, and moved his other hand up to her breasts. He was always gentler with those, like they'd break or something. She thought that was kind of funny, and almost wanted him to be rougher with them, because it felt sort of good when he was. At the same time, however, it was almost like a kind of reverence or restraint on his part, even when they were making out and getting all heated up and losing control. She thought that made a really nice combination, passionate but still affectionate and gentle.

Darrah took her mouth off his to kiss around his lips and chin, and let him settle back into her. He was still hard, but he wasn't thrusting up against her so much, but just kind of snuggling. *That's better, he probably won't get all frustrated and mad like he does sometimes.*

"I love you so much," she breathed as she kissed around to his ear.

"I love you, too." He paused. "You sure we can't do it? No one's around."

"I don't want my first time to be on the cold ground with a bunch of wet leaves up my butt, you big jerk!" She giggled. "I promise we'll do it. I'm just not ready. I know it's hard for you."

He pressed his bulge back into her a little harder, though he didn't hump and grind it like before. "You know what you do to me."

Darrah giggled one more time. "Yes. I think I can tell." She again held his hips to push him away slightly, though she kept kissing around his mouth. "Just kiss a little more, please? I love how it feels."

Their mouths settled together once more, tongues exploring more slowly this time. Darrah heard a creaking sound. Not like wood, but more brittle-sounding, the way ice on the pond would groan in the winter. She opened her left eye and saw the wood separating the panes in the window next to them bow outward, then contract back inward. There seemed to be a kind of breathing noise that accompanied this in and out of the panes, too.

She watched this for no more than two seconds. Although she was already plenty heated up from the kissing, she felt the temperature rise around them, like the breathing was from an evil furnace, and then suddenly plunge down, like they were being battered by a cruel wind in February. There was no rational explanation or plan in her mind, but somehow she knew to twist Cory to the right, as she turned her own head in the same direction and put her hand over his face. At the same time, she swept her right foot under his and knocked him off balance, causing them both to fall.

As her mouth popped off Cory's, Darrah could hear him give a little choking sound of surprise, but then everything was drowned out by the roaring explosion of glass and wood.

CHAPTER 28

Saturday, April 7, 2007 – The Sublunar Sphere

Christoph felt the evil presence intensify. It seemed to be growing stronger, as well as getting closer to him as he moved through the trees. The sensation was wetter than before, and itchy, too. It had changed from being like the taste of bad wine, to more like feeling oneself being cooked in a mixture of vinegar, sand, and dirty socks. How could people bring such feelings to light? Why couldn't they just deny them and keep them down in the dark where they belonged? How could they even stand such things – up close, in their own flesh - when the mere whiff of them made him nauseous and dizzy? People could be such a detestable mystery. After what he'd seen last night, he decided that blood was so much more simple, reliable, and pure. The uncleanness that was assailing him would definitely require blood to wash it away, to turn the horrible, seething blackness back into light... or at least, to that dim illumination to which he was now condemned. Christoph's anger boiled more vigorously, when he thought how he was trapped in this shadowy land, with much less reason than those who fanned such sinful flames as he now felt burning in the forest.

As strong as the impurity was becoming, for one moment it was blocked out by another presence. The change was so drastic and disorienting that Christoph had to stop moving in order to process this new information. This new collection of emotions, memories, and needs, was far less urgent and violent. It was more peaceful, but no less sensual than the other. Simple, was what it was, mostly. Simple and calm. Or really, a longing for calm, but without being so insistent on restless satisfaction and tearing, burning possession as that other, darker force out there. This presence did not agitate and enrage Christoph the way the other one did. It reached out and connected with him at some deeper level than the hurt and anger.

It took Christoph just a moment of confusion before he recognized Darrah's imprint on this new experience. She was feeling comfort among the things he had created in the Enchanted Mill Forest. The calm was more active, however, because she wanted to share it with others, the way Christoph had wanted to bring people here to see these things and be happy, if only for a little while. She wasn't feeling only joy, either, and that complicated the impression, and forced it on to him even more deeply. She was feeling the sadness and pain of others, together with a longing to heal those people and make them content.

Since all of this flowed from her as she walked among her grandfather's creations, the experience was consuming and intoxicating to him, as though he himself were causing, and then receiving back such a wide array of emotions at once. The feeling then moved on to something that Christoph didn't recognize at first, until he realized it was admiration and gratitude. *Darrah was feeling that for him.*

This rich, fulfilling, soulful mixture that had come upon him dissipated suddenly, however. Or rather, it seemed to Christoph, it was snuffed out, blasted to ash, like a small flower in the midst of a raging brush fire. No longer was there contentment or even the desire for contentment, but only a swirling storm of wracking hunger and clawing, grasping need. That was what he had sensed before, and it had grown much stronger, just in the few moments he'd been distracted. He could also tell, with increasing revulsion and even a sense of betrayal, that the overwhelming lust came from Darrah as well as whoever else was about. She had looked on all the innocent, pretty things he'd created, and then turned away to embrace this sick, depraved foulness? One might as well set candy and cakes before someone, and have the person toss them aside to eat garbage and filth. The girl was just like her parents; willful and conceited like her mother, arrogant and emotional like her father. And now she'd added that peculiarly feminine sinfulness of sensuality, on top of it all. Christoph had long known his grandson needed discipline, but now he was sure the girl needed it much more, and had turned out much worse, for the lack of it.

Christoph moved faster than before, more like a wind than a body. The taint of those two evil creatures; seduced and seducing, wallowing in their sinful pleasure, as though it were something beautiful and sweet, could not scream any louder through the trees, could not assail him with any more bitterness than it did now.

His vision was dimmer than ever before, as if he were in a hot, damp fog; it was all he could do to sense the presence of two bodies, yet both of them were radiating such energy he couldn't stand to be near them. To someone like Christoph, consumed with possessiveness and self-righteousness, their life-force looked like a bonfire consuming his world, threatening everything good and beautiful in it. His only reaction to this threat was rage, a longing to annihilate and brutalize this monstrosity before it took over.

Not just rage, he realized too late. Side by side with the burning desire to harm those who threatened him, there was the freezing cold vacuity of envy. The two sins embraced each other like a yin and yang.

In the church the night before, there'd been nothing but anger and disgust at some gross object out of place. But no one as sad and lonely and lost as Christoph was could be in the presence of two people in love and not feel jealousy, not feel his own emptiness take over for a moment and drive him to madness and spite. Worse, to despair.

He would've taken it back at that moment, if he could – the anger, the judgment, the sick, writhing envy – and hidden himself somewhere that he couldn't harm others. Merla had told him how dangerous regret was, for the things he'd done in life; she had not told him how useless it was, for the things he did, now that he was dead. Those thoughts and actions took on a life of their own, so they were far more potent and alive than he was now, and he could only watch them unfold, like those huge chains of dominoes falling when the first one is pushed over.

The blood this afternoon was not satisfying, mesmerizing, or cleansing to Christoph. When he saw it pouring from Darrah's torn, innocent flesh, the sight scalded and burned him; in his eyes, his mind, and his heart. He felt the glass slice into him with ten times the pain it caused Darrah. Christoph spun and fell to the ground, crumpled and flattened like a wet blanket that a high wind has torn from a clothesline and cast into the dirt.

As he lay there, he wished the agony inside could've been a hundred times what it was, if it would've spared her the pain of his sinful foolishness. Again, regret was futile, though perhaps he got a tiny bit of his wish when his weeping brought forth no tears, only a terrible, dry wracking of his body, worse than any stabbing.

CHAPTER 29
Saturday, April 7, 2007 – Northern New Jersey

Ruth turned off the burner and poured the hot water over her tea bag. It'd taken her a lot longer at the stores than she would've liked. That extra stop for Nat's cereal had bollocksed things up, with all the traffic on Route 23. The lines at the checkout were terrible, too. But still, she'd gotten a bunch of stuff for the week and it'd clocked in at less than a hundred between both supermarkets. The way those two kids ate nowadays, that was a fucking miracle.

She set the sauce pan back on the stove and turned to the grilled cheese sandwich Ben had just put on a plate for her. He really was unbelievably attentive and responsible, she thought as she took a bite and watched him put away dishes and tidy up. He was in a mood again, though, she could tell. Quiet, sullen, like he was about to say something nasty, or just stalk off to sulk. He had probably put on a good face for Darrah. He always doted on her too much, first born and daddy's little girl kind of thing, but with his wife he could always be counted on to be crappier and bitchier than any woman she'd ever known.

Ruth felt the bread melding into the molten cheese as she chewed, and she shrugged inwardly. It was probably that way with most men. It sure as hell was with Peter. *It's kind of flattering and a turn on at first, when the guy's idea of sexy talk while he's unzipping your skirt is to tell you how much better a lay you are than his wife, how much firmer your butt is, how much perkier your tits – but after a while of hearing him sniffle and complain about her, it's just fucking boring and demeaning.* Yup, boring and demeaning about summed up all men, most of the time.

"What are the kids up to?" she asked, trying to sound as innocent and inoffensive as possible. She'd make the effort for a little while longer, despite his mood.

"Nat's in his room," her husband replied. "He went outside with Darrah earlier, and cut his hand. It doesn't look too bad. Just a little thing."

Ruth put down the last bite of grilled cheese and wrapped her hands around the hot mug of tea. "What is it with that kid? Always blood all over the place. I just can't stand it sometimes."

"It's not his fault." His tone was getting brusquer, like he was going to lose it. *Too bad, he's been behaving better lately. Fuck only knows what set him off.* She hadn't done anything, that's for sure. *Still fuming over his suspicions that I might've gotten some on the side? And when was that? Seven years ago now? Statute of limitations was way up on that one, buddy. Time to act like a man and not some whiny cunt.*

Ruth took the last bite of the sandwich. "And Darrah?" Maybe he'd like that better, talking about his little princess. "I saw that kid's bike outside. They outside, doing God knows what?" Time for him to wake up and acknowledge what his precious angel was up to, and keep a better eye on her.

"Cory came over. They're outside. I think she knows to behave. More than some women do." He kept wiping the counter as he said it and didn't look at her.

All right, that comment iced it. She'd tried to be nice enough this afternoon. She didn't need to hear that shit. *Again.*

"What's that supposed to mean?" One hand on the counter, the other on her hip.

He squeezed the water out of the sponge and placed it by the faucet. "Same thing it's meant, every fucking time I say it, for eight long years."

"Oh? And what's that? You don't like how I behave? What'd I do wrong today, exactly? Hmm? Can't think of anything? That's because I didn't do anything wrong! I went shopping and was having a nice day and even thinking maybe you and I could do something in the bedroom later on, if those two hellions ever went to bed before eleven! That's all I did and I don't want to hear any shit from you!" Always feels good to go on the offensive. *There's nothing more offensive than his crap, anyway.*

Ben gripped the side of the sink, his knuckles turning white. *Fucker thinks he's the big Indian in One Flew Over the Cuckoos Nest? Probably. Guys love that bullshit, fantasizing they'd buck the system or stand up for themselves, when they fucking well knew they wouldn't. Bastard would grovel and beg for a section of freshman comp any day of the week, then bitch about the work when he got it. Isn't that something? Son of a bitch could think himself into a lose-lose situation over almost anything.*

"Nothing you did today. You fucking know what I mean."

Ruth wondered if he ever thought of hitting her at moments like this, when he was all wound up and pitying himself. There were enough patched-up dents and cracks in walls, along with doors that had been knocked off their frames and remounted, to attest to his temper. She never understood women who liked being smacked around, and she'd known a few, growing up, but she wondered about a guy who never even thought of the possibility, and just took it all like a fucking doormat. *Nothing wrong with some restraint, but to not even think of it? Guy had to be missing something in the balls department.* She'd thought of hitting him often enough.

"Yeah, well, that wasn't today, so you've got nothing to complain about right now. And you don't know anything, anyway. You're just making shit up and feeling sorry for yourself. As usual."

His grip relaxed a little and he wiped his right eye with the back of his hand before finally looking at her.

"All right, you didn't do anything today," he said. "I shouldn't have brought that up. I have other things on my mind, is all."

"Well, that's no reason to take it out on me."

Ruth relaxed some too, and took a sip of her tea as she eyed her husband. That was probably enough attack. She'd defended herself and put him in his place. She could afford a little gentleness now. *Besides, he's pretty lovable and caring most of the time. He just needs more self-control and self-respect.* Most days, she was pretty sure she didn't love him, but there was never a day she forgot how it used to feel, when she did. It was the happiest she'd ever been, before kids and jobs made life so damned messy and weird and frustrating all the time.

She put her hand on his arm. "You're right, Darrah's a good kid. Just keep a better eye on that walking pile of hormones she calls a boyfriend. Okay, hon? That's all I meant."

"Okay."

Ruth heard the front door crash open, and a breathless male voice shout, "Hello?" There was a huffing sound as well, and a little squeal.

"What the fuck?" Ben said as he pushed past her to the kitchen door. She was right behind him.

Cory stood in the living room, holding up Darrah. He wasn't wearing a jacket or long-sleeved shirt, only a t-shirt, which seemed odd on a cold day like today. Darrah's hair was down in front of her face and she was partly bent over, looking down at her left hand, which was wrapped up in something grey. They were both out of breath, but Darrah was the one making the extra huffing sound, the kind of gasping sound you make when something hurts, but you don't want to cry out, you just want to try to control it and figure out what just happened and get things back under control.

Ruth and her husband reached their daughter at about the same time, taking hold of her from either side and pulling her away from Cory.

"What is it, sweetie?" Ruth had her arm around Darrah, drawing her closer. It was instinct... besides, the kid deserved it. Maybe Nat had exhausted her mothering instincts and her patience, stretching her nerves and making her feel tired and inadequate, but to see Darrah in need and pain for the first time since she was a baby, that yanked Ruth's heart around and pulled her to her daughter like a magnet.

She felt cold, clammy. She looked at her mother, eyes red, face covered with tears. Her mouth hung open, still making that panting sound.

"I don't know. I'm sorry. It hurts!" Darrah dragged the last word out, leaning her head back and finally releasing all the frustration and pain in a long wail that broke down into a sob. She turned and put her face on her mother's shoulder. Ruth could feel her shake from the weeping.

She put her face in her daughter's hair. "It's okay, honey," she whispered. "You're okay now. I'm right here."

"I was scared, Mom," Darrah said in a snuffle only Ruth could hear.

She put both arms around her daughter. She hadn't held her like this in a long time; *hell, I can't remember the last time, to be honest.* It felt pretty awkward for a minute. *It was like riding a bicycle,* Ruth guessed. In a moment it was completely natural again, like she'd never let go, or ever want to.

"I know," Ruth whispered back. "I'm here. Don't be scared."

Ben rubbed their daughter's back and Ruth could see out of the corner of her eye that he looked as confused as she felt.

"What the hell happened, Cory?" he asked the boyfriend. Ruth didn't turn to look at the boy, but kept her face deep in Darrah's hair, breathing her in and holding her tight.

"I don't know," she heard the kid say. His voice was shaking. "We were by the one little house, the Seven Dwarves one. And the window exploded. I don't know how that could happen, but it just exploded. My face would've been torn up, but Darrah shoved me down and covered my face with her hand. That's how her hand got cut, from the flying glass."

"It exploded?" Ben asked. "I don't understand."

Ruth heard another voice from behind her. "What's wrong?" she could hear Nat ask.

"Your sister's a little hurt," Ben said. "You just sit on the couch and wait a second while we take care of her."

Ruth finally pulled her head up a bit and looked at Cory. *Kid looks paler and more useless than ever, but he'd come through.* She wouldn't have believed he'd be able to stand up to much of a crisis.

"Cory, we don't understand what you're trying to explain," she said as calmly as she could manage. Darrah had stopped crying, and was just shivering a little in her arms. "What kind of explosion? How did it happen? It doesn't make sense."

"I don't know. I don't know," he repeated. "It just exploded, right next to us. We didn't do anything to break it. It just... exploded."

Darrah turned her head, keeping the side of her face pressed up against her mother's shoulder and looking at Cory and her father.

"I could hear the glass kind of creaking right before it happened," she said. "And everything felt hot and then cold. I don't know, but I could tell something bad was about to happen, so I pushed him down and fell on top of him, right when the whole window exploded. You can go look for yourself. It exploded out all over the place."

"Are you hurt, Cory?" Ben asked.

"No, she got between me and the window. She saved me."

"I love you," Darrah sniffled. "I thought you were going to be hurt and I just couldn't stand it."

You know a teenager is really shaken up when she'd tell her boyfriend she loves him, right in front of her parents. Ruth waited, letting her daughter gaze longingly at her boyfriend for a second, until she calmed down a little. It was awkward, but Ruth knew the girl needed a second. She wanted to hug the skinny boy, too, for bringing Darrah home. They'd have to have him over for dinner sometimes. *If we keep him a little late after dinner, maybe his old man will be passed out by the time Cory gets home. Save the kid a beating.* She'd heard the gossip about that even before Darrah told her.

"Cory, can you get home to your parents, or do you want me to drive you?" Ben asked after the pause.

"No, I'm okay."

"That's good," Ben said. "Thank you for bringing Darrah home. You were very responsible, and we appreciate it, but I think we'd like to be alone with Darrah now."

The kid got that hang-dog look. Ruth could tell he hadn't slept with her yet, he still had all that longing and disappointment on his face when he was told he'd have to be away from her. Why'd that look have to go away, or ferment down to something sick and toxic?

"Yeah. Okay," he said. "I'll call you tomorrow. Okay, Darrah?"

"Yeah." She sounded like she was going to start bawling again in earnest.

Ruth loosened her grip and turned her daughter toward Cory. "Go ahead," she said. "Short clinch. No kissing. You two need it after all that."

The two kids shared a very brief and discrete embrace. Then as Cory headed toward the door, Darrah called out, "Wait, you'll be cold. I still have your shirt."

"It's okay, I got it," Ben said, as he got an old jacket from the hall closet and gave it to the boy.

"Thanks," Cory said, turning to leave.

Ruth reached for Darrah's balled-up hand. "All right, you," she said as she led her to the bathroom. "Let's see what we've got here and take care of it."

"Are you sure?" Darrah asked. "It'll be all bloody when you unwrap it."

She sounded pretty nervous. How could her daughter think she'd mind taking care of her, at a time like this? *I'm not Medea, for Christ's sake.* It was different with Nat, he was sick all the time, with endless doctor's visits, and never any resolution. Darrah was healthy as a horse, never sick or hurt once. Of course she'd take care of her. It was practically the only time she'd ever asked for any attention for herself in eight years.

"It's okay, sweetie," Ruth said, with a little catch in her voice from the guilt.

She held Darrah's hand over the sink and peeled away the grey shirt that encased her hand, the layers turning dark brown as she got closer to the center of the wad. *Oh boy, that was a bit more blood than I'd bargained for. First time the girl's needed me in forever,* Ruth reminded herself. *No time to get all squeamish and freaked out.*

Ben was beside them. Ruth thought he might feel her revulsion and weakness, because he put his hand on her shoulder to steady her.

"It's okay, Darrah," he said. "Your mom'll fix it up in a second." *That was nice of him to say. I need to cut him some more slack,* she decided.

Darrah's hand was unevenly coated in gore, and more blood flowed once her mother got the makeshift dressing off. There were little cuts and scratches all across the back of the girl's hand, but the main wound was a jagged hole between her thumb and forefinger. Ruth held it under the warm water from the faucet. *Damn thing looks like it went nearly all the way through.*

"How the hell big was the piece of glass?" she asked as she worked.

"It was big," Darrah said. "Long and pointy. It's on the ground somewhere back there. Oh no, there's probably some little pieces still in my hair. You didn't cut your face, did you?" Darrah was studying her mother's face, the deep gash in her own hand forgotten.

Ruth smiled at her. The kid was amazing; if things didn't always work out the way they were supposed to, or the way Ruth hoped they would, she'd still have to admit this kid had turned out better than she deserved.

"I'm fine, honey," she said. "Always worrying about other people, you big goof. Just let me get this patched up."

Ruth got the hand taped up with a layer of gauze underneath. It wasn't tidy, as she hadn't done it in years, but it looked like it'd hold fine.

They exited to the living room, where Darrah held up her bandaged hand. "See, sport, we match," she said to her brother. "You okay over there?"

"Yeah," he said. "I'm glad you're okay."

"Can you sit there another minute, sweetie?" Ruth said as cheerfully as possible. "We need to get your sister some tea and get her calmed down."

"Yeah. It's fine."

Maybe he isn't so bad, either, Ruth decided.

The three older members of the family went out to the kitchen, where Darrah leaned on the counter next to her father. He put his arm around her as Ruth made more tea.

"Honey and lemon in it?" she asked her daughter. "That's how I always like it when I'm feeling all cold and crappy."

"Yeah, that'd be great."

"You want some?" she asked her husband.

"No, I'm good."

Ruth put two tea bags in mugs and hunted in the fridge for the bottle of lemon juice.

"I don't know what could've happened out there," Ben said. "I'll go take a look later, but it doesn't make sense."

"We're telling the truth, Dad." Darrah almost never whined, either, but her voice had that edge to it. *Probably can't help it, under the circumstances,* Ruth mused.

"I know," her father agreed. "I wasn't saying you weren't. I just don't get it. It's weird." He fell silent for a moment before going on, and Ruth could see he was thinking something strange, that he didn't know how to put into words. "Weird how you both got cut the same day, on your hands. Well, at least you're both okay."

"Yeah," Darrah said. "I got the strangest feeling right before it happened. Not just like a premonition. I mean, I got that, too, an image of Cory getting hurt so badly. I could feel it and couldn't stand that happening to him, and I knew I could stop it if I tried, if I put myself in the way of what was happening." She paused. "But more than that. I got this feeling that someone was so angry with me they wanted to hurt me, punish me. They thought I'd done something wrong, but not just wrong. What's the word? Nat was asking me about it earlier. Unclean. That was the feeling. Someone thought I was unclean."

Ruth added the honey and lemon juice to the two mugs. She knew all about feeling dirty when you were with a man.

"You mean, you felt dirty?" Ruth tried to make it sound as innocuous as she could, following on Darrah's description, but she knew it still sounded like an accusation.

To see Darrah blush and stammer, though, she knew the girl didn't have anything to confess. Everything about her said "virgin," loud and clear. It was pretty endearing and lovely, too. *You give your kid the talk about the mechanics of sex and pregnancy, you buy her the condoms... but there were just so many feelings and hurts you couldn't warn her about, because she wouldn't understand those until they'd already happened to her.* Ruth hoped her daughter savored her life before all that adult bullshit hit her like a huge brown wave, but doubted that was even possible. Innocence was one of those things you didn't know you had, until it was gone. That was weirder and more regrettable than all her strange talk of premonitions and vague feelings of unease.

"No, I didn't feel that way," Darrah said. "I felt great, because, well, you know." She went a deeper shade of red. "I felt great because

I was with Cory. But I knew, somehow, that someone else was right there, thinking I was unclean. They even thought I'd made the place unclean. That I had defiled it. That's how they were thinking of me. Their anger was so strong I could feel it, like a wind, or even like poison gas." Ruth noticed Darrah shiver, at the vivid and terrible memory. Ben held her tighter. "It was weird and awful."

The water had boiled so Ruth poured it into the two mugs and stirred as she thought over Darrah's comments. Despite her career studying folklore, she always found talk like this boring or useless at best. People believed all kinds of crap; Lourdes, Medjugorje, shamans, snake-handlers, walking on coals, divining rods, seer stones, and probably a thousand other things she'd never even heard of. They could present it with the utmost of certainty and conviction, like their lives depended on convincing you it was true. But it was still crap.

Even Ruth knew, however, that you don't tell that to a scared teenager who thinks she felt something, and is using that as a way of understanding why she and her boyfriend were almost maimed for life a few minutes before. *You just play along as best you can.*

Ruth handed one mug to her daughter and smiled at her. "Well, you and your brother always were pretty perceptive about other people's feelings," she said. "But there wasn't anyone in the woods, was there, dear?"

"No." Darrah blew across the steaming tea. "But... well, Opa made that building."

Ruth truly didn't know where the kid was going with this. She'd gotten used to Nat's flights of fancy, though God knew they could still frighten her, but now Darrah was spinning weird, supernatural bullshit? *Must be Ben's side of the family,* she thought.

"Yes, he did," Ruth answered. "So?"

"Well, it seemed like he'd be the one to get angry, if he felt someone was disrespecting it, defiling it."

Oh shit. Is she going to tell me she had a fucking Ouija board next? And maybe the place was built on an ancient Indian burial ground? And when she walked home from the bus-stop the neighbor's dog talked to her and it was really Aleister Crowley? Whatever had happened, it must've really shaken the kid up, not just to be having these thoughts, but to be admitting them.

"Yes, I suppose he would," Ruth said, still as unperturbed and even as she could manage. "But he's dead."

Darrah sipped her tea. "Yeah. I know."

Ruth looked to her husband for some support, some gentle repudiation of the ideas Darrah was entertaining. Instead, he was looking down and nodding. He seemed quite intent on something, as though he were dissecting and analyzing everything his daughter had just said.

"All right," Ruth said as she nudged them toward the door. "Let's go sit and keep Nat company. We all need to take a break and regroup."

Great. Now the whole family has gone round the fucking bend. Although Ruth knew she could be a monstrously vain and self-confident woman, even she knew that if she were the sanest, most balanced one in the bunch, then they'd all have a very rough ride of it.

CHAPTER 30

Saturday, April 7, 2007 – The Sublunar Sphere

Christoph finally picked himself up from the ground. He knew Merla would be furious and uncontrollable, but he had no idea where else to go now.

As he neared the building where he'd left her, he could see the doorway was blocked with the tables and chairs that had been inside the room. That didn't make much sense, as he could just go through the wall, but it did seem to convey her message vividly, tangibly: he was not welcomed there.

"I'm sorry," he called over the barrier. "Please, I didn't mean to do that."

"Go away, you evil man," came the reply. "You nearly killed those two young people. How could you? And one of them your own family! I cannot tell everything that goes on here, since I'm not related to these people, but I could feel the poor girl's pain and terror. All because of you! If your God has followers such as you then I wish to know nothing more about him. He must be some being of darkness and cruelty, to create something as foul as you."

All Christoph could do was stay there and beg, he had nowhere else to go. "I didn't mean to. Please. I'm cold and tired. I really didn't mean to do anything bad."

"I'm glad you're cold. I hope you freeze and I'm rid of you. Or perhaps some of those other young people will come nearby and start their mating rituals. I sensed your fear of that, too. Good. You deserve to know fear and pain, since it's all you seem to want to cause in others. Their natural vitality and goodness might drive you away, to wherever it is fearful derelicts like you belong."

"I couldn't help it. I can't help it. Their feelings are so impure. They pollute everything. They drive me mad, when they're near. I'm sorry Darrah was caught up in it, but I couldn't help it. She had such powerful feelings, and they were so repulsive I couldn't stand it. Blame her. Blame that wretched little boyfriend of hers."

"I will not blame two young people for being in love. I'll blame a ridiculous old man for not minding his own business and harming everything and everyone around him."

"You told me to go out and see who was around!"

"I did not. I said it was your right to do so. I feared what you would do, but I'm not here to constrain you or force you to be good. No one can do that, not even whoever or whatever is in charge of this place, if anything is. Apparently my fears were quite well-founded.

"But the responsibility is yours. You had the right to investigate and protect. You had no right to harm anyone, least of all two people doing something good and natural, while everything you do is so unnatural, evil, and dead. That's really the problem, isn't it? I'm here to help you achieve the best life you can have after death, but you're determined to make everything around you as dead as you feel inside. I cannot abide that or help with it, and I'll stop you any way I can."

"No, I don't want to make things dead. I don't want to hurt people. But their feelings are so unruly, so out of control. They need to be controlled, disciplined. They need to be stopped."

"Not by you. I never said you had any right like that. And what is so unruly about them, anyway? You said you were married. You must remember what it was like to be young and in love."

"Well, yes, but not like that. They were acting like animals. We were modest and shy and kept such things private."

"Great spirits! Are you blind? So were these two! They went off in the woods to be alone! How much more modest can two young people be? Why can't you respect that? Why can't you let them have their turn to be young and foolish and alive? Are you as jealous and petty and stupidly unfair as all that?"

Christoph remembered the feeling he'd gotten right before the window exploded and hurt Darrah. He had seen within himself something uglier and more powerful than prudishness or embarrassment. He had realized how actively evil was his envy, and had felt the guilt and sorrow of having given birth to such a monstrosity. He remembered now that pang of conscience, but quickly and thoroughly shoved it back down to the bottom of his mind and soul to where it wouldn't bother him. He only thought of how it was their fault for making him feel that way. They'd made him jealous, with their sinful groping of one another. They'd made him lash out at them by invading and contaminating his property. This little heathen wasn't going to talk him out of that conviction, even if she did have the upper hand and he couldn't resist her or convince her of his rectitude.

"No," he said, his rationalization giving him some confidence. "But who are you to throw me out of my own place? You said a spirit had a right to defend his property. Why are you allowed to dictate to me where I can go, and keep me from this spot, if I want to be here? I made this place. Perhaps I should throw you out."

"Oh, I'd love for you to try, old man," Merla snorted. There then followed a long, incoherent howl. The girl really was a savage. "Oh spirit in the sky! Where did such a man come from? Who made him? He tries to twist the rules, but he has no self-control, no inner law. You made this place? What did you make? You created a son with a woman I now pity, and he only spurns and denies you. You had a small share in creating two beautiful grandchildren, creatures of light and gentleness, and you've hurt both of them. The girl you might've killed, though thankfully you avoided that horrible crime.

"You didn't create this life-giving fire here, that was made by some other power, and it drew me and you to it, because that is its special purpose. You had nothing to do with that. So what did you make? All I see are some silly figurines, taken from stories that don't even make sense. What's the one here? Some sort of hairless boar, dressed in human clothes? And it's using fire to kill a wolf, who's wearing pants? What kind of animals wear clothes? Or build fires? And why would a boar kill a wolf, when it's supposed to be the other way around? It's unnatural and absurd, like everything about you. You're a joke. No, worse. You're a disgrace, a monster. Now begone. I hope someone drops something big and heavy on you and you're gone forever to where I can't see you and I'm not responsible for your redemption. I don't think it's possible anymore. You're just not worth it."

Christoph could tell there was no arguing with her. That much had not changed between the world of the living and the dead, women were very difficult and frustrating to debate. They never fought fair. He drifted away until he was again by the wishing well and he sat down there. He knew he had done wrong and should pray for forgiveness, but he couldn't bring himself to do so. Why were other people so wicked and depraved, so much so that they had forced him to do the terrible things he had done? That question blocked out all other thoughts; a painful, unanswerable inquiry that could only bring him more anger and grief.

It was so cold and damp there, and would soon be dark as well.

CHAPTER 31

Saturday, April 7, 2007 – Northern New Jersey

Ben slipped out the side door from the kitchen. The cold air felt good, invigorating, like it would clear all the crap out of his head and let him see better. Everyone else was recovering from the day's excitement, but he just wanted to be alone and think through everything he'd discovered, as well as all the things Darrah had said. It now made an increasingly compelling, if strange, kind of sense to him.

He knew Darrah would never say anything fanciful or impractical, in that sense she was just like her mother, so if she talked about how she felt her dead grandfather's presence before she and her brother got hurt, then they should take her seriously. Ben still didn't know what he thought was going on, exactly, but he knew he wanted to be alone, outside, and face whatever it was before anyone else got hurt. *That's not a matter of believing, it's just being the man of the house and protecting your own. You don't send your kids out into the woods, telling them there was nothing to be afraid of there, when their injuries say otherwise. You go out there yourself to check it out. That's common sense, not superstition. What was that line near the beginning of Moby-Dick, when Starbuck's introduced?* Something about him having the sort of superstition that springs from intelligence, rather than ignorance. That about said it right for today.

Ben walked around to the back of the house and got the other wheelbarrow they kept there. He glanced around before pulling the bottle from under his jacket and placing it in the barrow. This was an investigation and analysis that required alcohol; there were a few tasks like that in life. Working up the courage to confront your spouse about her cheating, for example. The two or three times a year he got drunk, it had always been with that purpose in mind, but he'd never quite attained the appropriate frame of mind for that task. He had either just gotten weepy and passed out, or else punched a wall and went to sleep on the couch. Accusing your dead father of tormenting and injuring you and your kids seemed like a pretty analogous situation, so it would probably require a similarly skewed perspective and heightened emotional state.

Nobody in the house was much of a drinker, so it had taken a couple minutes of scrounging to come up with anything for this occasion. There was a nearly-full bottle of rum, from when his father had come over to make fruitcake, stollen, and mince-meat pies with Ruth, way back at Christmas. *Gal isn't much of a cook, but she sure can bake.* Ben thought it was something about all the preparation and setting up that she liked. He had grabbed that bottle first, but when he held the glass in his hand, it hadn't seemed like such a good idea. One had to have the right tools for the job, or at least, one didn't bring along something with such a poor track record. You don't bring a knife to a gun fight, as the saying goes.

More rummaging had brought up the 1.75-liter plastic jug of gin they'd bought last summer when they had some of Ruth's colleagues over for a cookout and drinks. Gin and tonic was a nice, summery drink, he had figured, but most everyone had opted for beer or wine, so the large container was still about half full. That was sure going to taste like shit without a chaser or mixer. This project wasn't about pleasure, was it? *More about pain and truth-telling,* Ben figured, *and gin is probably about as good a catalyst for that as anything else.*

He put a flashlight, hammer, and screwdriver next to the bottle; he had screws and nails in his jacket pocket. It'd be light for a little while yet, time enough for him to work. That had been his excuse for sneaking out, to board up the window for the Seven Dwarves, so the inside of their house didn't get damaged more by rain or animals. There were two sheets of plywood leaning against the back of the house, which he placed across the top of the wheelbarrow before picking up the handles and starting on his way.

To be honest, it looked like the rain might pass them, but that had just been an excuse anyway. The trip wasn't about preventing further damage, it was about determining the cause of the damage thus far. *No, that isn't completely right, either,* Ben thought as he stopped, looking around. He was right by the bridge with the troll. Trees and a hill were now between him and the house, and many more between him and the highway. He lifted the plywood and retrieved the bottle for a long, painful swig. *Yup, just as bad as I thought it would be.*

He paused, gasping from the burning sensation in his throat and stomach. *What am I doing, exactly? Better get that straight before proceeding.*

He was going to spend a couple hours deciding how he would interpret what had happened. That was getting closer to his goal. He gave himself a moment, then took another, smaller gulp. In a person's mind, there was always a sort of "official" version of events – "official" and definitive for that person. He was going to come up with his. He suspected from the way she'd talked, that it was a version he could share with Darrah. He was even more certain, given how the boy talked and thought, that it was a version Nat would understand. Seeing Ruth's predictable reaction to Darrah in the kitchen, she wasn't going to be on board. *Fuck her.* He had issues with her, but they were separate. This was a family thing; a fleshly, biological drama, driven by blood, shared by people who couldn't really disown or deny one another, no matter how much they'd like to.

You loved your spouse, maybe you even loved her after she cheated on you, though he himself went back and forth on that most every single day. But you *could* conceivably get rid of her, or she could get rid of you. Part ways. Untie the knot. Turn the page. Forget she ever existed. Clean slate. You might even fall in love with someone else, if you were lucky or unlucky enough, depending on how you looked at it.

It wasn't like that with parents and children, though. That really was forever, not even "'til death do us part."

Ben took another, smaller pull on the bottle, sucking his breath in through clenched teeth afterward. *So you're stuck with these people. They aren't going away, even dead. You have to decide what to think of them, how to look at them and the things they'd done, and remember, just saying "fuck them" isn't an option, the way it is with a spouse. That was the biggest lie of all, claiming you could just ignore them. You have to come up with an interpretation of events that you are comfortable with.* It couldn't be an interpretation that flew in the face of reality, though Ben knew it could skirt right around the edge of fantasy.

It was like when that Cory kid had a bruise, or any of the hundreds of times he had similar ones, growing up. You couldn't just say, "That's not a bruise." That was a crazy level of untruth. Everyone would know you were lying, and you'd know it yourself. But you could say, "That's a bruise I got when I fell down." That's believable. People fall down all the time. You can live with that explanation; other people will want you to as well. It might even be accurate, up to a point. Maybe you just left out the part about your dad pushing you down the stairs and kicking you after you got to the bottom. It was still true that you got the bruise when you fell.

Ben took a bigger swig this time, before capping up the bottle and putting it back in the wheelbarrow. Taking up the handles again, he proceeded down the path, feeling a little flushed and weak, but knowing that'd pass as a good, solid, roaring drunk took hold in an hour or so. He was going to get this investigation under way. *Start with interviewing the Seven Dwarves. Witnesses.* He snickered. *They probably drank too, so they wouldn't give the best testimony, but you have to go with what you had.* He'd end up at the other crime scene later, when he was nice and tight, and raising some hell would feel really satisfying to a desperate, middle-aged failure like himself. It didn't take a fucking ghost, or even believing in ghosts, to make him think that would be an interesting way to spend the evening, that he'd rid himself of some baggage he'd lugged around too long, and some he'd just recently acquired.

The scene at the Seven Dwarves was more unsettling than even Darrah's description. Ben got the bottle and took a swig as he walked around in front of the building, his shoes crunching the broken glass. There were no burn marks anywhere, and all the figures and furnishings inside the building were intact. So it wasn't like there'd been a fire or an explosion from anything like gas or gunpowder, but the placement of the shattered pieces was a worse riddle, it seemed to Ben. A little sip as he squinted at all the glass and considered the scene. *Okay. Suppose there was a sudden, cataclysmic drop in air pressure outside.* Ben thought he'd heard that happened during tornadoes, not that there had been a tornado there this afternoon, but again, just for the sake of argument. *Let's just suppose there was some kind of explosion, caused by some means, and obeying the laws of physics that prevailed here in northern New Jersey, a supposition supported by the clear, tangible evidence lying at my feet.* In any kind of explosion he could imagine, the glass should've flown outward in a straight line, or perhaps fanned out. Either way, the wood and glass remains should now be all over, in a big debris field in front of the ripped-apart window frame.

That wasn't how the bits of glass lay on the ground, however. They were focused in a dense, glittering, crescent-shaped puddle at the base of one of the wooden beams that held up the awning. It was like every bit of glass from across ten feet of window had all flown right at the one spot where the kids had been standing.

Ben shivered and took a long, angry swig from the bottle, thinking how both kids would've had their faces ripped off, if Darrah hadn't turned and knocked Cory down at just the right moment. *Hell, even with that stroke of luck, she would've still looked like she'd been hit with a blast of bird shot, if she hadn't been wearing that jean jacket.* That thought made him hate the person who did this even more.

There was the smell of sawdust, really fresh, but a little burnt. Just like Darrah had described earlier, there was that barely perceptible hint of cloves too, more stinging than the wood smell. There was about as much reason for those smells to be there, as there was for a window to explode. No *good* reason. One bad and crazy one, however.

Ben leaned the one plywood sheet against the wall, covering half the hole. He didn't feel like nailing it up, besides, between that and the awning, nothing was going to get in there until he had a chance to put in a new window. Even doing all the work himself, that shit was going to be expensive.

"It's crap like this that keeps making it harder and harder to keep this place, you know?" he said quietly.

Ben got a piece of paper out of his pocket. He unfolded it and spread it out on the sheet of plywood still sitting on top of the wheelbarrow, setting the hammer on the paper to hold it down. It was ancient – almost as old as he, to be exact – yellowed, crinkly, and curling at the corners. It was one of those forms with boxes that people actually had to use a typewriter to fill out. That's how old it was.

Even another swig of gin couldn't force what he was about to say into a logical category, or make it seem like the sensible action of an educated, rational person. But this evening was no more about rationality than it was about pleasure. Truth transcended both of those, didn't it?

"I found this paper, old man," Ben said. Not exactly shouting, but in a pretty loud voice; a cold, even, heavy tone. "Maybe you don't remember it. I sure never saw it before, so maybe you never looked at it in the last forty-four years. Maybe you decided just to tell me what it said, what you wanted it to say. Maybe you told it to me so much you believed it after a while. Well, let me point out the couple difficulties I've had with this paper, since I found it this afternoon. 'Date of Death – November 2, 1962.' Now there's the problem, see? I was told all my life that she died when I was born, and my birthday is in August. That's a little confusing, wouldn't you say?"

A deep, long drink, two big bubbles of air climbing up the neck and breaking inside the bottle. It didn't burn so much anymore. "And that brings us to this other problem I have. 'Cause of Death – Drug Overdose.' It doesn't say 'Complications related to childbirth,' or 'Hemorrhage,' or 'Infection,' or anything like that. Isn't that funny? That's what you always told me, that she died giving birth to me. Oh, and I think we both knew that meant I'd killed her, didn't we? Beating me, making me go to church and pray for her, telling me she'd be ashamed how I turned out... all that always implied I was to blame, I was the problem, I was the one that messed everything up and ruined your perfect life. I even felt sorry for you sometimes.

"Not anymore. She died. I can't tell from this whether it was suicide or an accident, but it wasn't me. And you laid that shit on me, day after day, year after year. You made me hate myself. You made me hate your stupid God for doing that to me and her. But now I see it was all you. I always thought you were just sad and lonely, but really, you were a liar and you got off on lying to me and making me feel like shit."

A smaller gulp and Ben checked the level – less than halfway there. It was good to be on schedule, even for such an unpleasant task. "I could still overlook all that. People make mistakes raising their kids. Shit, who would I be to throw stones over that, the way me and the little lady act around the house, the way we lay all our problems on those poor kids? No, you might still get a pass for that. But fucking with my kids? Look at this place! It looks like a fucking claymore went off here! Except your precious little bullshit figurines are still fine, and my daughter's cut up and lucky to even be alive, you bastard. That shit doesn't get a pass." Ben paused to catch his breath. "I'm not even angry anymore. I'm past that. I can't feel anything for you anymore. You're like a fucking disease that's passed on through the generations, and a man doesn't hate a disease. He just wants it to go away."

Ben put the paper back in his pocket and took up the other sheet of plywood. In the final rays of the sun, he leaned it against the other part of the hole in the wall. As he did so, he paused a moment to look at Snow White. In the dim haze, she looked even more alive than usual, like a real person, standing there in the twilight; tiny, delicate, but oddly blissful, as though she were quite happy there, unperturbed by the evil pursuing her.

"How could you make such beautiful things, and be so ugly inside?" he whispered as he walked away.

CHAPTER 32
Saturday, April 7, 2007 – The Sublunar Sphere

Even before it got dark, Christoph felt the temperature around him plummeting. Ben must be about. Christoph wondered how someone who was so angry so much of the time could make such an imprint of freezing cold. The physics of this place seldom made sense to him.

The orb of the sun was touching the horizon, and it had gotten so cold Christoph felt himself literally frozen to the spot. How could he have been so foolish as to leave Merla? She would've taken care of him. He would have just needed to figure out the right way to implore her, convince her, work on her sympathies, but instead he'd gotten angry and accusatory. Now he was out here freezing from his son's hate and spite.

At least the boy had some reason this time. That made it a little easier to accept. He must've seen how hurt and frightened Darrah was, but how could he have known it was Christoph who caused it? Ben probably wouldn't have been able to figure it out on his own. It wasn't, after all, the sort of conclusion to which one normally jumped. Darrah and Nat were more perceptive about spiritual and emotional matters, however. Between the two of them they might have thought to suggest their grandfather had something to do with what was happening. Although Ben was disinclined to such speculation, he would be apt to believe them, especially Darrah. He had a special love and trust for her, as a man should have for his firstborn and for a daughter. The boy knew some things about familial love, at least. If it weren't so damnably cold, Christoph might've even felt grateful for his son's enormous love for Darrah and Nat, but he was now too focused on his own pain.

Kim Paffenroth

Through the searing cold, the memory of his wife suddenly hit Christoph like a punch in the stomach. Even though Christoph didn't breathe anymore, this new invasion of his conscience created a sensation similar to what a living person would feel if he had the wind knocked out of himself, that catching and spasming, right in the middle of himself. As though his center were gone, or not under his control. It was not an image of Rachel that thrust itself on Christoph, not a smell or taste or sound, unfortunately, but just a desiccated phrase he had worked so long and so hard to banish from his mind: "*Cause of Death – Drug Overdose.*"

How can that be a cause of death? Sadness, anger, jealousy, greed, hate, revenge... these are the kinds of things that cause people's deaths. Those sorts of things explained what happened to the person, and why. This maddening phrase accomplished nothing but more torment for him. How could that horrible man who filled out the form sterilize and evaporate all her anguish and suffering down to that pathetic, meaningless phrase? She'd always been moody and unpredictable, but after the baby was born she was sad in a way Christoph had never seen and couldn't understand; weeping, incoherent, and inconsolable. Back then they didn't call it depression like they did now. They even had a cute name for it then, "baby blues," and all women talked about having it, and how they eventually got over it. Back then, though, the doctors were so eager to prescribe drugs for it. Damn them, their smugness, their condescension, their quackery.

Christoph had never really known if she had deliberately taken her life or not. The wretched man who had filled out the form said he would leave it open, and just put "Drug Overdose," rather than the more troubling "Suicide," though he wouldn't go so far as to add "Accidental" before the description. He wouldn't give Christoph the comfort of an official ruling, just more ambiguity and doubt. Damn him, too.

Now Ben possessed that cursed, twisted, incomplete information. It was staggering, numbing to Christoph, to think it had come to this. *No, blame me for the beatings, of course. That makes sense. I deserve that hate and blame, for having been an angry, bitter fool who pitied himself more than the poor child entrusted to him.* But no, he

—206—

shouldn't be blamed for hiding the truth of his wife's death. No, that was done to protect his son, to keep the shame from him, to let his thoughts of her be the natural, softer sadness of grief, and not the cutting, poisonous blame the boy might've attached to his mother, if he believed she committed suicide. But oh, he had shielded her from her son's blame, only to bring it on himself. It wasn't fair. It didn't make sense.

Christoph wanted to get closer to Ben, to show him somehow what had really happened, to explain his reasoning. He really was frozen to immobility, however. Even if he could have moved, there was no way for him to do such a thing as communicate with the living in a way they would understand, and he knew it. The time for that was long past, and regret remained as futile and maddening as ever in this realm.

There in the dark, it was purely and simply as cold as hell, before the flames began and a wholly different pain assailed him.

CHAPTER 33
Saturday, April 7, 2007 – Northern New Jersey

Ben left the wheelbarrow behind, and slipped the hammer and screwdriver into his jacket pocket, leaving his hands free for the flashlight and bottle. He was still walking straight, but his thoughts were starting to jumble in that first giddy rush, the frenzied mental activity of a good drunk, just before you settled down into dull numbness.

It was time to get shit done, the investigation was complete. That had not been a normal explosion back at the Seven Dwarves' place. *That's some shit that isn't supposed to happen in the normal world, and it needs to stop.* That piece of paper was some shit, too, even if it was old and supposedly over and done with. It could've been over and done with years ago, if some old German asshole had just put it out there in the open and not made up shit to suit himself and his fucked-up version of the world. All that had been laid out now. The charges read, the evidence presented, the verdict passed. Now it was time for some punishment.

Ben took a moment, standing in front of the chapel on the hill, and took two long swigs from the bottle; it had that nice sloshy sound as he put it back down. It gave him a feeling of accomplishment. He hadn't really thought through this part of the evening, he wanted to make a point to the criminal out there, he knew that, but how to do that was a bit mysterious. He took another long gulp. *You just don't go around thinking about how to harm the dead every day. It's an interesting experiment in thought.*

All right. Enough of this bullshit. Time to just do, not think. The gin was making the thinking part harder with each passing minute, anyway. Ben set the bottle down on the ground, and brought the hammer out of his pocket as he took a few quick strides to the side of the building. Each of the three windows on that side got two blows from the hammer. Ben slipped around the back of the building and did the same to the three windows on the other side. It was too bad, he liked the way they looked in the day. *Sometimes punishing the wicked requires a sacrifice,* Ben thought, retrieving the bottle and stooping to step inside the building.

"I really don't fucking care much if you kill me with your breaking glass trick," he said as he ducked into the doorway. "But not before I make my point."

The flashlight beam found the rabbit remains, and the heap of broken glass beneath it. He got up closer to it, and like Darrah said, it was gross. Fur and blood in a kind of chunky paste. The way the gore glistened, it looked like some glass was embedded in it, straight through to the wall, too. He examined the smaller stain above it, which looked like it was just blood, no fur or flesh. It wasn't part of the rabbit mess, but looked like it had dripped down the wall from another point.

Is it Nat's? That didn't make sense, but maybe the kids hadn't told him everything that'd happened. That was okay. It wasn't their fault; it wasn't their job to process and deal with this shit. They had enough trouble with their selfish, living asshole parents making their lives difficult. They didn't need a dead asshole too, with all his hang-ups and now an obvious tendency toward violence.

Ben set the flashlight on the front pew and took a drink before setting the bottle beside it. Finding a non-bloody spot on the wall to put his hand, he got out the screwdriver as he leaned down to look at the bottom of the wooden cross. He'd examined it closely before. The workmanship was amazing in every way. Even the mounting to the wall was elaborate and careful. To keep any non-decorative parts like nails or screws from showing, his father had mounted a thin vertical piece of wood on the wall. He'd then cut a groove in the back of the cross to fit over this piece. The only screws on the cross, therefore, were two counter-sunk ones at the top and bottom, so that all the visible parts were pristine and pure, just the grain of the wood and the intricate shapes in it, nothing mechanical or artificial. Ben ran his fingers along the surfaces of the carving and marveled at it again.

"Well," Ben said as he leaned down again and started working on the screw at the bottom of the cross. "As I was saying. I'm going to make a point. And my point is that this place is mine. Anything I like here, I'll keep. Anything I don't like, or that I think you were especially fond of, I'm going to destroy it, if you fuck with my kids again."

The one screw fell into Ben's hand. He slipped it in his pocket, then fitted the screwdriver to the other one.

"I thought of the Evil Queen," he continued. "Burning down her and the Jonah-woodsman would really fuck with you. Snow White looked pretty tempting, too. But I just couldn't bring myself to do it. So you're still at something of an advantage, old man. I like so many of the things here, it's hard for me to do too much damage. But I'll work on it. One more scratch on either of those kids, and I'll find a way to make myself destroy every fucking thing you ever made."

The other screw was free. Ben pocketed it along with the screwdriver. He wrapped one big hand over the mysterious shape in the center of the cross, and lifted it from the wall. He cradled the carving, considering it for a minute. The thing was so damned heavy. He had a strange urge to kiss it, partly because of the Catholic overtones and how that might cause some pain to the old man, wherever he was in the Great Beyond.

But Ben was like his daughter in that respect; gross acts of impiety didn't really appeal to him, and he knew that coming from him, the gesture would be meant as an insult. He had more interest and attraction toward blasphemous thoughts, but actions of desecration still struck him as wrong... not so much morally, but aesthetically. They were ugly, is what they were, while the thing in his hands was the opposite. It could've been an object of fear or veneration, but it was just so damned beautiful it had to be respected. He felt unworthy to hold it, let alone kiss it.

"That's funny," Ben said as he smirked. "I just thought how I'm not worthy to hold such a beautiful thing. Maybe not. But you're ten times more unworthy to have made the thing in the first place. You didn't deserve the talent you had. You didn't deserve the beautiful things you made. You couldn't even appreciate them. And you sure as fuck don't deserve to be anywhere near my kids."

Getting the flashlight and bottle, Ben awkwardly carried them along with the cross as he ducked out of the church. He leaned the cross and the bottle against a tree. Glancing back at them, he smiled. The moon had come out, and the two seemingly incompatible objects looked strangely balanced and graceful in the light, even though he'd just set them down without thinking anything of their placement.

With a jerry can of gasoline from the shed, he walked around the church, splashing gas on all the sides of the building. Striking a match, he lit one corner, and the flames quickly spread all around the base of the church. The ground and leaves were wet enough that he didn't think the spreading would be a problem. The church would be gone in a short while, and his point made. *Tomorrow'll be a bitch explaining it to Ruth, but sometimes shit has to be done.*

Ben sat down next to the cross and took up the bottle again. Gazing at the flames, he sipped more than gulped. *You kind of have to get a running start with a drunk, then you can coast along.*

He sunk into a sullen silence for a moment, then perked back up. "So, anyway," he started up again, "like I was saying, it's hard for me to destroy the things around here. But I'll make sure I do it, if you don't leave us alone. You can count on that. This stupid little church I thought was a fine place to start. You always had to drag me down the road to go to that one of yours, didn't you? I laughed my ass off when it closed a few years ago. Nobody as backward and hateful as you to go there anymore. Thank God. And now I'm getting rid of your little version of it."

He turned to look at the cross as he took a sip and smiled. "Oh, but I did know just the thing to keep, just the thing to threaten you with, until you learn to behave." The flames had grown enough to cast a nice orange glow on Ben and the cross. He again ran his fingers along it. "This'll be here forever. I'll force myself to tear down or burn down or blow up every fucking thing in this forest, no matter how beautiful it is. But this'll be here forever. I'll look at it every fucking minute of every fucking day and think of you. There won't be one thing left that you ever made. Except this. This'll be your legacy, your only surviving work. Won't that be great?"

Ben checked the bottle before taking another drink. About three or four fingers left.

"So, from now on I'll be watching. Those kids so much as stub their toes out here, and I'll start wrecking stuff. One more window cracks, and I'll smash them all and replace them with plastic. That, or I'll just sell the place and they'll pave it over and put up another dentist's office, or gas station, or another mini-storage place, full of people's ugly, useless crap." He took a sip and lowered his voice a little. "But if you can behave yourself, I'll take care of this place, and the kids will love it the way they always have, and maybe one of them will want to take care of it when the time comes, and it'll be here for another fifty years. I'm here and I'm ready to do it, whichever way protects my kids. It's up to you."

Ben had no idea if all this made any difference, or even if it made any sense. Three sheets to the wind, and with his anger burning far more furiously than the conflagration in front of him, it certainly made perfect sense to him at that moment, and for a few minutes, that could be all that mattered.

The church was really blazing now, the roof the only part not fully engulfed in flames. The heat washed over him, smoky and kind of damp. Although Ben relished the destruction and felt in control for the first time he could remember, it was still a strangely unsatisfying feeling.

CHAPTER 34
Saturday, April 7, 2007 – The Sublunar Sphere

Christoph could feel the flames. Not so much the physical ones, of course, but the anger that prompted them burned fierce enough to carry between the realms with little loss of its force and violence. Now it wasn't cold, venomous, sickly hurt for the past that gripped him, but the active, virulent blast of a soul that wishes to harm another. Christoph writhed from the torment. He felt within it something more than just anger and hate, and he suspected this was increasing its strength.

As with everything he felt, it took a moment to untangle it from all the other confused feelings, but he eventually identified it as a kind of righteous indignation. His son's wrath could wound more; they both knew it had some justice to it, the primitive, rough fairness of retribution, and also the added dimension of protecting the innocent and punishing the guilty. This made it hurt more, but it made withstanding the ordeal easier. Christoph could not cry out against this as unfair and incomprehensible, as he had the accusation about his wife. This was deserved, and that forced even someone as misguided as he to welcome it in some way.

The suffering was exquisitely complex this time. There were so many hurts and desires mingled there, and little by little Christoph could pick them out and experience the burning and stabbing of each one, or of various combinations of them. First, he could tell Ben was destroying the church building. Christoph could feel all the shame and disappointment that place represented to his son. More importantly, he felt no urge to blame or prevent his son from having these feelings; he simply knew them as one knows unpleasant facts. The act of destruction seemed necessary, even as it wounded him deeply. Just as importantly, Christoph could tell that setting the fire and seeing the structure burn did not just cause him pain and his son pleasure, he could feel a subtle ache from Ben, something almost like regret.

Finally, Christoph felt the calculation and rationality: Ben knew what he was doing, even if his thoughts were muddled and scattered, they were moving forward in a plan and not just lashing out in a frenzy. He wanted to communicate something to his father, though of course, the actual words could not pass between the realms. Despite all the pain and rage reverberating between them, however, Christoph wanted desperately to know what was being said, and so he continued to try to figure it out.

The image of the building Ben hated so much faded somewhat. Christoph suspected the structure was gone, or well on its way, and his son was turning his mind to other things. Burning down the church was a warning of some kind. Over and over, Christoph felt his son's protective love for Darrah and Nat, the love that is devotion and sacrifice, rather than desire or affection. Ben must be releasing all this destruction in order to hurt him in retaliation for what had happened to the children. *Good. That makes sense. That was fair.* He welcomed punishment for that, but there was that regret again in his son's soul.

The boy felt he had hurt and failed his own children as well, and that redoubled Christoph's pain in a new way, as he couldn't console his son. He knew it was only old fools like himself who would judge others, rather than focus on their own punishment. All he could feel for the suffering or guilt of others was compassion. His own suffering fascinated and thrilled him now, just as the pain had before, when he'd felt it together with Nat. This felt cleansing and liberating and he did not want it to end until it had done its work in his impure soul.

Weaving in and out of these feelings was yet another, and this one had that cold edge of spite to it. Christoph couldn't make it out at first, but then he realized it was the cross from the church. He'd forgotten about that. Now he could tell Ben had saved it from the flames to spite his father. For a moment, Christoph could feel anger at such a diabolical, mean-spirited ploy. The funny thing was, however, that without the hated symbol in front of himself, he could now only feel and experience the cross through his son's mind. For the first time, Christoph could feel the warm, erotic beauty of the thing; the curves that drew one's eyes upward and cleared one's mind like a perfect insight into some certain but painful truth; the dark, forbidding, beckoning wound in the middle that made one gasp and weep and beg.

No, this is not the first time I've felt this, Christoph realized. *The first time in decades, yes, but not the very first time.* He had experienced this when he'd held the thing in his hands and created it. All these years his son had seen perfectly the beauty of the symbol, when he had not. His son had felt this inspiration and longing, that only now came to his misguided, dim-sighted father when it was almost too late to do any good. Though it stung inside his mouth like the bitterest poison, to know how much his son hated and blamed him, seeing such beauty finally revealed still gave Christoph some hope amidst all these various torments he was experiencing. He could even feel something, faint and just barely detectable, akin to what he had felt earlier that afternoon with Darrah, before he made everything ugly and hateful. This was more grudging and there was little joy in it, but it was still something like admiration, or even respect. *This, too, is better than I deserve,* he thought.

He felt something warm and heavy placed on his numb shoulder. With difficulty he turned his head to see Merla.

"Christoph?" she said very quietly. "Are you all right?"

He nodded. It felt like the bones of his neck exploded as he moved, they were so frozen and stiff, even though he'd been pounded by the flames for what seemed like hours. He moved his jaw a tiny bit, resulting in a similar sensation there.

Merla rubbed his shoulder and gave her funny, noncommittal little smile. "I think we both know I can't carry you. I can barely roll you over when you get like this. But it's time you came back to the hearth. You have suffered in a good way, I hope?"

"Yes," was the first word Christoph managed. It hurt, but was a relief.

"That is a good sign. I had feared the suffering might've destroyed you. But then, if it had, you would not be the kind of creature I could help, or one that I would want to be near. So it was bound to work out, either way. You have failed some tests, but this is an important one you have passed. I am glad. Now come on, you."

She got her hands under his shoulder and started to pull him up. As his legs straightened, it felt like his knees were being hit with ball-peen hammers and his thighs were giant rubber bands already stretched beyond their limit, so that they now snapped from the exertion. He staggered and fell into her, but she kept him upright. They began walking slowly back, Christoph shuffling his feet and holding on to the tiny girl like a blind, lame man.

"Your son made you suffer?" Merla asked.

"Yes, in many ways, for many different things," he replied.

"Good. I did not sense he was completely righteous and innocent, as I sensed with your granddaughter, but I felt the most important thing – that you both suffered. It was not torture, I hope you know, but something complicated and necessary between two people who know each other intimately."

"Yes. I suppose so. But some of it was unfair."

"I told you about that before, Christoph. It is the lesson your grandson learned. Suffering is blind. There is nothing intrinsically just about it, there is no suffering you cannot benefit from."

"All right. I'll try."

"Good. But tell me about the unfair suffering, so I know. I can't tell everything that goes on, especially the thoughts and descriptions. It is just the feelings I can sense."

"I had lied to my son about his mother. I said she died when he was born, when really she died later. I told him that, because I wanted to protect him, I didn't want him to suspect she killed herself. I don't know how it is where you come from, but in our society, it brings a terrible shame on a family, if a family member kills herself. I wanted to save him from that, and not have him blame her, either."

"I see. You tried to protect him from being hurt, and caused a different kind of pain. This is common. Tell everything, Christoph. I sensed even more blame from him toward you, than just that."

The freezing inside increased again, though Christoph struggled to keep moving. "He thought I blamed him for her death."

"And did you?"

"I don't know. I didn't mean to." Christoph slowed and could barely continue.

Merla pulled him along with difficulty. "Say it. Whether you meant to or not is not what I asked. One feels what one feels, and one must atone for it, if necessary. Did you feel blame? Did you put that on him?"

"I think I did. A little. I blamed her, too, but that was too painful. She wasn't there. She'd already punished herself. He was still alive. So I had someone to blame, someone to take it out on."

"All right. Keep moving. We're almost there. And for that terrible blame you put on him unfairly, he wanted to make you suffer now?"

Christoph could move a bit more easily now, though every step still hurt and was a monumental effort.

"Yes," he said.

"And did you blame him for wanting to do that? Did you feel like it was his fault, punishing you that way?"

"No. Not anymore."

"Good. That is a good start. Tell me what else."

"He blamed me for hurting Darrah and Nat and wanted to hurt me for that."

"And you were accepting of this punishment as well, I hope?"

"Yes."

She led him into the room they had occupied before. Christoph closed his eyes and soaked in the vital warmth, filling himself with comfort and healing and calm.

They sat down together again on the large chair. "Was there anything else?" Merla asked.

Christoph didn't know how exactly to explain the cross to her. It was mysterious and complicated enough, even to him, both the symbol itself, and the confusion surrounding his son's reaction to it. She'd come out and retrieved him from the deadly cold, and she had the power to help save him, so he felt he should be open with her now.

"I made a carving long ago, of the most important symbol of our religion. I never thought it looked right, and always wished I'd never made it. I thought it would offend my God. My son is not religious, he does not even believe in God, but he loved this carving, for some reason I never understood until tonight. Tonight I could see it as it appeared to him. I could see its beauty for the first time. I don't know what it means, but I know that for a moment, just seeing that beauty with him was enough."

She leaned up against him, even slipping her arm under his, to pull him closer. "I will never understand your strange talk of your God, and these different religions that you think lead to him, or lead one away from him. It's all too complicated and bothersome, over something that should be so simple and peaceful. What happened tonight seems like a good thing to me. You and your son saw and understood the same thing, even if just for a moment. That is a great vision for two people, whatever else they've been through.

"You should rest now. I have a feeling there will be other things revealed, perhaps even more tonight. Things seem to happen so fast with you people. Your whole family is so headstrong and unpredictable. I don't know how you all managed to stand each other, when you were alive. It must've been exhausting."

He smiled a little and leaned back against her. "Yes. It was. But now I don't mind it as much as I did before. Sometimes it was a good kind of exhaustion."

"I'm very glad for you. We almost lost you."

Christoph stared at the flames, and even risked a glance at the rusting metal hatch on the other side of the room. That was still a mystery, but he suspected would not remain so for much longer.

CHAPTER 35

Saturday, April 7, 2007 – Northern New Jersey

It didn't take long for the whole structure to burn, the collapsing roof blowing out what was left of the walls with a huge sigh. As Ben had suspected, everything was too damp for there to be much danger. All the sparks that went flying away from the pyre fizzled wherever they hit the soaked leaves and wet ground.

All that remained now of the church was a jagged, smoldering heap, with a few small flames still dancing on the larger pieces. Most of it was now reduced to nothing more than glowing embers.

Ben saw two flashlight beams bobbing across the park, headed toward him. *Shit.* He'd assumed dealing with Ruth was for tomorrow, not tonight. *This is going to be an awkward encounter, me blithering drunk, with my ass frozen from sitting on the ground and stare-eyed from the gin and staring into the flames.* Well, nothing ever went according to plan and he'd just have to face the music on this. Who was with her, though? He certainly didn't want the kids to see him like this, even if they were more likely to understand what he'd done than his wife was.

Ben quickly brushed the cross and the bottle under some leaves, then stood up and turned on his flashlight. He took a few steps down the hill, towards whoever was approaching, having trouble keeping his balance. He really hoped it wasn't the kids with Ruth.

Crap. The only thing worse than seeing your kids when you're shit-faced, is seeing a man in uniform. One of Hallicott Mills' finest was coming up the hill with Ruth.

She got to Ben first. He thought he almost saw concern or even fearful devotion on her face, just for a moment, before it went hard and angry. She didn't embrace him, but she made sure to take a position between him and the cop. *Smart gal. She can stir shit up at home, but she knows better than anyone how to defuse a situation with strangers. Fucking would've been fucked if the cop had come up here on his own.*

"Ben!" she said, "What's going on? Sheriff Bagley came to the door and said there was a fire in the woods."

"What?" Ben said. "Oh." *Shit it was getting hard to talk. This is going to go badly.* "Yeah. When I was fixing the other building, I saw the fire. It was already mostly burned down when I got to it, so I just stayed to make sure it didn't spread. No big deal. Just the one little building. Don't know how it could've happened."

Flashlight beam right to the eyes, with one of those eighteen D-cell jobs the cops used. *Fucking things must be made to burn people's retinas to a crisp. They fucking teach them to do that in cop school? Blind the citizenry every chance you get? Let them know who's boss?*

"You all right, sir? You look a little... shaken up," came the voice from behind the mini nova in front of Ben's face.

Like the bastard gives a shit what condition I'm in. Or like he'd have any doubt, given how Ben must be reeking like a fucking distillery. No, he was sure Sheriff Bagley only cared that he'd been rousted from hitting on the Indian lady at the donut shop on Route 23. No doubt he was further pissed by having to do some actual fucking work tonight, besides giving out tickets and chasing teenagers who were skateboarding in some store's parking lot.

"Oh, yeah. Fine. Just was a little hot by the fire."

"Hmm-hmm," came the smug reply. At least he put the fucking light down. Now all Ben could see were orange and purple spots. "No idea how it started?"

"No," Ben said. "Most of the buildings don't have electricity, so it can't be that. No idea."

"Smells kind of like gas," said the cop.

Smug, so fucking smug. Not even accusatory, just smug, as if to say, "Cut the crap. We both know I can fuck up your night for bringing me out here. Go ahead, smart guy, and give me an excuse to do so." Ben didn't think they had to train them in that attitude. He just thought the people who signed up to be cops were little bullies and tyrants in the first place, ones with perpetual wood from the power trip of a gun and a badge. *Fucking good thing I came part way down the hill. Smelled a hell of a lot more like gas up at the top there, Sherlock.*

Ben's vision was starting to return, so he could see his accuser. Why did cops always have mustaches? Sheriff Bagley must be pushing the limits of department policy, too, with that walrus-like one. What was the guy? Five-eight? Like some cops, he obviously had a barbell in his hand every minute that he wasn't holding a donut, but still. Ben was big enough and drunk enough to think – like every drunken man who'd ever lived – how satisfying it'd be to take a swing at him. Catch him off guard, get in a few good shots to the head. Everyone in town would see the guy with a nice shiner, maybe two, for a few days. That'd almost be worth the pepper-spraying and merciless beating that would inevitably follow.

All right. Enough thinking shit like that. "Oh, well, I guess I left the can we use for the lawn mower and stuff up there," Ben said. "Maybe that helped spread the fire. Sorry. I should've been more careful."

Sheriff Bagley grunted. He took a step forward and that urge to punch him in the face just about overwhelmed Ben once and for all. *Fucker even sticks his chin forward, like he's daring me to do it.*

"Yeah. Definitely be more careful," the cop said. "And maybe it'd be best if there wasn't any insurance claim about this. That might not be a good idea, under the circumstances. You know what I mean?"

Ben had one fist clenched, the other so tight on the flashlight he thought he could hear the plastic cracking. *Out here, in the cold and dark, trying to protect my family, and this little piece of shit's accusing me of something? Fuck.* Ben decided he'd lay a beat down on this fucker that'd be worth the jail time.

Ruth was between them. Subtly, but Ben knew her well enough to realize she'd seen what the two testosterone-soaked idiots were up to, their increasingly threatening back and forth of male bluster, one high on authority, the other smashed off his gourd.

"Oh, you're so right," she said in her perky, cheerful voice. Even had that little twinkle of flirtation to it. "I'm just so glad you came and got me, Sheriff, so we could straighten this out. We're so sorry to bring you out on a cold night like this. We'll go right back home and you won't hear anything more from us."

They hung there a moment. Ben could see the cop thinking if he needed to say anything more to put these two uppity college-types in their place. But Ruth's charm, and the siren call of the donut shop lady won out after a minute.

"All right," Sheriff Bagley said. "You be more careful. Good night."

"What the fuck is wrong with you?" Ruth said through clenched teeth as the beam of the sheriff's flashlight bobbed away off to their left, and their two beams began following the trail back toward their home.

"Nothing." *Fuck.* He was going to waste another perfectly good drunk and not say what needed to be said to her.

Ruth walked beside him. That was probably a good thing, as he kept bumping into her, and if she hadn't been there, he would've stumbled and fallen off the path. Probably would've woken up in the middle of the night, face down there in the dirt, his pants stuck to him with frozen piss. He kind of laughed, but it came out as a cough, when he thought how Ruth, of all people, could be a steadying influence to him, save him from such embarrassment, just like she had with the cop. *No, any humiliation for me, she'd want to be the one inflicting it, but otherwise, she'd help him out. Funny shit, that.*

He could tell she was wound up and wasn't going to let it go at that, however. She grabbed his arm. Gal had balls, he had to give that to her. Him, obviously drunk and whacked-out over something, her probably one-twenty and all of five-five, and she *still* had it in her to grab him and stop him. Balls. He respected her for that. He wondered if he could ever love her and long for her again, as he knew he once had.

"No. Really," she said. Not yelling, but definitely getting louder. "I need to know what the fuck is fucking wrong with you, you fucking drunk. I'm dragged out here in the freezing cold by some cop, because you're burning the fucking place down? I have two kids in the house. Tell me what the fuck is wrong with you, or I swear to fucking God I won't let you back in the house with them, you sick, crazy fuck."

Bringing the kids into it wasn't quite fighting fair, but he knew she had a point. "What's wrong with me, Ruth? Something old, and something new. Or really, no. Something old, and something older." He couldn't help giggling at that.

She let go of his arm and stalked toward their house. "Fuck. You're too drunk. You're a fucking child. Drop your sorry ass on the couch and sleep it off and we'll talk in the morning. Or not. I don't really give a fuck."

This time he grabbed her arm, none too gently either. She looked suitably surprised. Not scared, exactly, but it definitely got her attention.

"No," he said. "You asked. The old thing that's wrong with me is you fucked someone else. Not once. *Lots.*" The last words came out all spitty and slurred, like Sylvester the cat would say it. Fuck, it was hard to say this shit sober, but it was harder to say it blind drunk. Now he had some momentum, at least, and the words could spill out on their own. "And then you and I made it a hundred fucking times worse by not talking about it, pretending like it didn't happen, fighting about it all the time anyway. There. Now I finally said it."

She glared at him. She tried to pull her arm away, but not hard enough to break his grip. "You don't know anything," she said. "You bring this shit up all the time, even if this is the first time you came out and said it. You know what? It's fucking tiresome. I don't give a flying fuck if you think I fucked somebody else. I was always there for you and the kids and that's all that should matter to you. So now you said what you wanted to. You made your huge accusation. Whoop-dee-fucking-do. Now can you stop starting fires, for fuck's sake? Are you fucking happy now?"

He stared back at her, as steadily as he could with the ringing buzz in his head. *Besides having balls, the gal was a looker, he had to say.* She looked so damn fine in the dim light coming up from their flashlights, still pointed at the ground. Together with the fog of their breath, she looked like some fairy or demon queen an Arthurian knight would think he saw in the mist as he searched for the Grail. So fucking cold and beautiful and intelligent, you couldn't believe she was real, and you'd let her have your soul, if that's what she wanted.

If this were a film, they'd kiss now. *Hell, if this were a porn movie – well, that'd have a really happy ending.* But this wasn't Malory or Hollywood. This was New Jersey, so they just stood there, cold and tired and hurt.

"Happy?" he said. "Not really. Not sad... but not happy. I think I'd be happy if I could love you again, Ruth. What about you? What would make you happy?"

She finally wrenched her arm free, but she didn't just walk away this time. She stared at him, her eyes a bit softer than before. She probably hadn't expected that question.

"I don't know," she said. "I haven't been happy for a long time. And it wasn't just you that was making me unhappy. I don't know what it was. Lots of things. Stress, boredom, money. Everything. I don't know. Nothing, really."

"I know what you mean."

They should've talked more before. She made a lot of sense. Ben swayed a bit from the booze and she reached out to steady him. Sometimes she was good about stuff like that, too.

"Ben," she said, "let's just get back to the house and put you to bed, okay? We'll talk more in the morning. I don't know what the fuck you were thinking with the booze and the fire, but let's just get back to the kids. That's all that matters now."

He took a staggering step forward, and she caught him. They walked slowly arm in arm down the trail.

"Ruth," he said as they walked along with faltering steps, "that thing's been bothering me for a long time. I should've said something about it sooner. I'm sorry."

She held him a bit tighter. "It's okay. It's nothing to be sorry about. It's hard to say things sometimes. I know."

"But there was something else tonight. It didn't have anything to do with you. I was going through my father's stuff. I found my mom's death certificate. She died two and a half months after I was born. It said 'drug overdose.' He'd always said she died in childbirth."

She squeezed him again. It was good to have her here, even if she didn't believe him or understand. Just her physical presence was enough sometimes.

"I'm sorry. That must've been hard to find that out. But maybe he was afraid you'd think she committed suicide or that she abused drugs. People get really ashamed about suicide or drug use, especially way back then. It might not have been a mean thing on his part."

"Maybe. I don't know. You know he did a lot of shit, hitting me and stuff. This seemed like his excuse to do it."

"I know. He had no excuse for the hitting. I understand that. But maybe your mother's death is different. Maybe he was thinking of your feelings, trying to protect you. You can't be sure."

"Maybe."

"It's too bad you couldn't talk to him about it."

"I don't know how far we'd get with talking, if he were alive. But that's why I came out here tonight, to send him a message."

She loosened her grip on him. That hadn't gone over well. He should've known it wouldn't.

"What are you saying? That's why you came out here and set a fire? You're not making sense. I know you're drunk, but that's really not making sense."

"Well, it started with finding that out, but mostly, it had to do with the kids getting hurt today."

"What does your father have to do with that? You're not talking about that stuff Darrah was saying after I bandaged her up, are you?"

Fuck it's hard to follow the line of reasoning, the track of the conversation. Thing was like a moving target and he was swaying back and forth.

"Yeah. I think she's right. It's something with my father out here. I don't know how to explain it. He's out here. And I needed to send him a message. Let him know we know it's him and we want him to leave us alone."

They took a couple steps in silence. "Ben, you were upset. I was upset about the kids. I understand that. You got drunk. You do that a couple times a year. I guess you've been doing that because of the other thing you mentioned, right?"

"Yeah. Pretty much."

"Okay. So sometimes when you get upset you get drunk. That's not too weird. Lots of people do that. Fuck, two-thirds of the Philosophy department's half in the bag, some of them even during class. So I don't mind if you need that once in a while. But I don't know what I'm going to do if you're out here talking about ghosts and communicating with dead people. I mean, I can't handle that. That's too much. Normal people don't do that."

"Normal people just get drunk or have affairs." *Shit. Shouldn't have blurted that out. That wasn't going to help anything.*

They were almost to the house. She turned and faced him, taking his arm again. *Shit. She'd been acting nice.* Now he'd pushed her button. She didn't look mad though. Confused, but not angry, even just a little gentle.

"Yes, normal people have affairs," she said. Pause. "I don't really want to talk about that anymore. I don't really want to talk about this ghost stuff, either. I just want to go inside." She leaned a bit closer. God, her eyes were amazing. "Ben, when the cop came to the door and I realized how late it was and you were still outside, the only thing I could think of was how you might be hurt, and that scared me to death. I couldn't stand the thought of you being hurt, and there still being so many bad feelings between us. Is that enough for you, for now? That I'd be scared to death something might happen to you? I guess it's not much, but it's something. It's all I have, right now. I'm too overwhelmed with other stuff to give you more than that."

"That's kind of a big something, I think."

It was still New Jersey and not Hollywood, so they only hugged rather than kissing passionately, but Ben thought his wife's body felt so reassuring in its vitality and vulnerability. Then Ruth held him at arms length, brushed him off, and fixed his hair a bit, so he wouldn't look like such a fright when they went in to present their weak, confused, broken, and middle-aged selves to their children.

CHAPTER 36

Sunday, April 8, 2007 – Northern New Jersey

Darrah couldn't sleep, even though the clock next to her bed said 12:37 a.m. She certainly felt physically exhausted and wanted to tune out all the weirdness for eight hours or so, but she just couldn't shut her brain down, make it stop thinking about what was going on. Worse, she was trying to figure out how to fix it, and that didn't seem like something she could solve anytime before daylight.

At least the whole thing with the cop hadn't gone too badly. Mom had pitched a pretty small and understandable fit when she realized it was dark outside and Dad was still out there somewhere, and now she had a cop on the front stoop, telling her there was a fire on their property. But Darrah had only had to endure a few minutes of worrying what the two adults were up to before they came back in, looking surprisingly calm. Mom seemed kind of affectionate toward Dad, even though he looked pretty trashed. *Damn, their moods are impossible to figure out.*

Mom had just put him to bed, then come back down and done the same for Nat. When she was done, she had sat next to Darrah on the couch. "Darrah," her mother said, "I can't believe I'm asking this, but do you really think your grandfather is haunting the place? Do you think he's out in the woods, and he tried to hurt you and Nat?"

Darrah had considered the question. She still wasn't sure of the answer, but she knew her mother's statement wasn't far from what she believed.

"Something like that, Mom," she answered. "I know it's crazy, but it's just something I felt out there. Like when you say you get a bad vibe from someone, or you have a bad feeling about how something's going to turn out. I know I can't explain it or convince you to feel it, but it's still real and I can't shake it. I'm sorry."

"All right. I guess I can understand that a little. But you've got your father convinced of it now, and he went out and set fire to the little chapel on the hill. That's what that was all about. He thought that was a way to get rid of your grandfather, get him to go away."

"Did it work?" Darrah had known immediately that wasn't the right thing to say to her mother.

Her mother turned to her and grabbed her shoulder. "Darrah! How can you say this stuff? Your father was out there, setting fire to things, and you ask me if it worked at scaring away a ghost? What's gotten into you?"

Boy she had a hard grip for such a small woman. "Sorry Mom. I didn't mean Dad should've done that. But it would've been nice if it had worked, at least."

Her mother had just stared at her, her mouth a little open, blinking. Ruth's eyes had started to get wet and she relaxed her grip on Darrah's shoulder, rubbing it a little.

"Darrah, please. I don't know what to say. I love you. I don't want anyone to get hurt anymore, because they're running around outside doing crazy things. You should've seen your father. No, actually, you shouldn't have. You shouldn't see your parents when they're like that. But just believe me, I know when he's going to lose it, and he was so mad he was about to hit that cop. And then what? Bail? Trial? Do I look like I need all that shit? I'm sorry." Her mother had turned her head and sniffed once before turning back to her. Her eyes had really been full then. "You want to find out what the kids at school say after your father's been in jail?"

"No, Mom."

"All right. Then please, please help me out here. You've got to help me keep an eye on Nat and your father. If you want to think your grandfather's ghost is out there, I can't stop you. Light a candle. Hell, say a prayer, if that's what you're into now. But help me keep this family together. I know you've always had too much to do around here. I know I haven't always been... I haven't always been good to you. I'll work on that, I swear to you. Just help me through this."

"I will Mom." She didn't remember her mother ever begging for anything like this, from anyone in the family or otherwise. She'd just go out and get what she wanted. Or make do without it, and make sure everyone around her knew how pissed off she was. It was almost a little scary, to see her like this.

Her mom had hugged her after that. "Thank you, Darrah. I love you so, so much."

"I love you too, Mom."

Her mother had gone to bed soon after that. Darrah had stayed up a little longer, flipping channels and not paying attention, before she went upstairs. But that had been hours ago, and sleep had not come to her. There was just the ticking of the clock, the occasional car on Route 23, and all the mad jumble of thoughts rattling around in her head.

She could hear her bedroom door opening, but it was too dark to see anything. Darrah gave a little gasp as she sat up and pulled the covers up to her chin.

"Darrah?" came a whisper from across the room. "Turn on the light. Be quiet."

Darrah winced and looked away when she flipped on the lamp by her bed. Nat came in and silently closed the door.

"What're you doing, you spaz?" she whispered to him as he walked over and stood beside her.

"Can't sleep."

"Me either. But that's no reason to walk around in the middle of the night scaring people." She scooted over and he sat next to her.

"Sorry. Dad tried to scare Opa away?"

"Yeah. Mom told you?"

"No. I figured. And then I heard her talking to you."

"Nosy. You were at the top of the stairs?"

"Yeah. He didn't do it right. He just made Opa feel bad."

"Oh?" she said. "How do you know that?" She'd only been able to sense what their grandfather was feeling when she was with Cory, and their grandfather's emotions were directly related to her. Nat was claiming some more general knowledge of what was going on, and that frightened her.

He shrugged. "I don't know. I just felt that, when Dad was outside. Not like when you and your goofy boyfriend were outside. Then I could feel Opa getting angry and scared. This was more like him being hurt. And it was good for him, it was teaching him something, but he needs something else before he'll go away. He needs to feel good, too, and not just bad. He needs to know we're all right. He needs to know he did okay and didn't mess things up too bad."

Darrah nodded. That made more sense to her, actually.

"All right," she said. "What will make him feel that?"

"I think he came close when I cut my hand."

Okay. Enough of that noise. That whole scene had been way too much for me. "No, Nat," she said firmly, even grabbing his arm. "I'll call Mom right now if you talk about hurting yourself again."

"I promised you I wouldn't. I don't need to. We both got hurt. You got hurt too. I heard you talk about it when Mom was bandaging you up. You were protecting your boyfriend, you said."

"Yeah. So?"

"You got hurt for someone else. And I hurt myself because I wanted to." He looked at her expectantly. "Don't you get it?"

"No, Nat. I don't understand what you're trying to say."

"Okay. I didn't get it at first, either. I've been in my room thinking about it, trying to figure it out. It takes both. Don't you see?"

"Both what? I don't understand."

"Both kinds of hurt. That's what makes the difference. That's what makes it something good, and not something bad, like what Opa did to the poor rabbit, or like Dad tried to do to Opa. You have to be hurt because you want to, and because it's for someone else. That's what makes it work. The pain isn't wasted. But you have to have both."

Darrah stared at him. Maybe it was exhaustion, but it was frightening how much sense he was making to her right now. Still, the way he put stories together without skipping a beat, maybe it wasn't so crazy, that with a couple hours alone in his bedroom, he could come up with this. He took a bunch of disconnected events and treated them like they were the pieces of a puzzle, just waiting to have their pattern detected and revealed. What anyone else saw as random and meaningless, Nat saw as a challenge to be overcome.

"All right," she said. "So we have the two kinds of suffering between the two of us. I guess that's a nice way to look at it, but how does it help Opa?"

"Only he knows that. We don't know everything that happened in his life. He'll have to figure it out. But we have to show him how the two go together. It's not like he's sitting here, listening to us. He just feels things. So we have to feel, really strong, how the two kinds of pain go together."

"And you promise you won't hurt yourself again?"

He looked very intently at her. "Yes. I do. I promise. I couldn't stand it, if I scared you like that again and made you cry."

"Thanks, Nat."

"It's okay."

"So what do you think we should do?"

"I don't know. I was hoping you'd have an idea."

Shoot. Kid hadn't figured everything out. Too bad. Darrah hardly felt up to the task of coming up with a way to send signals into the ether, or wherever it was. Most everything had centered on the church, so that seemed like a good place to go. *But I promised Mom I'd behave and not do crazy stuff. Well, this wasn't really crazy, even if Mom would probably think it was.* Darrah had promised to keep an eye on Nat, and clearly she was fulfilling that part of the promise by going along with him. She decided she could do this with a clear conscience.

"Let's go to the church," she said.

"Right now?"

"Neither of us can sleep. And we want to get this done sooner rather than later. Pull some clothes over your pajamas and let's sneak out and get this over with."

"Okay."

A few minutes later they were making their way up the hill to the smoldering ruins of the church. Darrah had a flashlight and the moon was out, so it was pretty easy picking their way along. Among the charred wood, some spots still glowed red. They stopped at the edge of the wreckage and just stared, Darrah waiting for some further inspiration, as this part of the plan she hadn't figured out yet.

"Well?" Nat said. "Do you know what else to do now?"

"No. Sorry."

"It's okay. You'll think of it. You're smart."

She smiled. "Thanks."

The place reeked of smoke, the smell of gas faint. Mostly it had the heavy, kind of wet scent of a dampened wood fire. Darrah tried to concentrate, think of what should come next.

"Didn't they used to think blood purified things, made them clean?" she asked.

"Blood makes a mess. Mom hates it."

"I know. She hates it because it's special somehow. It means something. It's not just like mud or grease or something. Didn't they use it to clean their temple in the Bible?"

"I don't know. I'm just a kid."

Darrah could barely keep from laughing. Everything was so surreal, being out here in the middle of the night, and Nat would think to say something as simple and funny as that.

"I thought you read it, silly," she said.

"Not the whole thing. You seen it? It's like a bajillion pages."

"Well, I think they did. They definitely thought it had some special power. And everything's been about blood that's happened here, the rabbit, you, me. Not the fire, but that was Dad trying to solve it, and I think you're right, it's not the right way." She paused, then held out her left hand and unwrapped it. "Take the bandage off yours. We'll put them together. I guess that's kind of literal, but you said that was the point, to show how the two kinds of hurt go together, how they're both necessary. So maybe we can hold our two hands together over what's left of the fire."

She helped Nat with his bandage, and took him a couple steps into the rubble, hoping they wouldn't step on a nail. *A trip to the emergency room for a tetanus shot would finish Mom off.* Darrah thought how she'd have to remember to hide their shoes when they got home and clean them up tomorrow. *The blood will be harder to take care of,* she thought, taking her brother's hand. But at that moment, she was completely convinced of Nat's analysis of the situation. Everything he'd said made perfect sense. More than just sensible, what was the word? It was hard to focus out in the freezing cold. She tried to think of it as she clasped Nat's hand between both of hers. *Sublime, that was the word.* She took a deep breath.

"Okay, put your other hand on mine," she said. "And just squeeze until it hurts."

It started out as a dull ache, but stayed that way only a moment. Darrah could feel the scab crack and the pain shoot up her arm. She sucked her breath in through clenched teeth as she felt her hand getting wet.

"You okay, kid?" she said.

"Yeah. I'm sorry it hurts you."

"It's no big deal. I'm sorry for you."

"I hope it works."

"Me too."

Darrah bowed her head. She thought of what her mom had said about saying a prayer. This seemed like a great time, but she had no idea how to go about it. She just thought how tiny her brother's hand felt in hers, how frail her mother had seemed when they hugged, how weak and old her father had looked when he'd been led off to bed. Her memory reached back further, to the bruises she'd seen on Cory, the black and purple stripes from a belt. She thought of all their collected misery and reveled in the blood as it flowed through her fingers, so much warmer and thicker than the tears she shed at the same time. She hoped Nat didn't see those. It'd make him feel bad. He might even think he'd caused them and that'd upset him more.

The heavy, red drops sizzled as they hit the embers, steadily enough that the sound became an undulating hiss. The smell crept up to Darrah, as mysterious and familiar to her as her own heart.

CHAPTER 37

Sunday, April 8, 2007 – The Sublunar Sphere

"What is it, Christoph?" Merla said beside him. "You are sensing something from your grandchildren?"

It was a diverse, but very strong feeling. "Yes, I suddenly realized that Darrah saved that boy. I only felt her pain before, when she got hurt, but now I feel the love she has for him. It's calmer than it was then, not so urgent and confused. It's sweet and affectionate, like she just wonders how he is and whether he's happy and when she'll see him again. She can remember the terrible fear she felt when she thought he'd be hurt, though now she also feels safe and joyful that he's all right. Everything is so natural and peaceful about how she feels now."

"She is strong. She values what she did. She values the pain she felt for him and the sacrifice she made. So should you."

"I do. But I'm so ashamed I caused her that. I don't know why I couldn't see before how right she was, how normal and good. It's so clear now."

"You were misguided. People in their physical life often are, and their vision sometimes becomes even more clouded when they come here. They're not used to this place and its rules and they're thrown into terrible confusion. I'm sure she forgives you. It's in her nature to do so, I think."

Christoph drew himself up a bit. "Oh. She's feeling pain again, real physical pain combined with her fear for the boy. It's funny, though, the sharper the pain, the less she thinks of it, or of herself. She's thinking so strongly about her family and the boy she loves. She's weeping for their pain, not her own." He swayed slightly, feeling dizzy and emptied by the impressions he was getting. "The feeling is so overpowering I can barely stand it. She feels a longing to take away their pain. The desire's almost physical, it's so intense and deep. It is stranger than anything I've felt."

"Good. These are good things. The children are together? Are they doing this deliberately?"

Christoph steadied himself and tried to concentrate. "Yes. Nat is with her. He is feeling like before, when he hurt himself. He's so intent on the physical pain, but his focus makes it not hurt. He doesn't notice that. It's... it's almost like when you look at a photograph from too close. You see such tiny details, but not the whole picture. That's how he's keeping the pain from hurting. It's so different from Darrah, even though they're together and feeling the same thing. She's focused on others, and he's focused on himself, on how this is his pain and he doesn't want anyone else to feel it. It's his and it's not thrust on him, and that makes it all right, in his mind. The two together are remarkable, overwhelming."

"Yes. They are. The two children are sharing something profound with one another, even though they're so different. I don't think you need to fear for them. They are wise, and I think the girl child will keep the boy from focusing too much on suffering. She is a good influence."

"Oh yes, she is. I know." Christoph felt more clarity opening up for him, like clouds parting or the sun rising. "Wait, you said he focused too much on suffering?"

"I said it was a danger, yes, especially in one so young."

"Yes, I think you're right. It can be dangerous. Can it be dangerous not to focus on suffering enough?"

"Oh, yes. I think I've seen that problem much more often. People will avoid pain, but only end up suffering more in the end, or suffering in a bad way, a way that is demeaning and deadening."

"They are trying to show me the right way to suffer, aren't they?"

"I think that's quite possible, from what you have said. But only you can say for sure, or even guess what it's about. I know these people only very dimly, like images far away, or in a fog. To you they are intense and specific. Concentrate on them."

"I am. They've shown me how wrong I was. I made my son suffer. I knew it was wrong, even at the time, but it was easier than facing all the pain I had from my wife's death. I made him suffer more, even when I was trying to shield him from something unpleasant. He is right to hate me."

"He is right that you treated him badly, but your grandchildren have shown you that hate is not the right response. Hate wants another to suffer. They have shown you that suffering is only right when it is accepted for yourself, not forced on others. It is the most sublime when it is accepted for yourself for the sake of someone you love."

"I cannot suffer for the living, can I?"

"No. Your tie to them is very tenuous now. They can pray for you or try to show you things, as they have done now very admirably. But you are not really a part of their world, and can have little effect on them, and most of it will be negative, I'm afraid. When you have suffered here, you have made them suffer as well. Even when you have felt some fond regret, they have suffered. That is not your place now."

"So if I am to suffer the right way, it would be for another dead person, wouldn't it?"

"I think you've known that all along, though my heart soars to hear you say it."

She actually leaned forward, to catch his eye, so he would see her smile. Her joy was so spontaneous and unrehearsed. *If she were a savage, then civilization was much to be regretted,* he thought.

Christoph could only nod and feel relief at this realization. He looked at the rusting hatch on the other side of the room. "I think it is time for me to open that," he said.

"Only you can tell. And I hope you know I am glad if you stay here with me a little longer."

"Thank you. I now see why that thing is here. It is ugly and I dread it more than anything else here, more than any flames of hell that I might have imagined before coming here. I've sensed that since I first saw it. It leads to a place of cold and loneliness and despair. In the weeks before my wife died, those were the only things she could feel, and I couldn't share that pain with her. I didn't know how. Or maybe I wasn't supposed to then. I don't know. But now I can. She is somewhere past that barrier. And now I'm ready to join her and free her."

Merla stood up, still smiling, and extended her hands to take his. She pulled him up, then walked hand in hand with him across the room.

"I don't see the things you do in this room, Christoph," she said, "but perhaps you should tell her of it. She might like that."

"I think you're right."

"I can help you turn the latch. It looks like it might be difficult."

"Yes, thank you."

When Christoph took hold of the metal, it still felt deathly cold, but did not burn as much as it had before. He tried to focus on Nat and Darrah and how they wouldn't have minded the pain.

"Will you stay here?" he said as they both struggled to move the wheel about an eighth of a turn.

"Oh, probably not for long. A woman nearby will be murdered by her lover, or a child will be run over by one of your vehicles, and they'll need me to help them." The latch yielded some more. She smiled more broadly at him. "Or perhaps another foolish old man will die in his sleep."

The latch had started to turn more easily, hand over hand. Christoph smiled back at her. "Oh, well, I don't know if you need two such difficult assignments in a row."

"It would be a great pleasure and honor, if his journey ended as well as yours, my friend. To suffer for one's beloved is one of the finest fates a man can have."

The latch gave a clunk as the wheel stopped in the unlocked position.

"Here, Christoph," Merla said as he turned toward her. "Take this."

She held out an object about the size of small pear, though flattened and not as thick and round as that. Christoph took it and studied it more carefully. It was a piece of dark wood, crudely carved in the shape of a turtle. There were two small holes in it.

"What is it?" he asked.

"A whistle. I carve them sometimes when I'm alone and no one needs my help. I finished it last night, even though I was so angry at you, because I hoped you'd come to your senses. I thought the turtle suited you as soon as I met you, because you needed to learn his patience and persistence, and not rush into everything. If you need me, you may blow on it and I will come."

"Thank you very much. That's very kind."

Christoph still did not know the decorum of this place, but he could not deny himself the simple pleasure of bending down and hugging her to him for a moment.

The hatch swung toward them with a rush of cold air.

"Goodbye, Christoph."

"Goodbye, Merla."

The passage beyond the hatch reminded him of the inside of the whale he had created for poor Jonah. Even as Christoph cursed himself for ever having thought this a very appropriate place to put someone else, his footsteps eagerly splashed down the dark, wet tunnel.

CHAPTER 38

Sunday, April 8, 2007 – Northern New Jersey

Ruth rolled over to see her husband sitting up in bed. He was turned to the side, his feet hanging over the edge of the bed, facing the window. She blinked. It wasn't all the way light yet. She checked the clock; 6:34 a.m. She'd put him to bed pretty early, but still. He really should sleep more after getting that wasted. Sometimes there was no telling your body what to do.

Ruth turned back to Ben and touched his side, running her hand up to his shoulder and down, just lightly at first. He had on old, plaid pajama bottoms, but his chest was bare. He still looked pretty good, considering either last night's debauch, or his forty-four years. At that moment, Ruth couldn't tell why she'd thought of him as old and useless, big and oafish, for so long, or why she'd stopped thinking those things this morning. Right now he just looked regular, and right now she just felt regular and wanted that feeling to continue for a long time.

"Can't sleep?" she said.

"No. I didn't mean to wake you up."

"No, no, you didn't. Don't know why I woke up now."

She sat up and risked some more touching, with both hands on his shoulders. He didn't pull away, shrug or grunt. That was a good sign. But at the same time, it made it more difficult, since she'd grown so used to those reactions. If he did those things, then she could get angry and that'd be the rest of their morning covered, scrapping. But now she didn't know what the next step was. It wasn't like with Darrah earlier, where the clumsiness of hugging her for the first time in years wore off in a second.

This got more awkward the longer she did it. She had some dim recollection from years and years ago, that making up used to just happen. You didn't even have to think about it, exactly, you just sort of let yourself forget what you were being pissy about and everything fell back into place. But things had been out of place so long, that now being out of place was their normal condition, and jamming them back into place was a real chore. *Damn. This was why I put this off so long, it takes some real effort and thought. But so what?* When had she let herself get lazy, on top of all her other faults?

Shit. Somewhere between having her daughter be too scared to show her a cut hand, and relying on the poor girl to do all the heavy lifting around here, physically and emotionally. *Somewhere along the way you pick up every bad habit and vice,* Ruth guessed, *and doing the right thing looks like more trouble than it's worth.*

The sun creeping in, the warm covers, his smell of smoke and booze, mud and leaves – dirty and gross, but simple and direct, just like him – everything combined in some way to make her not want to roll out the other side of the bed and go make coffee. Ruth sat up and got behind her husband, wrapping her arms and legs around him, pushing her t-shirt covered breasts against his bare back. She wriggled a little bit, snuggling her panty-clad crotch against his butt, as she laid her head on his shoulder.

"Oh I have ta'en too little care of this," she whispered.

"What?" He stirred a little. "Oh. That's a funny line to pick. What made you think of that?"

"I don't know. I just remembered how Lear was your favorite Shakespeare play. Remember that time we saw it up at Boscobel?"

"Yeah, that was something. I haven't cried like that at the theater ever."

"We should have done stuff like that more."

"Yeah."

"We used to talk about stuff like that, too. Our favorite plays, the books we're reading. We shouldn't have stopped doing that."

"I guess not."

He wasn't getting his usual sullen or exasperated tone, just kind of tired, like how she felt. That was okay. It was her turn to do some of the work. She held him a little tighter and ran one hand up through the hair on his chest. He stretched a little bit, bending his neck, rolling his shoulders, running his hand up and down her calf. Not aroused, exactly, both of them just kind of moving their hands around as they talked. It helped, though it was still tough going, trying to get the words out.

"How much do you remember of last night?" she asked.

"Most of it, I guess. Once we got here it's hazy. I don't remember getting into PJs or into bed."

"So... everything before that?"

"Yeah. The fire. The cop. Walking back here. What we talked about."

"No more fires, Ben?"

"No. If I have to wreck some more stuff, I'll use the sledge hammer. But it feels different here this morning, like he learned his lesson. I'll ask Darrah later what she thinks, if it feels different to her, too, but I think he got the message."

Definitely not the answer I wanted to hear, but maybe it wasn't too far out there, Ruth thought. Lots of people believed in ghosts and stuff. What would she do if he became a holy roller or something? Going to church all the time, maybe wanting her and the kids to go, too, trying to save everyone's souls. It could happen. Lots of people did crazy shit like that when they hit middle age. That'd be a lot bigger strain than this. No, if he and the kids wanted to believe they'd driven off a ghost, she could live with that. She nuzzled her face against his shoulder.

"Yeah, you should talk to her later. She was shaken up, but I think she'll be fine. But the other thing, Ben... I just... I don't know how to say it."

Ben turned as Ruth scooched to one side. It was an awkward tangle of their bodies for a second, but they ended up partly facing each other, her one leg draped across his one knee, him still caressing it, her still touching his chest and shoulder.

"I'm ashamed of what I did," she said. "I'm sorry. I don't know what else to say."

She knew she'd deserve it if he told her to fuck off. He didn't look like he was going to, but she still thought it. And she knew that if he did, this time would really count, not like all the times he'd told her to do so in the previous eight years. But he just looked into her eyes and nodded a bit.

"I think I could love you again," he said very quietly.

"You mean... you don't?" It was hard not to get that whiny, accusatory tone, like it was his fault if he didn't. Fuck, she sounded like a school girl again. Darrah knew as much about loving a man as she did. What a fucking painful embarrassment she'd made of her life.

"I don't know." His voice was steadier than hers, but still tired and weak. "What about you?"

"I don't know. I..." *Shit. How do I say it out loud, when I'm not mad at him?* How'd you make it sound as tepid and meaningless as it was? "I didn't have the affair because I didn't love you. But since then... it's just gotten so messy and complicated. I won't lie to you more. I don't know how I feel."

"I think not lying is a good start." His one hand went further up her thigh, and he ran the fingers of his other hand through her hair. "I know I want to love you again, Ruth. I've wanted that for a long time, but I couldn't bring myself to say it, and I didn't know how to do it."

"I want that, too."

"Maybe you can help me figure out how to."

"I'd sure like to try."

His hand at the back of her neck, he pulled her to him and they finally kissed. Softly, just with their lips. It wasn't like the old days; she didn't feel herself heating up instantly, like she would've back then, but it was nice in its own way. Comforting and soothing, more than urgent. She focused on the act more, pouring all her vulnerability and need into the kiss, all her fear of losing him and her disappointment in herself. She hadn't felt this scared and weak with a man since high school, and the feeling was strangely, unexpectedly exhilarating – like pouring out all the bad stuff in your mind and soul, and just being left with a light, ringing emptiness inside your head and heart.

"It's so early," Ruth whispered. "The kids probably won't be up for a long time."

"I know."

She giggled. "You're a mess. Let's do it in the shower."

"Sure."

He grabbed her hand and yanked her off the bed, his roughness making her laugh again. A little more laughter as they got out of their pajamas, and then the hot water was flowing deliciously down her body. The kisses then were just a little more like the old days, with one of Ben's hands on her breast, as the other went between her legs. Ruth decided it wasn't like riding a bike, unfortunately, but it seemed like something she could relearn.

ABOUT THE AUTHOR

Kim Paffenroth is Professor of Religious Studies at Iona College. His books include the *Dying to Live* series (Permuted Press) and the Stoker Award winning *Gospel of the Living Dead* (Baylor University Press).

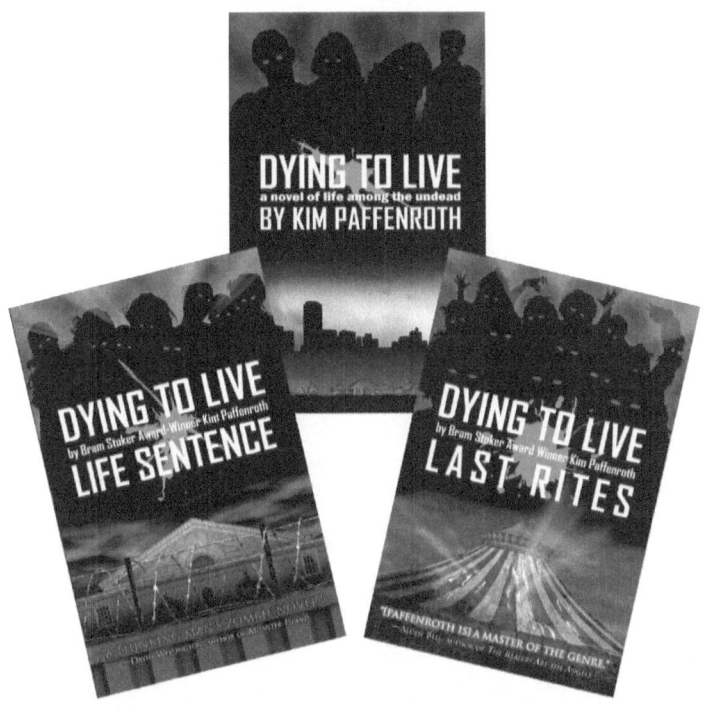

www.ingramcontent.com/pod-product-compliance
Lightning Source LLC
Chambersburg PA
CBHW031313170626
46807CB00001B/401